SHUT THE DOOR

SHUT the DOOR

amanda marquit

st. martin's press ⚏ new york

www.stmartins.com

ISBN 0-312-31929-0
EAN 978-0312-31929-8

First Edition: January 2005

10 9 8 7 6 5 4 3 2 1

To Mom, Dad, and Adam,
for being the family upon which this book is based—just kidding

The harbor is still,
the silence is screaming.
Dreams seized untasted,
beckoning them nearer.
Water is deep,
an endless circle;
the pattern cannot cease,
for someone is waiting.
Anticipating.
The demise.
I can see it in your eyes.
Clear,
transparent,
still as an empty harbor,
endlessly guarding deep waters.
Striving,
yet hopelessly failing to protect
your daughters.

AMANDA MARQUIT, 1998

SHUT THE DOOR

Beatrice

She felt awkward without him there. As if her movements were newer, more different, emptier. Blind and without meaning. And she had never known about missing him before. He had always just been there, asking nothing of her but his breakfast, the paper, a cup of tea (he never drank coffee). And now he was gone.

She pretended not to notice the emptiness. The silence. She switched on the radio, hoping to fill the empty seat with music that would replace the concave shape his body had left in the cushion. Years he'd sat there. *Just yesterday he'd sat here.* She had made her coffee already. Sat noiselessly in her seat, sipped, and stared at nothing.

She stood up and began to boil water on the stove.

It was routine. She'd been doing it for the last eighteen years, and would continue to do it for her entire life to come. No matter what happened, he'd be there, and she'd be there. She would make his tea, and he would smile that same weary, worn-out, drab smile that was almost too familiar to her now. But she loved it. She loved the monotony. Longed for it. She knew he would smile at her in the morning. She knew it every morning she had woken up fifteen minutes earlier than he had, to cook his breakfast. She knew it when they were newlyweds. And when they had gone to bed angry. She knew it when he was overtired, when he was stressed. And although she always knew he would do it, sometimes there was a slight tinge of fear that he wouldn't.

He always does.

And there was nobody there.

She laid the mug down at his place. *Just where he likes it: the left side of the plate.* She laid his paper on the right and waited. She waited as if she were expecting him, as if he were only late or in a traffic jam or caught in the rain. But it was sunny outside, and he was not there. He was not in the house. Was not outside. He was not in the garage or off to work early. He was not there.

Bea never prepared breakfast for Vivian and Lilliana. They always managed to feed themselves, or went out with friends, she supposed. She didn't really say very much to them in the morning. Sometimes she didn't even see them, but it didn't matter. As long as he was there, everything was fine. Harry, drinking his Earl Grey and reading his paper in the same way every time. And giving her that halfhearted smile that seemed to consume more and more of his gradually depleting energy with each day that passed. But that was enough. *More than enough even.* All she wanted was that, but this day, she couldn't have it.

She stared across the table at the cup, the paper, the clean white plate, and the emptiness. She wasn't hungry, but decided to cook breakfast anyway. She never ate it; she was always on a diet. But he did, and often he finished the scrambled eggs that she had only picked at, after he had cleaned his own plate. "This is good," he would say.

She made French toast and scrambled eggs.

At first she felt funny dumping the food onto the white china, but then a sense of comfort, of regularity, seemed to guide her through the familiar movements. It felt good to have a routine. To be involved in something she knew so well. To continue things as they were meant to continue. And she sat in her seat, and stared at the plate of food that she knew would not move until *she* moved it. She filled up her own plate as well, and picked at the eggs, waiting to give him her half-eaten meal.

He wasn't there though. She knew it. She saw the empty space, the full cup of tea, the plate, the neatly sectioned paper fresh with the morning's headlines. And she smiled back at him. She smiled as she did when he gave her his weary grin, and suddenly, as if the words had taken on a life of their own and sprung from her lips, she said, "Glad you like it."

For a moment, her breath caught in her lungs, her heart bounced in her chest, her eyes bulged. He was not there. *Harry is not here.* But it had felt good to speak. To carry out things the way they always were—and always had been. She'd felt the familiar sigh of relief when she'd said it. He'd liked the breakfast. He was eating the breakfast. He was drinking his tea, and he'd just smiled at her. And she always replied in that same way.

She spontaneously ran to the kitchen door and swung it shut. She didn't want the girls to hear this. She didn't want anyone to hear. She didn't want anyone to see, so she yanked down the shades on both windows. Switched on the harsh white lights, and took her place again. She was safe now. Safe from the world. Safe from her daughters. Safe from prying neighbors, from people who might wonder. She was just there, living. Alive. *Getting on with things that need to be done.*

She checked the date on her watch. Thought about how he'd never been away for more than a weekend. He'd be back from Cleveland in ten days. She missed him more than she'd missed anything in her whole life.

Lilliana

She stared silently at the clock on her dresser. He was supposed to be there. He was supposed to have been there ten minutes ago. *Whatever. Some guys like to keep girls waiting. Fuck them.*

She smiled at nothing. Contemplating. Waiting. Waiting to exercise her power, smile her captivating smile, stretch her beautiful limbs, and peel off her outermost layers, layers that seemed so suffocating in the presence of a member of the opposite sex.

Because this was *fun.*

Because he wants me. They want me. A conquest.

It seemed that things had always been this way. She had always been loved, some way or another. Unconventional love, but love nonetheless. And she didn't care. Lilliana didn't care. *I'm in it for the fuck. They should know that.* And that's why the stupid ones were best. Or the old ones. Or at least the old*er* ones. Who were too transfixed by her youth and strength of character to realize that they were being so easily and copiously manipulated.

He should be here. They're usually on time. But this was nothing special. This meeting. This was not a date. *This is nothing special.* This was entertainment on a Friday afternoon. Just something to do. *Just someone to do.* She did get impatient. She wasn't ashamed. *She'd* invited him in the first place. To study, she'd said. She'd asked him to study.

God, she loved being cruel. Making them want her. She loved tearing away their masks of masculinity, stripping them of all disguises. Dismantling their egos and looking at what was left. A scrawny, pale, sorry-looking boy. One with no confidence, with no strength, no awards, no pride. *What a trip.*

Because everything was somewhat boring, and no guilt was involved. Because she *could.* Because she had the ability and because she had power. And poise. And something else that was indescribable. Allure. Or something.

She wondered what he would think, as she heard his footsteps in the doorway.

"I really, really like you. You know that, don't you?"

"Sure I do."

"So . . ."

"So . . . ?"

"So I've been waiting to say this pretty much forever, and now that I have, I guess I want to know what you think of me. . . ."

"Can you press Play, please? I mean on the CD player by your foot. . . . (silence) You know, I'm not sure, Jake."

"Oh, I totally understand. I mean, I didn't think you'd . . ."

"Look. I just want you to know that I'm going through a rough time right now—you know, with school and parents and everything. So I'm not really looking for a relationship. You know? I'm not looking for a boyfriend. . . . (silence) Why are you afraid?"

"I'm not."

"Then why can't you look me in the eye for more than, like, two seconds? (silence) That's better. That's more like it. You should look at people when you talk to them, Jake."

"I know, I . . . Everyone says that to me."

"Well, it's true."

"Yeah."

"You know what?"

"What?"

"I know what you want."

"What?"

"I said that I know what you want."

"You do?"

"And I think that we should quit this small talk, and just get it out."

"Okay, but what do you mean?"

"Basically, the truth is that I don't really care if you like me. I just think that

if we're gonna fuck, we should do it now, because it is a good time and everything. And you can't leave too late, right?"

"You . . . Say what?"

"You heard me, Jake. It's what I want. What about you? Isn't that really why
you came over anyway? Because that's why I invited you. . . . (silence) I mean,
you didn't actually think that we were going to study, did you? You came over
here for something else, didn't you?"

"I . . . well, yeah. I mean, I guess so. I . . . I . . . mean that . . ."

"Look. Shut the door. Shut it, and lock it."

Harry

The plane trip had been his first in a while, and while cramped in the con-
stricting business-class seat and drinking inexpensive, lukewarm chardonnay
out of a plastic cup, he had never been so happy. In fact, he'd hardly even
thought of Bea the entire plane ride, and for some reason, he was proud.

An accomplishment.

He knew she was thinking of him, though. Pining for him, really. He slowly
made his way through the Cleveland airport. For once he felt free. And he
loved this feeling. Good and new. He was no longer a family man. That rainy
day in Cleveland, he was just a man. A man without a wife, without daughters,
without a house or a car of his own. He was just living. A person in the world.
A solitary, alive, single unit of living, working organs. And that was it.

At the baggage claim, he stood silently watching the anonymous pieces of
luggage move slowly in and out of sight. He traced the bags to their owners.
The nameless people who matched their suitcases perfectly. A businesswoman
(tightly packed black suitcase with wheels), an unshaven man with two gold
chains around his neck (gray plastic suitcase wrapped multiple times with a
strip of duct tape), a girl with an array of facial piercings (a bag with assorted
patches, and a cardboard box, scribbled over with a permanent marker). They
all seemed to struggle in their own way.

He was in Cleveland for business. They'd flown him to Cleveland. Cleveland was so far away from home. He would stay in a hotel in Cleveland. Eat

Cleveland food, and watch Cleveland people for two weeks. Work in a Cleveland office, and live a Cleveland life.

And out of his peripheral vision, he saw a woman in a little black skirt and a red blouse.

She must be twenty-five . . . maybe twenty-eight, but that's stretching it. He watched her slink to the front of the carousel, and wait . . . and wait. *If Bea had been here, she never would've let me look away. I might've never even seen her!* He was looking at the woman then. Thinking about the woman. And although Bea could never get inside his head, she always seemed to have some way of knowing what he was thinking and having a large and crucial impact on it.

But now, Bea was not there, and he was free. He was free of her, free from her stares and her need of his constant approval of everyday tasks. He could be careless. Smile when he felt like it. And he did feel like it, for the first time in a decade, it seemed.

And he let his fantasies contaminate all pure thoughts his mind had harbored that day, and the woman at the baggage claim was the only thing he wanted. He couldn't have asked for anything more.

He had grabbed his own luggage five minutes before, and so he pretended to look for an alternate piece, which most definitely did not exist. She hadn't gotten her bag yet, and he edged over toward her. *God, those legs!* He'd never liked Bea's legs. Never liked them in stockings, and even when they'd been tan in the summers, he always wanted to turn away at the sight of them. Two pillars that held up the shapeless upper body that he had lost interest in so long ago. But this . . . this new body. This was a body he'd like to hold. To explore. To touch. He could've stared at those legs forever. . . .

Vivian

She smiled awkwardly into her mirror and fixed her hair. She turned up the music in order to drown out her sister's noises.

She hated hearing Lilli like that. The walls were thin, especially since the renovation, when one wall, merely a wood spine overlaid with plywood and

Sheetrock and then wallpaper, was put up as a divider in what was once an enormous bedroom. She wondered why her mother hadn't had a more expensive wall installed; they could afford it, and it would have blocked out some of the noises that emerged from her sister's lair, be it Nirvana CDs, or quarrelsome telephone conversations, or the types of sounds she was hearing right then.

She was thinking of herself, though. She hardly ever thought of herself.

Sick of herself.

She thought that if she dyed her hair, it might change something. *A valuable change. A much needed, much awaited change.*

Maybe I'll do red. How about that? A redhead. She'd always wanted to be one. *And everyone does blond. And red is different, and unique, and mysteriously beautiful, and seductive.* These were all the things that she was not.

Maybe if she'd had Lilli's hair, things would've been better. Lilli's hair: silky and ideal. Her hair: uncooperative. She could straighten it and dye it red. *That would be the best thing to do.*

She heard a high-pitched sigh from next door.

And then, as usual, the bed began to slam against the thin wall, shaking her posters ever so slightly, her dresser, her jewelry in her jewelry box. The mirror that she had been looking in at that moment.

Her features began to quiver, and she watched the girl, the ugly, unwanted girl stare back at her. "God, I'm definitely doing red," she whispered to herself. She looked at her closed bedroom door.

She looked past her face, down to her midriff. *Fucking fat girl.* She got down on the floor, and began to exercise. For a moment, she wished that she were her sister. Her beautiful, carefree sister, carelessly fucking in her own bed, in the house in which she had been born. In the bed she'd slept in as a child. In the sheets that wouldn't be changed until Monday.

The carpet felt rough against her back.

It all seemed to die down after a while. And then the silence came as the last song played, almost louder and more prominent than the moans that had escaped through the wall only moments before. Vivian was happy for a moment; she could sit in peace. She could sit and do nothing at all, and not have her sister's sounds scream at her. It had been enough for an evening. It had been enough for a lifetime. But then again, she thought this every Friday night anyway. Things just seemed to lose importance.

Harry

The Cleveland air was full of cold water, it seemed. It threatened rain, but didn't. The cab, however, was hot and stuffy, and he could hardly focus on keeping his things together. He could hardly remember the hotel address, hardly comprehend the tasks at hand. His fingers clumsily fumbled over the dial on his watch. *It's only an hour difference. It's not that big of a deal.* The woman, the black skirt, the legs, the mystery of her consumed him, and already he felt unexplainably sorry that he had not gone over to assist with her bag, or ask what she was doing in Cleveland, or where she was staying, or for her coveted phone number even. . . .

God! He was getting carried away. *I have a wife; I have kids. And now I'm just letting myself go, acting like a teenage boy, like a goddamned kid.* "Snap out of it, Harry," he whispered to himself. He rolled up the windows and shut the divider between himself and the driver. "You have a wife who loves you, and two beautiful girls. Now why are you so infatuated? Huh?" His voice grew louder, sharp, bouncing angrily against the walls of the constricted space. The driver eyed him suspiciously in the mirror.

"I don't know. I really don't." He shook his head. *God, I'm so fucking confused. I never should've left them all. I never should've gone on this trip and left Bea and the girls. They need me.*

This is not normal.

Real men don't talk to themselves. They don't yell at themselves, accuse themselves. No, they don't. He'd get to the hotel and do whatever he wanted, whenever he wanted to. If he wanted to, he *could* think about that woman. *It's only thinking. Come on, I mean, Bea can't see into my head. She can't see my fucking thoughts. And she's not here.*

He was at the hotel minutes later.

The room was average. Average bed and an average TV. There was an average bathroom with a shower and a bathtub and sink. There was a night table with a lamp, and there was an alarm clock. There was a full-length mirror and a closet with metal hangers that were permanently soldered onto a pole that reached from one end of the closet to the other. *As if I'm going to steal the fucking*

hangers. *What kind of a person do they expect you to be?* There was a telephone.
And there was Harry, and he was alone.

He thought of the woman.

"Stop it, Harry!" he yelled into the mirror. But *she* was there. She was present and prominent. That nameless woman. That woman in the black skirt and red blouse. That woman, grabbing her suitcase and walking away.

He turned on the TV.

There's no reason to be scared. All men fantasize. All men do all kinds of things. And all you're doing is thinking. Think away! Bea's not here. She's not here. She's not here. . . .

Beatrice

She'd seen him go out the back, belt unbuckled, considerably frazzled. Sprinting away, as if he had had some experience that was either too good to be true, or that he wished to forget forever. Maybe it had been both.

Lilliana. Christ, I'd tried. I'd tried! And she'd thought about it all the way to and from the store, and knew what was happening. *She's sixteen. I should be able to leave her alone. I shouldn't have to baby-sit her all night. I shouldn't have to worry.* She decided to pretend she hadn't seen him, because that would rid her of the responsibility of talking to Lilli about it—and that would make Bea feel less guilty.

She felt very guilty.

She hoped that Lilli wasn't sleeping with them. *Maybe she's just experimenting with them. You're only young once, I suppose.* Experimenting. She hadn't smelled anything more than the sweet perfume of fragranced candles in Lilli's room the last time she'd been in there. She'd found no mysterious white powders or pills. She'd once searched every square inch of her daughter's room after a parents' meeting about drugs at school. Of course, the search had turned out negative, though her suspicions had not completely ceased to arise. *I searched practically everywhere except in her tissue box, for God's sake.* She hadn't even found condoms! Or should she have found condoms? She wondered which was worse. . . . It didn't matter though. She did not condone this behavior in her house; thus she refused to bring it up at all.

But she hadn't done a search in a long time. She felt guilty searching. *I have the right to know though. I want to know.*

Right.

She'd picked up two of Harry's shirts from the dry cleaner. One of them was his favorite. It was blue with a tiny pinstripe in white. She laid the shirts out on his side of the bed when she went upstairs. Went back down, and began to fix dinner.

She was going to make brisket, Harry's favorite.

The girls hated brisket. They detested it, in fact. Vivian had stopped eating red meat for health reasons a year ago, and recently, after a loud row about burgers that were too charred to eat, Lilli had declared that she was becoming a vegan. At first, Bea had thought it was nothing but a rage-induced declaration of defiance, but now, nearly six months later, her daughter had not touched a piece of animal, including fish, and insisted on a tofu- or soy-based dish nightly.

And Bea did not feel like making tofu.

The rest of the family, including herself, had learned to eat it. It was good for you, supposedly. And Lilli no longer drank cow's milk either. Everything was soy, soy, soy. *Just to be difficult.*

But tonight, she was not making tofu. She was not boiling soybeans, and she was not pouring soy milk. *I am making brisket, Harry's favorite, and they will all eat it.* She didn't care how much of a fight Lilli would put up; but by God, she was making dinner for Harry, *not for the girls.*

She stuck the meat into the oven, and smiled as she sat down at the kitchen table. The shades were still drawn. The door was shut and latched. She looked over at Harry's seat. "Guess what? I'm making brisket tonight, your favorite!"

Lilliana

It was done, and he had gone.

He'd been all right. Nothing special. A bit too afraid. It was funny how he'd exuded such confidence in school, but was so clumsy in bed. *Inexperienced in bed. Very inexperienced.*

She wondered if her mother had seen him go.

She'd heard the door open before he was all the way downstairs. She reminded herself that her mother probably would pretend not to notice, even if she had. Sometimes Lilli flaunted her conquests, leaving little clues around her room for fun. A boy's boxers had once been left crumpled on her floor. Plainly in sight. Clashing violently with the pink carpet. Magazines, face down, with every sex article clearly marked. A half-used jar of Vaseline. And her mother never said a word.

Never.

She wondered about her sister for a minute. *Poor Viv. Is she lost or what? Now this . . . this is life. This is fun. This is how it should be.* She convinced herself. Convinced herself? She'd never had to do that before. She'd always just been happy, or disturbed, or inexplicably sad, but never had it crossed her mind that this was not fun.

She thought of her first time.

Now that hadn't been very special. But what was the point? Did it really need to be so great? It only gets better. She remembered lying there, in his room, on his bed, naked in the dark, while some unknown local rock band spun countless times on his CD player, and he had felt around for all of the right places, but had never ended up finding them.

She didn't know his name. Or she'd known it then, but didn't remember it now. She remembered that it had been at a party. All of her friends had been downstairs, and they'd been dared to do it. She'd sort of liked him. Thought he was sort of cute and sort of nice, and if he hadn't had acne, he might have been good-looking. They'd been dared to just fool around. *Really innocent stuff. I guess it seemed like a big deal then.* And then things had gotten out of hand, and seven minutes turned into an eternity, and she was not a virgin anymore.

And somewhere in that moment, bathed in a haze of Lava Lamp light and sweat, she'd decided it hadn't been so bad—a little painful, maybe, but it would only get better. It had felt good to be past the wonderment of losing it. And not having to make decisions. And not having to anticipate the unknown. Because there was no longer an "unknown." It had all been revealed to her. All that societal pressure had dissolved and blown away into nothingness. She could do it an unlimited number of times. She could fuck whomever she wanted, wherever she wanted, and not have to worry about making it special or perfect, or even nice. *Just satisfactory. That's all I ask.*

Technically, she'd lost it on a dare.

A fucking dare! Viv still has time. She can pick the when, and where, and with who, I guess. But it's not like I can take it back. And it's not like I ever would. At least I got it over with then. And you've just got to get it over with.

Vivian was so much wiser than Lilli had been. And she wasn't thirteen either. *Viv is a virgin. An inexperienced prude.* Did Lilli wish she could switch places? *Nah.* She was loved. She had so much of it too. But did they love her body? Did they love *her*? Did they love the rumors that spread like fire the next day through school? *No handcuffs. Wild, maybe.*

But that might have been the reason why. It probably was, for all she knew. And she'd had guys tell her they loved her. She'd had guys fall in love with her mystery, her sex tricks. And she could have returned it if she'd wished. But it was so unrequited on her part. She could never imagine falling for any of the men she slept with.

She heard her mother call her for dinner, and decided to go.

She brushed her hair, put on some makeup, and latched the door behind her.

Vivian

She knew that her mother was home by the smell of dinner cooking downstairs. It was brisket.

She hated brisket, but had never been brave enough to say it. In fact, she despised it, and wondered why her mother was making it at all. It was her father's favorite, but Bea usually didn't like it very much either.

Tonight, I will not go to dinner. I will skip dinner, and go to the drugstore, and dye my hair red.

She glanced in the mirror again, and decided that red would most definitely make a change. An important change. A well-earned change. She had always been the good one. The one who followed all of the the rules and ate whatever was on the table, no matter how bad, or overcooked, or slightly stale. But now it would change.

She was going to go to the store to buy the dye, and nobody was going to stop her.

She heard her mother call them for dinner.

She was not going to dinner that night. She would not eat that awful dinner. She was going to change. She took one last glance at the mirror, and then decided to go out through the back, so her mother wouldn't interrogate her.

"Well, it's about time you came down here. I've only been calling for the last five minutes. Where's Vivian?"

"I dunno."

"Well, go and sit down. *Vivian!*"

"Mom, she'll come down soon."

"Vivian!"

"Mom, she'll . . ."

"Viv! *Vivian!* Vivi . . ."

"You know, she can hear you fine, and if she's not planning on coming down, there has to be a reason."

"Yes, thank you so much for informing me. Now go and sit down."

"Where's my soy stuff? Where's my tofu?"

"I . . . well, um . . . we don't have any tonight. This is our dinner. It's brisket . . . and you're going to eat it."

"You're joking. I asked for fried tofu tonight. Didn't you hear me?"

"Yes . . ."

"So why didn't you make it?"

"We are all eating this tonight, Lil."

"I refuse to eat that piece of shit! That dead animal!"

"You will eat it."

"I will not. And this is not my milk! What the hell is this? Why the hell are you, like, all anti-vegan all of a sudden? Suddenly you refuse to let me eat what I want? What the hell are you trying to do?"

"Sit down and eat it."

"Fuck you. I'm going out. I'm not staying and listening . . ."

"Don't you dare say that to me, you little tart! You come back here."

"I will not eat this fucking cow or lamb, or whatever the hell it is. And you know that. I'll go up to my room then, but I won't sit here and have you expect me to conform to your cannibalistic ways. That's it."

"So go. Leave, fine! But you're not getting anything else. Oh, and by the way, the last time I checked, I was not a cow. It would really only be cannibalism if you eat your own kind."

"Really? Doesn't seem like you've checked in a while."

Harry

And he wished he'd gotten her number.

He hadn't asked for a woman's phone number since he met Bea. And Bea had consented immediately. She'd never put up a fight, which was part of why he'd liked her in the first place. He'd never liked the tricks women played. He'd never liked the games, and the strategies, the bitchery, the tactics employed in capturing a male specimen and keeping him. Rearing him and branding him with a special seal, and wrapping his left ring finger in gold to say it. Hindering his movement. She had known none of these things when they'd met. *Simple. That's how she was.* Even when he'd expected her to flatly refuse to give him any personal information, she had consented happily. And so their relationship had begun that way. Simply and consensually.

The room had been stuffy that night. *A stuffy party room. A dance.* And he hadn't been sorry then. He hadn't even *known* her. And she had become his wife. Bea. Fixing up everything and arranging it just right. No changes because things didn't need to change. Theirs was a comfortable marriage. There were no complaints. There was nothing *wrong* there. He didn't care what other people thought of them, how well they seemed to think that he and Bea worked. He liked being known as part of a working thing: a family, a machine.

Because there's so much divorce these days, and he was doing just fine. His family was fine.

He was happy about that.

He really had liked Bea for a while. He'd loved her too. He'd told her all the time. But he never really felt that way now.

He didn't really feel much at all.

But he knew what to expect from the people he lived with. He knew that he couldn't hope because hoping wouldn't get him anywhere. *Realism is best. Even if it is a letdown sometimes.* He'd tried to instill that sensibility in his daughters. He didn't know if he'd succeeded.

He'd never dreamed after he'd met Bea. He'd basically forgotten how. Just endless dead nights. Stretches of hours lost in liquid darkness.

He slowly let his eyelids slip closed while the TV blared nonsense in the background. Behind them, he expected to see an image of Bea that first night at the party. Perhaps he could, because he was no longer at home. No longer lying next to anybody to steal it away. And so he fell into a dream. Vivid and hot. He walked up to the girl in the cornflower blue dress and tapped her on the shoulder. She did not respond. He tapped her again. "Excuse me." She turned around, but it was not Bea. It was the woman. The blue dress was gone. She was wearing her skirt and blouse. The band played in the background, melodic and soft. Her red lips parted into a smile as he looked down at her endless legs. She said nothing. A sly smile crept across her lips like disease. "It would be such an honor to get your phone number. . . ."

Beatrice

The food had been good, but a disappointment overall. She noiselessly cleared the four plates. Two were unused, one had been picked at, the other was heaped with food that would have been eaten under normal circumstances. She wondered why Vivian hadn't come down for dinner; she'd always been the first. She was too tired to call for her again, too tired to go up and check, and Vivi was the good one anyway, so she didn't worry. But now, Lilli was angry at Bea, and maybe she deserved it. She knew perfectly well that Lilli had asked for fried tofu, and she hadn't made it. *It was a terrible thing to do. Just awful.*

She aimlessly hand-washed the dishes, even though the dishwasher worked perfectly and could've made her job a lot easier. *Maybe I can bring up some tofu for Lilli later. Try to make amends.* She paused and looked at the dirty dish in her hands. *Maybe not. She's a big girl, and she can get it herself. I shouldn't have to do everything for her. Besides, I don't condone her behavior lately. What a loose girl. What kind of mother am I? What kind of daughter do I have?*

She closed the door of the kitchen with her slippered foot, and watched it swing shut.

She looked up from the running faucet to Harry's seat. For a moment, he was there. Alive, breathing, having already eaten. Looking discontented with what he was doing. He took his reading glasses out of his pocket and placed them on his face.

"Did you hear the news today, Harry?" She whispered at first. Turned back around to the sink. Smiled as she went on washing. She didn't wait for a response. She knew that she wouldn't have gotten one anyway. "Well, Mrs. Taren got that rosebush replaced, the one that was wrecked by the station wagon . . ."

She swung around to look at the door. She thought she'd heard the slight shuffling sound of a teenage girl in the doorway, but there was nothing. She wondered about Vivian for a minute. Let her mind leave Harry's seat. And then, suddenly, she realized that she didn't love her daughters half as much as she did her husband. She was always silently wishing that they'd stay at school a little while longer, study harder, be more willing . . . yet she had to wish nothing but good fortune for Harry. And she did her best for him, which usually seemed to be sufficient. But not for the girls. Everything was too much, over the top, or not enough at all.

She hadn't even really wanted children to begin with.

But he had. He'd wanted them, so she'd had them. Didn't even put up a fight. Didn't even dispute it. She'd always been much too ashamed to disclose the fact that she did not really want a "proper" family. Just the two of them would be best . . . but appeasing him was the only thing she cared about. And therefore she had launched into motherhood reluctantly, however readily.

But he'd wanted boys.

She knew it; he knew it. He always talked about it when she was pregnant:

the little boy to play catch with, to teach to ride a bike, to join the baseball team, to go to an Ivy League school, to start a family of his own, and to eventually become just like Harry. *Just like him. The son he wanted.* But she hadn't given him that boy. She hadn't created the perfect son. She'd brought two baby girls into the world, a year apart, and then they had given up.

Neither of the girls had even wanted to learn to ride a bike.

So Bea always felt awful seeing them walking around in high heels. Reading women's magazines, cheap romance novels. Seeing the contents of their trash cans turn bloodstained every month. Seeing them leave their dirty little underpants on their bedroom floors, and buying and buying and buying. Push-up bras, skimpy tops, skirts that showed generous flashes of bare thigh and threatened to show a peek of underwear depending on the wind that day. Dirty makeup sponges, lipstick stains, perfume that was way too strong, too sophisticated, too much . . . They weren't both this bad. Really, Viv was a lot better than Lilli.

If she'd had another daughter like Vivian, she wouldn't have minded as much. *He wouldn't have cared as much if they were both agreeable, nice, intelligent, studious, pretty, likable girls.* But even Vivi had her moments and could not be classified as perfect. Bea had always loved perfection.

Harry is perfection.

Vivian

She'd felt awful all night. Very hungry, a little afraid. But most of all, she felt rebellious, because that's what she was. *Rebellious.*

If there had been one adjective that she would've picked if asked to describe herself, "rebellious" would've been the very last one that she would've considered. She would've said something like "demure," "compliant," "studious," "dutiful," "responsible." . . . Even "worldly" was too much for her. She had really never rebelled before. Never done anything rebellious in her life. *Except for now.*

She felt safe behind the locked door.

She looked at the pretty woman on the box. Her straight red hair billowed in an artificial wind. Superimposed on a cloudlike backdrop, the girl looked unexplainably happy. Elated. Imprisoned in a state of pure, sedated ecstasy on a box of dye for all eternity. And she wondered what could make her feel that way. What could make anyone feel that way. She felt that if she wanted to smile like that, there had to be something else present in addition to the new, permanently colored hair that was destined to adorn her head in a matter of minutes.

She began to shake as she emptied the contents of the box onto the bath mat. A vial of dye that looked like black blood rolled against the clean whiteness. She pulled out the instructions, stood in the bathtub, and began.

Please don't let Lilli come in here.

She emerged an hour later. Hair the color of a "Violet Raspberry," smile pasted to her face like the smile of the girl on the box. And a sense of freedom that she'd never felt before. *Never like this.*

She glanced in the mirror, and dumped her towel and bath mat in the laundry. Each had been stained the same berry color as her hair. She was in love. *Look at this! What a high! Oh God, I look so much better. Mom's gonna kill me. Who gives a shit though? I look good. Almost as good as Lilli.*

The smell of the dye had permeated everything.

She looked down in the stained bathtub, and thought about how it glistened with all of that nice redness dried against the sides. She didn't run the water to rinse it away; it looked too special. A prize. When she washed her hands, the water that swirled down the drain turned a transparent red. Her fingertips were stained. Dangerous.

She wondered how different she'd feel when she walked into her bedroom.

She gently twisted the knob on the bathroom door as it sprung open to reveal the last place she'd been. Constant, unwavering, childish room. And now, she was the variable. She was new. She was important. She was different. She had begun to grow up.

Harry

He woke up in a panic, only twenty minutes before six-thirty, when he had planned to meet a partner for drinks. Steve Verchon. *Rich bastard.* The largest and most influential client with whom Harry had ever dealt. Harry's face was coated in sweat; his suit was creased. He needed a shower, but didn't have the time to take one. He had been thinking of *her.*

It's not a good time for this. I can't do this. He was in Cleveland on business. Important business. Legitimate business.

When Bea had asked him, "why now?" he had told her it was important. "Important business matters" was all he would say. It *was* important. It really was. *Fucking finally.* "We need the money, Bea. I need the promotion."

He tried to banish the woman's persistent image from his mind by staring at his wallet-size family portrait from a few Christmases ago; when Bea was wearing a red dress (that she no longer fit into), and the girls were still young. He looked at his daughters: fair skin untouched by makeup, dresses with high necklines and low hemlines, heels that did not exceed an inch. *God! Things had been so different!* And things weren't that way anymore. His family did not look that way; their smiles were not genuine any longer.

Bea. *Christ, she's obsessed with me. She loves me to death. Would give me anything. Anything. I should be more appreciative. So hard to be appreciative.* And he'd been married to her for eighteen years, their love decreasing with each one that passed until he was sure there would be nothing at all. They would just stay together, live together, hold up the facade together, eat together, sleep together, and probably die together. For some reason, he didn't feel like dying with Bea.

We're all liars.

He washed the sweat off his face in the sink, and for a moment, *her* reflection flickered in the mirror.

He turned around to face a blank wall. "Jesus, Harry, you're going nuts." And he dried himself off, and went to get his briefcase. He locked the door behind him, and was out in the world. *You can't fuck up.* The world rested on his shoulders.

Lilliana

Stupid bitch. It didn't make sense. *She's just fucking weak. She doesn't even understand what she's doing to us. She doesn't know how she's fucking us up.* The last person who Lilli wanted to respect was her mother. *How am I supposed to look up to someone who does NOTHING? Like, really nothing. Just sits around and lives vicariously through everybody else. It's fucking sad.*

God, I feel dirty. She decided that her sex life shouldn't be a problem. She'd been fucking forever. She'd never felt this sorry before. Not once.

She looked at a crumpled shirt that lay on the floor.

She remembered when she'd gotten it. It had been plain black, and she'd cut it, glued little red rhinestones to it. Slit it down the sides, safety-pinned the seams. Worked hard, really hard. Maybe for the first time. Dragged razor blades roughly opposite the grain of the fabric. Shredded the bottom hem, and had written on it with metallic silver markers. It said, "Make Me." *Lame, stupid shirt. Juvenile, trendy, stupid, poser shirt. Freshman shirt.*

And she got up off her bed, and picked it up off her carpet. "Make Me." Make Me? She remembered what she'd been thinking at the time too. Make Me. Hah. She unclipped one of the safety pins from the seam, examined its perfect point.

Safety pin. Haha. Safety pin. "Here goes. Ugly bitch. Slut. Cunt." And she took the nice skinny point, and dragged it across her upper arm, near the bicep. It made a nice rosy streak, and when she did it again, the streak turned from rose to garnet as it seeped liquid.

She sat there on her carpet, and leaned her head back. Euphoria. So easy to fix it all up. All perfect and equal outside and in. She made another line on her ankle. Watched the redness explode over the edge. A privilege.

The blood from her arm dripped onto her carpet, and she watched it seep into the fibers. Finally, she felt a part of her room. This was her own room, and she'd never felt at home in it before. Not with the pink carpet, and flowered curtains, and classic, calculated, overdecorated beauty. Now she did. She'd tried so hard to make it her own. She'd worked so hard to erase her mother's notions of beauty. *Clichés. Everything is just a fucking cliché.*

The bleeding began to cease, and the drippy redness turned into crusty brown. Everywhere. On the carpet, on her skin. She wished that blood could always stay red. Red and wet and special. She smiled at the straight line on her bicep.

She felt so much better.

"Hey, Harry! How are ya? Haven't seen you in what? Years?"

"Steve! It definitely has been a while. Maybe not years though. We saw each other last July."

"Well, take a seat. Don't just stand there."

"Right."

"So, what do you drink again? It's really been so long."

"Just a vodka on the rocks for me."

"Alrighty. Waiter! Waiter. Uh . . . Grey Goose on the rocks for the gentleman."

"I'd actually like Absolut."

"Absolut? Okay, whatever you say, Harry. You know, the French stuff is better."

"I like Absolut."

"Fine. Fine. Make it an Absolut. And I'll take a Bombay Sapphire and tonic. So, how's the family?"

"Great."

"Just great?"

"Super."

"Well, don't sound too excited. You know, Daisy is better than ever."

"Is this number three?"

"Number four. And I think this one might last. You remember, I had qualms about her at first. But she's been pretty swell. At least she hasn't thrown anything at me yet! You remember Georgina, right? You know, the brunette?"

"Uh huh."

"Well, she'd throw stuff all the time. Anything she could get her hands on! Just chuck it right at me. Real expensive stuff. Dishes, lamps! Couldn't argue for shit. That's all I have to say. I like a woman who argues. Just not one that's physically argumentative. You know, the intellectual ones."

"Uh huh."

"Not to say that they have to be Einstein or anything, but they have to know how to defend themselves. And I'm talking about verbally, not physically. I never laid a finger on any one of them. *They're* the ones who get all out of whack. None were as bad as Cleo though. Remember Cleo? She was the first."

"I . . ."

"Well, the thing about Cleo was that she was gorgeous. Just all woman, and I was young and naive, and I went for her for the wrong reasons. We lasted two, three years maybe. God, she was a big spender. Took my paycheck and turned it into sawdust! Got the apartment in the end too. Christ. She was a mean one but, boy, could she argue. Smart cookie. Just a real smart—"

"Steve—"

". . . cookie. She was great in the sack too, if I may say so. I used to call her Cleopatra, ya know. She liked that. But what a tyrannical bitch! Just impossible. So it ended, but while it was going, boy, was she something else. And then there was Sophie: she was number two. Great rack—"

"Steve—"

". . . terrible sense of humor. I swear the girl had a heart of concrete. Couldn't squeeze a single laugh out of her for beans. And eventually she—"

"Steve!"

"What? I'm trying to tell you about my unsuccessful marriages. I mean, Christ, I'm a successful businessman, but hell, I always pick the worst women."

"Steve, I'm going to the john. Excuse me."

"Harry! Your drink isn't even here yet!"

Harry

The men's room was the deliberately pretentious kind found in fancy restaurants. There was no sign on the door, but an iron relief of some Greek god hung in its place. And the ladies room had some sort of goddess hanging on its door. When he walked in, he noticed the sink was marble and the toilets were clean.

He felt sick. Not violently sick, but a sickness that underlay everything he did and said and thought about.

And he knew it was the woman.

Why can't she just leave me the fuck alone? I don't want this. I don't need it. But it was too late. He had succumbed to his vision of her. Long, long stockinged legs, leather heels. Short black skirt. Red blouse. *What a body!* He splashed water onto his face. Looked squarely in the mirror. "Harry. This is all in your head. Just go back out there, and have your drink with Steve, and you'll be okay." *Fuck, I'm talking to myself again! Fuck! Jesus fucking Christ, why can't I just go out there? I will go out there. Okay? I will.*

He turned off the faucet, and decided to return to the table. He took one last look at the god on the door.

He wondered what it would be like to be a god.

He turned to walk away, but then he saw it. He saw *her*. Her! In her red and black forbidden beauty. She was real. Alive now. Her eyes gleaming with the pain she'd been causing him. Her lips smiling with the torture. Her legs gently swung back and forth with her carefree stride. Her dark hair billowed, even though the air was still. She wore sunglasses on her head. Her leather shoes made music on the lacquered wood that he'd found so slippery and much too shiny only minutes before. Heels clicking like a clock. Counting down to something. And she opened the door to the room with the goddess on it.

He turned to watch her go. And he realized that her smile had not been for him. He turned to see where she'd been looking. And she'd been smiling at the Greek god on the door. Right over his head.

Beatrice

She wondered why he hadn't called.

Maybe it's the time change. He probably forgot to set his watch. He'll call any minute. I know it. She'd been thinking this for an hour.

Maybe he's gotten into an accident.

Suddenly, Bea could envision Harry in a smashed-up airport taxi. She could see the paramedics failing to save his life. She could see his body bag being driven away from the scene in an ambulance whose sirens had been turned off because the drivers knew that the weight that they carried within it had failed. It was nothing, and it was everything. Maybe he'd electrocuted himself in the bathroom, or had been mugged and stabbed on a side street, or had choked on a piece of food. She was sure that he was dead. Dead and gone. And she would be alone. Left with the girls by herself forever, alone, to rear them and steer them in the right direction to the best of her ability.

"I can't raise them alone. I told you, Harry."

If he were dead, the police would've called already. You would know by now. But Bea was completely convinced that Harry was harmed or ill, or had died, painfully and prematurely, in a torrent of noise, blood, and shattered bones.

Maybe he fell, and his spinal cord snapped. Just snapped. Like a branch.

The phone didn't ring.

She grew expectant. The police would call her any minute. Give her a synopsis of her husband's evening leading up to his demise. And she would scream, "I knew it!" into the receiver, through tears of hysteria. Then she'd break down and . . .

This is ridiculous. He'll call. Now you have to shut up, Bea.

She was sitting on the bed. She glanced over to Harry's side. He'd slept there. He'd woken up there. He'd been there. And she'd been there next to him, and now he was gone, and he hadn't called. *Maybe he's out for dinner, talking about important business matters. What's the time difference in Cleveland?*

She decided that she might as well go to sleep.

She thought about the girls for a moment.

Ten years ago, she would've gone in and kissed them goodnight. It was only nine o'clock, but they would've been asleep by now. She would've done it earlier. She hadn't seen Lilli since their argument. Hadn't seen Viv since the morning. And ordinarily, she would've gone in to make amends, or admit her wrongdoing. But she hadn't. And she didn't intend to.

She got into bed and turned out the lights. "'Night, Harry." She looked at the sliver of light that crept underneath the door. She closed her eyes as they began to well up with tears.

She was sure that he'd died. *What time is it in Cleveland?*

She fell asleep to the sound of metal and glass crashing into brick.

Vivian

She stared in the mirror, transfixed by her own reflection. She couldn't believe she'd done it. She'd gone through with it. And there it was, permanent and obvious.

She wished that she could go show someone.

Her mother was sleeping by now though, and she'd look pretty stupid going into Lilli's room just to show off her almost-purple, unnatural hair color. After all, Lil had gone through so many boxes of dye on her own that she could care less about her sister's own attempts at bettering herself.

Vivian hadn't had a real talk with her sister in something like forever.

Lilli hardly ever came to her for advice. Viv didn't think she was in any rush to. They were embarrassed by one another. *I'm the older one. I can be mature. Maybe I will go and show it to her. Or, better yet, I'll ask to borrow something, and I'll show it to her like that. I'll ask to borrow a CD. Okay. Okay. I'll do it. I'll just walk in and act like nothing's wrong, and then she'll notice.*

Sometimes Vivian wished that she were the younger sister. So she could have a free ride once in a while.

She combed her hair with her fingers, and began to braid it. *Braids? What the hell am I? A six-year-old? Jesus, I can't show Lilli in braids. I'm such a nerd.* She jammed her fingernails through the braids and began to part her hair on the side.

For a moment, she felt sorry that she'd dyed it at all.

Don't feel sorry. Don't. It looks good. It looks fine. And Lilli will appreciate my rebellion. She smiled at the word: "rebellion." She enunciated every syllable into the mirror. "Rebellion. I'm a rebel." And she walked to the door.

Lilliana

It was almost one A.M., and she was starving. She didn't want to go to the kitchen, though. She didn't want to resort to eating potato chips, and she was sore all over anyway. Her cuts had scabbed already, and the stain on her carpet was pleasantly noticeable. Simply beautiful. Simply human. She smiled when she looked at it.

She looked at the bra she'd been wearing earlier.

It was crumpled on the floor. Black lace. She couldn't remember the last time she'd worn white underwear.

She got up off her bed to look in her underwear drawer.

Under everything, there was a single pair of white cotton underpants.

She slipped them on. She felt different. *This is what Vivi must feel like. This is how it feels to wear this white cotton shit. You don't feel sexy at all.* The panties didn't hug her curves. They sagged in the back. She decided that she liked them. She really, really liked them. She kept them on.

The white looked very pretty next to her pretty scars on her pretty arm and her pretty ankle.

She'd never felt this way before. She didn't feel like herself at all. Stepped out of her skin and into someone new. Everything she ever hated and wanted all at once.

She looked at the CD player in the corner.

She remembered how he'd looked when he'd reached down toward it. So unsure. A little boy, and she had been the adult. The manliness had fallen away like a sheet and revealed the truth. There would be no battle, no fight for the survival of the fittest. He had been afraid. All of the muscles on his arm had looked out of place. His tan skin, his slightly stubble-ridden face had revealed a boyish newness. A sallow skinny boy who couldn't read, couldn't tell time. Couldn't do anything. And then, as soon as he'd pressed the button, the music had exploded from the speakers. Triumphant, strong and dark and meaningful. And that music had given her the energy. It had given her the power—and the poise. And she'd taken charge then. And she'd said to herself, *I bet he's a virgin.* And went through with it.

She looked away.

"Hi, Lilli."

"Hi."

"Um . . . can I borrow a CD?"

"Yeah. Which one do . . . Oh God. Your hair."

"I just, you know, felt like dyeing it. Do you like it?"

"I, well . . . it's sort of purple."

"I like it that way."

"Okay. What CD?"

"Well, aren't you surprised?"

"Yeah, sort of. You could've picked a different color though. It doesn't really match your skin tone. It looks fake."

"I like the color."

"Great. You like it. You asked my opinion though. So, what CD do you want?"

"I . . . I thought you would say something more about it."

"Like what?"

"I dunno; I just thought you'd be more surprised."

"I am surprised. There. Happy? Now tell me the CD."

"Well, you're supposed to go on about how I'm such a rebel or something."

"You'll never be a rebel, Viv. Please just tell me what CD you want so I can go to bed and you can—"

"What's that on your carpet?"

"What?"

"On the carpet right there. Is it a stain?"

"I guess."

"What is it?"

"I dunno. It doesn't matter. I can always get it out and—"

"Is it blood?"

"Blood? Why would there be blood in my room?"

"It looks like blood to me."

"It's not blood."

"Yes it is."

"Look, it's not blood!"

"What's this from?"

"Stop checking out the fucking stain! It's not blood!"

"Okay, okay. Please be careful though."

"I am careful."

"Sure you are."

"What's that supposed to mean?"

"Nothing. I just want you to watch out."

"Watch out for what?"

"Just don't do anything stupid."

"I never do anything stupid. And I never do anything that I regret."

"Okay, right. I just want you to think things—"

"And I just want you to stop trying to be my fucking mother."

"Fine, Lilli."

"Yeah, fine. Your hair looks really hot. And fuck you."

Harry

He could never be a god for anyone. *Except Bea.*

Not even if he tried.

Not even if he exerted himself beyond the boundaries of humanity. Not even if he did more than what was crucial. For once.

He realized this as he stood outside the door to the ladies room, waiting for her.

He wondered if she knew he was there.

He'd tried to be a god before, and all of his attempts had come to nothing. Except for Bea. He was Bea's god. Bea could worship him all she wanted, but he didn't care. He didn't want to be her god. He didn't like it when she venerated him. It only seemed to magnify his flaws. Expose his mistakes.

He didn't have much of an ego to speak of.

He suddenly felt young and helpless again. *It had been so easy with Bea. So self-explanatory.* She had agreed to nearly everything he asked. He had, after all, taught her everything she knew, or would ever hope to know, about sex. She wasn't difficult to get along with. She cooked for him and tended to him and served him—and she *liked it. She likes being told what to do. Taking orders.* Made him feel large. Too large for their house and their life and their world.

Like a giant, a master. But now, Bea was gone from his frame of mind. And he stood there and waited.

He couldn't help thinking about what she was doing in there. He'd always wondered what women's bathrooms were like. He'd always wondered why women went to the ladies' room in pairs and threesomes, emerging twenty minutes later looking a bit more put together than before. A bit more tidy, with more lipstick and more powder laid upon their faces, creating some form of colored beauty out of otherwise pale banality. But essentially, they were the same. Underneath the new layers. Still, there seemed to be something magical about ladies' rooms.

He didn't think that anything erotic happened in them.

At least not anymore.

When he was a teenager, he had been convinced that ladies' rooms were one big orgy, excluding the male race definitively. He had never had the courage to actually *ask* a woman in order to verify his assumptions, most likely out of fear that his fantasies would be confirmed false and laughed at by someone whose opinion mattered. Regardless, his mind had been clouded with images of leather-clad restrooms, with women lying in heaps on the floor. Then, after they'd had their fill of midmeal pleasure, they would straighten themselves up and join the males once again. Refreshed, rejuvenated, and coated with fresh lipstick. Smelling like perfume from department store counters. Hair freshly combed like the girls in the shampoo ads who he'd been ashamed to admit he loved so much. The girls always got to have all the fun.

But when Bea had come along, his bathroom fantasies had faded with her snappy realism.

He could never picture Bea joining in a bathroom orgy. He would've liked to, but he couldn't. He remembered the day the fantasies went away. Just like everything else that was fun, or naughty, or out of bounds. It all gave way to a more proper, censored version. *The acceptable route. Sometimes you just can't get it all back once it's gone.*

He desperately strained to hear moans through the door, but nothing was apparent except for the flushing of toilets, sinks running, and womens' busy chatter. He wondered if *she* was chatting. He had never heard her voice. Bea's voice was demure, indecisive, sugarcoated to hide the tartness underneath. He prayed that hers was very different.

He did have to get back to his table.

He had been here for what? Ten minutes? Fifteen? This was where gender determined what was and was not acceptable. This was not acceptable. A fifteen-minute bathroom break. For a woman, fifteen minutes is nothing.

She'd been in there for ten.

Beatrice

She was in the kitchen making breakfast for him again. And his tea was already hot at the table.

She looked back at his seat and smiled into the emptiness.

I'm such a good wife.

She was frying bacon. He loved bacon. He loved everything that the girls hated. Golf, meat, bicycles. And she loved those things just because of him. She loved them even more now that he was gone.

She remembered he hadn't phoned.

I'm sure he's all right. He has to be. People can't just die. I would've heard about it. The time change probably got to him. He'll call today. She felt like a teenager. She felt like she had when she'd sat by the phone as a girl, willing it to ring, hoping for someone, anyone, to think of her long enough to remember her phone number and actually dial it. And now she felt anxious like that again. Harry didn't seem like he was really hers; he felt like something that she wanted, but couldn't have. He felt like something that she was desperately trying to keep.

Do wives normally feel this way?

The thought had never crossed her mind before. She had never thought she was anything but the average, admirable, quintessential suburban housewife. She had never wanted anything more. She had never wanted anything else. Anything different or new. She had never dreamed beyond the boundaries of their town. Sometimes not even beyond the walls of the house. Had never asked Harry to move into the city. She had never drained her husband's pocket on the avenue, and had never embarrassed him in public. And for all of the things that she was doing correctly, at least in her own eyes, *this* was a new black cloud over her entire being. So constricted. So judged. So moral. So uninteresting.

Bea hardly ever asked herself if she was happy. Was she? *Am I? Yes. Of course. I could never ask for more. My life is perfect. Complete. And Harry loves me.* She'd given up her life for him. Not that she'd had much to sacrifice in the first place. But ever since she met him, she had always been willing to banish any part of herself that he didn't like to the furthest corners of the darkest closets. She was always ready for change for the better. She took his advice. She cooked his meals. He must be happy. *She* was happy. *She* felt complete. *How much more complete can you get? I have everything. I don't want anything more. Except Harry. I want Harry.*

Harry was hers.

But Harry *was* hers. By law. The papers said so. The pictures in their wedding album said so. The rings on their fingers said so. And yet he felt so far off. *It's because he's in Cleveland now. That's why I feel this way. I'm missing him. I miss him more than anyone. I love him more than anyone or anything.*

But he was not far off any longer. He was right at the kitchen table. Living there, and loving her. Just like things had always been. Just like things would always be. And in just a few days, he would really be there again. Sitting, sipping, reading. He would be there with her, and maybe she wouldn't feel so unsure. She wouldn't feel as if she had to confirm his presence all of the time.

Vivian

She wished it had gone over better. But what could she expect from Lilli? *What was that on her carpet?* Lilli wasn't exactly the most hygienic person in the world. In fact, Vivian wouldn't have been surprised if her sister had soaked right through her clothes and just hadn't bothered to clean up after herself. But she'd made an excuse. *Lilli would've been the first to say that it was her period if it had been.*

She ran her fingers through her hair again, and looked at her clean face. It was very clean. She'd worn the same makeup since eighth grade. The same drugstore staples: the chalky baby-pink blush, the vanilla-flavored ChapStick, the thick foundation generously dabbed on skin afflictions that needed hiding. She'd never really needed change before. And now she did. She thought of Lilli. *She wears eyeliner; black eyeliner. Not to look like a Goth or anything. It does make her look better though. What about lipstick? Red hair and red lipstick. Think about that!* And she did think about it.

She removed a black eyeliner pencil from her drawer. She was almost surprised that she owned something so dark. So dangerous and new. She remembered buying it. She'd worn it for Halloween the previous year.

But it wasn't Halloween. This was an average day in an average place. Just like every other day and like no other day. She didn't need a holiday to allow her to look different.

She drew a black line on one of her eyelids.

She'd never loved this feeling so much. Finally alive, encased in blackness, their drab sheath seemed to have fallen away and revealed a new luminescence. Finally, something about her could stand out. Two eyes. Two innocent eyes encased in black. Two virgin eyes pretending they'd seen it all. So deceptive, right? *I'll do this every day. Just like Lilli does. Lilli wears it, and I'll wear it, and it'll look great. I'll look great. Maybe I'll get a boyfriend now. Or at least a little more attention or something.*

She painted her lips crimson.

Suddenly, her face was alive and forbidden. Suddenly, her features exploded; not necessarily in a beautiful or professional or classic way, but in a way that made a difference. At least you could see them. At least they didn't melt into one another like a failed experiment. Something to be discarded in the trash.

She wondered if she had any black lace underwear.

Lilli has some.

Lilliana

She had come back from the music store, Max Records (the name sounded much larger than the actual compact store itself). It always made her feel so much better to go there.

She went on the days when she couldn't bear to come straight home. She didn't care much about her homework. Of course, she'd rather be blowing her money on music. But the merchandise wasn't the only reason she liked the store.

She'd never realized until now that she liked to go there because of Paul. That was because Paul wasn't classically good-looking, or reputable, or connected, or anything that she supposedly cared about or sought in a man. He wasn't the type that stood out much. And he wasn't arm candy. He was a little mysterious. Nonchalant. He had a way of looking past you when he spoke to you sometimes. This was not what she usually liked. She *never* liked these attributes.

Paul was smart, and he played in a rock band. He talked to her sometimes. He was just one of those guys who was nice to talk to. Lilli had never thought about manipulating him or playing games with him. She didn't even think that she could. He was in college. He was too smart for her. He could see right through her scheming little mind. She knew it.

He's just a guy. He's not cute even. I dunno. Not my type. Did she have a type? She didn't seem to go for one certain type of man. Well, there were the obvious requirements: slightly oblivious, completely enamored by her, highly attractive . . . Were those even valid qualities? *It doesn't even matter.*

Paul was nice. *Paul is nice.* That's what she thought. *Nice nice nice. Nice Paul. A nice guy.* And she never seemed to venture beyond that.

She looked down at the scab on her arm.

She remembered the previous night. And suddenly she felt very . . . remorseful. She wished she could pretend that it never happened. Take two hours and cut them up with scissors. Slash them sideways with the X-Acto.

She'd never felt this way before. She'd never felt rational. Maybe this wasn't rational. Maybe this was irrational. When had she ever felt sorry? *I don't feel sorry. I don't. I never feel sorry.* "I never feel sorry," she whispered as her eyes began to blur.

Harry

He was getting his things together. The briefcase seemed too small. He was nervous. Sweating. Things were slipping from his hands. His pen had leaked and stained his fingers black. He'd gotten a spot on his white shirt. He didn't like being jittery. Didn't like the adrenaline rush. *But this is your chance. You get only one chance. And this is it. This trip. It's your chance!* He liked working, but he didn't like when things were at stake. Big things. Things that meant something. Things that meant money. Money that would buy things and pay for things and make him feel guilty and greedy and gluttonous and happy all at once.

Hadn't been away on business in ten years. Hadn't been alone.

He'd had the chance. He'd had it before. The boss had asked him, and he'd declined. Because Bea had begged him not to go, held onto him, her solid fingers gripping his flesh firmly. Pleading with her eyes, her body, her entire being. Letting herself stay rigid for once. Saying, "Don't leave me. You don't know what will happen if you do. I can't do this alone." Silently, of course. Holding him close, making herself think that if she held him long enough, tightly enough, she would keep him there. And she did. *She did.*

So he hadn't gone. *Because I was scared.* She had made him afraid.

"You don't know what will happen if you leave."

And it was the truth. He didn't know what would happen.

But the girls had been young then. The future had seemed uncertain. Everyone had just been walking around unsure of where they were headed, and everyone had been in the dark and knocking into walls at full force. And everyone had been falling and crying and getting bruised. He couldn't have left then. But certainty was nice. *Because we all know ourselves now, and everyone knows what they're doing. There is no uncertainty anymore. There's no chance. It's just BORING.*

And he'd known what he was doing too, until now.

Because now there was a variable. An unknown that could fuck up everything and ruin the maps that had been so meticulously drawn for him. All set up and he just had to walk the trails. He didn't have to dig ditches for himself. He didn't have to find his own way through the woods.

But now, every time he thought of Bea, of home, his mind was blocked by *her*. Thoughts of her and a longing. A longing that hurt and bled like a wound. *I hope it doesn't stain my clothes. I hope it won't show.* Can't let secret wants become too obvious. There's a reputation at stake. There are so many things at stake.

If I'd just waited . . . He had had to get back to his drink. *You stupid fuck. You could've waited. You missed your only chance. Who even knows where she's staying? Who fucking knows?*

"You blew it, Harry," he whispered as he lay his head in his hands. "Fucking asshole. Fuck fuck fuck . . ."

Beatrice

He still had not called, and she was worried. Now she was not only sure that he was dead, but that he had died an even worse death than she had originally feared. He had been brutally stabbed, chopped up into a thousand irreplaceable pieces, cremated, and dispersed in a river or reservoir, but the authorities hadn't phoned her yet because they had not found the body. *Because there IS no more body.* She was certain of this. More so than anything else in her life at the moment.

They're not going to call me. They're just going to wait. This is what happens when you travel alone. Accidents happen. Horrible things happen. I never should've let him go. I could've gone with him. Taken a little vacation. No, no, no. I couldn't leave the girls here. Lilli would turn this place into a whorehouse if I weren't careful. I have to be careful.

Tears ran down her face, hot and feverish.

Bea hated crying. She hated it more than anything. She hated it more than tofu, more than soy, more than dirty underwear on her daughters' carpet. She tried to stop it. *Stop it. Just stop. You have to stop it now!* Yet every time she thought about Harry and his horrible death, she grew more and more inconsolable. "Harry!" She was whispering his name now. How could she have ever not enjoyed saying it? She'd tried to appreciate every single day he'd been there, from their wedding day onward. She'd smiled at the appropriate times, been congenial, hadn't done anything wrong. Or at least she didn't think so. "Harry! Harry, I love you." Her sobs became violent. Painful.

And then, she saw Lilli in the doorway.

"Mom?"

"Oh, Lilli, uh, I was just getting ready to make dinner."

"No you weren't."

"What do you . . ."

"You were crying."

"I have allergies."

"You were crying."

"I should really get some Claritin or something."

"The Claritin's in the cabinet. Not in the drawer."

"Oh, that's right. Whoops! Do you want tofu?"

"Duh."

"How do you want it?"

"Fried."

"Fine."

"Fine."

"Where were you this afternoon?"

"I was . . . at a friend's house. Studying for the . . . trig thing. The test."

"You know, Lilli, you shouldn't lie. I can see right through that little act of yours now. You should know better than to try it with me."

"I'm not lying. You can't accuse me of lying if you don't know the truth yourself! And I am telling the truth. I *am*."

"Well, if I catch you in a lie, you're going to be in deep trouble. It's not like I haven't caught you before, you know."

"Oh yeah? When was the last time you caught me in a lie?"

"When you said you were going to Jennie's—"

"Jamie's."

"Okay, Jamie's house for the weekend, and you went to that all-night teen club."

"Oh yeah, Mom, that was in eighth grade."

"And I wouldn't want to know what you're doing if that was how bad you were then. I can't imagine what you're doing with yourself now. And I am not gullible anymore. I know your tricks, and you will be very sorry if . . ."

"Oh great. More punishments. And now you're punishing me for things I didn't even do. You're accusing me of things that you don't even have a fucking idea about."

"Watch your language."

"It's just a word."

"A word with a disturbing meaning."

"It means sex. Is that disturbing?"

"I'm not getting into this."

"You know what? I don't give a fuck about . . ."

"That's it. I don't care if you're lying or not. You'll go upstairs and think over your language and your tone. You sound like you come from the slums of . . ."

"Slums of what? Now you're being racist and prejudiced!"

"How's that?"

"Okay, where's the largest African American and Latino population? In the slums, or more correctly, the lower district. And you're also being prejudiced against both of those minorities by directly associating them with the negative connotation of the word 'fuck.' That's only to you, by the way. Also, you're basically saying that we suburbans are better. And we're so not."

"Sure, Lilli, sure. You think that you just know everything about everything. You go on rambling about all of these . . ."

"That's because I'm right."

"And I'm not arguing anymore!"

"And I can't believe I have a racist mother!"

"I am not RACIST!"

"You are."

"I think it's time that you go and think over your—"

"This is disgusting."

"Get the hell upstairs!"

"Oh no, Mom. You swore. Now you're really going to hell. What an awful person you are!"

"Just go."

"Fucking hypocrite."

Vivian

She heard them arguing downstairs. The one thing she knew was that she couldn't ever be argumentative. She could never be argumentative.

She'd never had a fight like that with her mother. And Lilli had had about a million. They didn't seem to matter much anymore. They occurred almost as often as normal conversation. Maybe more often.

Couldn't stand up for herself yet.

She'd snuck into Lilli's room and stolen a pair of her underwear. The dueling voices downstairs had served to cloak her deed.

She had carefully stepped over the mounds of laundry, assorted wrappers, and magazines that formed a snaky obstacle course through Lilli's space. She had glanced at the stain but veered her eyes away from it. It had grown darker, more dry with time. She had noticed that Lilli had made no attempt to remove it. She had felt guilty slipping her hands into her sister's drawer. Smelling her sister's perfume, looking at the posters on her walls, her twisted untucked sheets. Yes, they were only a few feet away. Just across the bathroom. But it seemed so much further. The cold tiles had stung her feet on the way across. The three minutes spent in Lilli's room had felt like hours. They stuck in her mind like pins.

Vivian was a size or two larger, but she could fit into Lilli's underwear. *Something to work toward, a goal.* It was a black lace thong. She'd never worn a thong before. For some reason, it never made sense to her that underwear that covered half as much could cost twice as much. However, now she understood that aside from banishing worries of panty lines, it was the *feeling* while wearing thongs that gave them their allure. And that feeling was valuable enough to spend a few extra dollars on.

It wasn't comfortable by any means. It wasn't warm or soft. In fact it was pretty scratchy; it made her itch, even gave her a rash. Or at least it felt like one. But it wasn't the material that made it special. It was just the fact that it was actually a thong, and it was actually black, and it was actually lace, even if it was synthetic. Yes, it was lace. And the sight of her in this piece of lingerie didn't look anything like the girl that she had known.

What did women in thongs do, besides wear tight white pants?

She imagined Lilli, in her own bed. Lilli with some boy or some man pressed on top of her. His strange large hands slipping this underwear down around her ankles, then onto the floor. Or Lilli performing a striptease for a willing subject. Or doing a table dance. Or a lap dance. Or sandwiched in between a male and a wall in some dark club. Or bending over innocently while the thong protruded loudly and obviously over her jeans, creating a drastic image against the whiteness of her skin. This was not a mistake. Saying it. *This is not a mistake because I want you to think about me. And if you're not going to think about ME, at least think about my ass for a little, maybe even about how I'd look naked on your floor. . . .*

And it all happened in *this* underwear.

And now *she* was wearing it.

There was something disgusting about it. Something erotic about it. Something dangerous, and something strangely and unusually normal about it. It felt like growing up. It felt like moving on. A sort of rite of passage into womanhood. And it felt like the best feeling she'd felt in a long time.

Standing there in nothing but underwear in her room.

She had never let a boy see her in her underwear only. She was seventeen. *It should've happened by now. I should've at least gotten comfortable with the idea.* But somehow, she never had. Until now.

She wondered what it would be like to have boys up to her room. To have a male lying on her bed next to her or sitting in her desk chair. The last time she'd had someone of the opposite sex in her room had been for her science project, and there had been nothing even remotely sexual or even romantic about it. She'd felt nothing; he'd felt nothing. She hadn't daydreamed about the two of them lying down together after studying, or even flirting over their textbooks. And he had come and gone. The project had gotten an A–. And it was fine. Her room was probably the most chaste place she'd ever known.

Still, she couldn't imagine how Lilli could do it.

She couldn't see how Lilli could do it *and then feel nothing.*

Lilliana

Can that woman get a fucking life? Jesus Christ, she's so goddamned close-minded. She's, like, trapped in the fifties. She's just an airhead who thinks that she knows everything about everything. Fucking bitch! So what, I did lie. So? It doesn't really matter. I mean, I wasn't doing fucking lines or anything, I was at the fucking CD store.

She thought of Paul, and wondered why.

She wondered why thinking of Paul made her feel better all of a sudden. She'd just talk to him. He'd fix it. He'd help her. He could.

She smiled to herself as she got into bed. It was the earliest she'd been to bed in a while.

But then, she felt something against her leg.

It was something made of plastic. Something that crinkled and cracked as it was manipulated by her toes as she pulled it out from under the twisted sheets. It was the wrapper from a condom. For a minute, she just stared at it. Examined the way it had been ripped (with her teeth), and the colors of it (blue and white), and the warnings and the directions and the title and the name. She looked at all of these things, and then she felt the heat rise up in her eyes.

You know, you really shouldn't feel like this. Why is it that you feel so guilty all of a sudden? It's not like it's your first fuck. It's not like it even mattered to either of us. Maybe to him, but it doesn't . . . it shouldn't matter to me.

But her first fuck hadn't been anything either.

She wiped a tear off her cheek as she swiped a pair of scissors off her night table. *Now I'll have a good excuse. When it bleeds in the bed, I'll just say that I got my period.*

It took longer with the scissors. A lot more pressure, a lot more rubbing. The edges were dull and thick, unlike the skinny pin that delivered a quick sharp pain. But when the skin broke, the cut was deeper, thicker, redder. More exaggerated. More real. Present. Bleeding into the present. In it. More vivid than the brightest of the world's colors laying asleep next to one another.

She watched it spill out of her body and onto the sheets. *I've got to get over this remorse thing. I mean, since when have I had a fear of sex?* She picked up the phone. *Since when am I so into self-pity?* Looked through her address book. *The only way to get over this is to try it again. I just don't get why I'm feeling so guilty these days. It's not a big deal.* And she dialed Nathan.

Harry

He sat on his bed, his head throbbing, his senses dulled by alcohol, his mind pulsating red and black. Sipping slowly. Slowly so that he could feel the burn and taste every facet of the alcohol. It sucked into the cracks in his lips. *Even if things are common, there's more than one side to them. I like to think about that. There's more than one side to one-sided things. One-sided people too . . .*

His mind had been torturing him ever since. She was always there. His old ladies-room fantasies had returned, filled with pink toilet paper, full-length mirrors, and silken female flesh. He dreamt of what might've happened had he stayed.

And then he thought of Bea.

Bea, Bea, Bea. *I should love her. I'm married to her for Christ sake. She's crazy about me.* But when he pictured Bea, he was no longer attracted to her at all. He wondered if he ever was. And if he had been, he wondered what about her had grabbed him. Had it been her body? Her face? Her mind? She was no rocket scientist, no intellectual, no artist. She was no beauty, no supermodel. He could see nothing in her that he wanted any longer.

How had he ever loved Bea?

I know she's worrying about me. She's probably going nuts. I haven't called. I should probably call, just in case the girls are worried. She'd keep me on the phone forever though. And I couldn't stand talking to her for more than five minutes.

He wondered how he'd slept with her, how he'd looked at her, and watched her, and put up with her bullshit, and ate with her, and had never gone away before, and hadn't ever complained. He couldn't believe how oblivious he'd been. Marriage was simply a regimen; he'd fallen into a pattern that was easier to live with than live without. He'd been blinded by the monotony; his voice had been stifled, stolen by Bea. She was responsible; she was at fault. And so was he. He was too. Even if he couldn't see it.

He closed his eyes.

He tried to remember one time when they had all been happy. Each and every one. But he couldn't see them any longer. Their faces and bodies were faded, weathered. Their shapes were indefinite, constantly shifting. They were not the same people. New colorless silhouettes of people whose lives had come and gone, the shadows merging, giving birth to a new shape, a new body that was the future. And she grew and grew, and became more vivid and bright, and there she was. Blindingly beautiful, stunningly real. Immersed in her colors. More present even than the present itself. A fusion of past, present, and future. A new twist of lemon in his drink.

The fact was, she had pried her way into his life. The woman. She wasn't going to leave. Her influence was permanent.

I haven't made any Freudian slips, thank God.

He tried to think of how it had been before he'd left. When he'd thought only of Bea when he wanted love or sex—or anything else, like food and drink. When he'd thought only of the girls. Vivian and her mind, and Lilli and her problems. *Issues. She's got issues.* He'd once asked Bea if she thought Lilli should "see someone about, you know, stuff." Afraid of the word "psychiatry." And Bea had said no. He could see the pain in her face then. The fear. "Oh no, that wouldn't be right. It just wouldn't." *She'd said no because she didn't want to change things . . . how could she not see that she was hurting her? She's just afraid of everything.*

But the alcohol was bringing his mind to a focal point. And nothing could sway it. *I should be thinking about work. I should be thinking about Steve and the big fat-assed deal that I'm going to cut. I shouldn't be thinking about this . . .* person.

He decided to call home.

Maybe because he needed reality, even if it was inevitably disappointing. Harry knew what reality was, and what the reality of the situation was. Maybe Bea's voice would bring him back. Snap him out of it. Put him back on track and make him say, "This is it." In a reassuring way, of course.

He didn't even have to think of the number; his fingers automatically guided themselves through the necessary motions. He hadn't even heard a full ring; it had only just begun. He'd been looking forward to the lengthy sound that provided nothing except anticipation. He'd wanted to anticipate. And then there was Bea's voice on the other end.

"Hello? HELLO!"

"Hi, Bea."

"Harry?"

"Yep."

"Oh God, Harry! You have no idea! I thought, well, I . . . I . . ."

"I'm here; there's nothing to worry about."

"But, I was sure that you . . . I just . . . I thought that you were . . . Are you okay? Because—"

"Calm down, and pull yourself together."

"Okay, okay. Just give me a second . . . Okay, I'm a little better. How's Cleveland?"

"Fine."

"Is your hotel all right?"

"Yes, it's fine too."

"And the food?"

"The food?"

"Well, do you miss my cooking?"

"I guess so."

"I'll make a brisket when you come home. I promise."

"We'll see."

"It's your favorite. It is. Right?"

"Sure."

"Harry, if you don't like it anymore, I'll gladly make you something else. Just say so."

"It doesn't matter. Brisket is fine."

"As long as you're sure. If it's fine with you, then it's fine with me. . . . (silence) And how was your meeting?"

"It was fine. Just fine."

"Good. Well, I'm so happy that you're all right. I was so worried. Is the time change getting to you? I said it must be the time change."

"No, I'm fine with the change."

"Well, you didn't call. You haven't called since you got there."

"I'm calling now. I was just very busy."

"I know, I know. I'm being very selfish right now. I hope that you forgive me. I know you're very busy, and I'd be a nuisance if I bothered you. I hope you understand that I don't mean to be . . ."

"Bea, it's fine."

"Okay, as long as you—"

"How are the girls?"

"Well, I haven't really had much to do with Vivian—she likes to keep to herself lately—but Lilli is impossible, as usual. We had another fight. She's always been a little bit tougher to deal with, as you know, but never this bad. I hope that this is a phase, her and all of these boys."

"Why don't you tell her she can't have them up to her room anymore?"

"She does it when I'm out. I see these boys running out the back whenever I come through the door."

"Have you talked to her?"

"I can't talk to her. She's impossible."

"Well, it's a phase. Just let it run its course. She knows better than to risk her health."

"That's true. You're always right about these things, Harry. You don't know how much I miss you. You don't know how hard it is for me here, alone. It's as if I'm missing half of me! I don't know what to do with my time. I don't know how to deal with this sort of feeling. With being alone."

"Well—"

"And I hope that you aren't too lonely there either. In that hotel, all alone. It seems like we were never apart before, and now, all of a sudden, you're gone. I'm sure that you're lonely too."

"I—"

"You don't even have to tell me. I can hear it in your tone. I can sense it. That's what happens when you've been living with someone for almost two decades. You know them so well; you know how they feel. You know what they're thinking, even though they're not there with you."

"I'd really like to—"

"It must be so lonely with no one to keep you company. I guess when you're so alone, your mind just wanders. You just think of things that you never would've thought of if someone else had been there."

"Bea?"

"Yes, Harry?"

"I have to go now."

"Do you have a meeting to run to?"

"Well, no, but—"

"I know, the time change is tough, but you'll adapt."

"I *have* adapted, okay? I'm going now."

"I love you, Harry."

"I really have to go."

"Okay, I love you! Harry, why do you sound so—"

"Bye, Bea."

"Wait! *Harry!* Don't you want to talk to the girls?"

Vivian

She'd been to the mall and back in an hour. It was the latest she'd been out in a while. Finally, *defiance.* She'd gotten a ride from a friend, and now it was after midnight, and she'd spent her money. All of it, or at least most of it, on some things that were more valuable than the laptop she'd been saving up for. She hadn't even been close to being able to afford one; she'd only had a couple hundred dollars saved, and now there was only a twenty and a five, crumpled in her generic, synthetic wallet.

It hadn't been a waste though, because this was *a new life.*

Her mother hadn't seen her since she'd dyed her hair; she hadn't gotten the reaction yet, the threats, the dry forceful hands pushing dark brown dye back into her hair in quest of her natural shade. None of that had happened yet. And she'd taken care that it wouldn't happen for a while.

She wondered how much longer she could go without her mother knowing. She'd passed her a few times in the last few days, head cloaked in hoods or hair twisted on top of her head, stuffed under a baseball cap. She hadn't gone to dinner in a couple of nights; she would just call down the stairs that she'd eaten earlier. *Mom is so gullible! She'll find out soon though. Once she sees me walking around like this. She'll see it, and she'll have to love it. Whatever. I don't care anymore. I don't give two shits what she says or does. I'm almost eighteen. In seven months I'll be eighteen, and then I'll have the ultimate excuse for everything. I'll have an excuse for whatever I want.*

She took out the skirt, the pants, the shoes, the three tops, the new bra and underwear set. And she looked at her empty wallet again. She was happy. Just fine.

She slipped on the new clothes. The skirt wasn't short enough, so she took scissors and cut the hem at upper thigh, letting jagged chunks of thread and shredded fabric dangle where it had been forced apart. *I could get on my knees and . . .* She slipped on the shirt over her new lingerie. *Why should I hide myself . . . my body? It's mine to show.* And her shoes, higher than anything she owned. Made her legs look a million miles long. *Why didn't I ever do this before?* She ached to show herself. Present herself under soft lighting, hair burned straight, eyes, lips, cheekbones: all separate entities, all begging to be noticed. All colored by number. Arranged to create one package that screamed, "Fuck me! Pick me! I'm willing!" Speaking silently to the onlooker. "Please look at me! Want me! Take me! Kiss me; make me yours. I'll listen to you. I'm free, and I'll listen."

For once, she felt special.

I'll do what you want. I'm willing to try.

And she had barely eaten in two days.

It was a great feeling to know that she didn't need food. She didn't need to be like her mother; she wouldn't turn out that way. She wouldn't have saddlebags and flabby arms if she took care of herself. She would be skinny and sexy and beautiful in her new clothes, new hair, new makeup, new body, new person. A whole new mood.

It was all so easy!

It hadn't been difficult at all. In fact, she'd hardly realized that she was doing it until she had gone until four in the afternoon on a piece of toast and a banana, and then she just kept convincing herself that she was full and she was fine. She drank a little water sometimes. To trick herself. So easy to slip into. *Like nothing. Like getting undressed and actually liking the reflection.*

She smiled demurely at her new self. *Finally, much closer to perfect.*

Beatrice

He's alive! He's okay! And he's your husband! He's yours! It seemed that she'd never been so elated. She'd taken their conversations for granted, and had felt so sorry. No, more than sorry. She'd felt like the worst person alive.

But it was all better. For the most part.

She didn't care that he'd sounded rushed. She didn't care that the time change hadn't been the reason. *He'd been busy. He'd been busy making money. His mind was on other things. He had obligations.* And he'd been busy being loved by her.

Her entire day had become a million times better.

"Harry! Oh! You saved me! You saved my life!" She realized that she had cried this aloud, and she shot a look over to the kitchen door that was carelessly open, framing a slice of the immaculate dining room outside. Light flooded onto the floor. She ran over and shut it. The room was dark. The light was gone. Things were better. Softer. More forgiving. She was alone. They were alone.

"Harry, I love you. I love you, I love you!"

She walked over to the table.

Now I have him all to myself. I can talk to him all night. Harry's with me. He's right here, and he's with me.

"Harry, you're my husband, and I love you." She laid her head down on the table. "I just want you to know that." She couldn't even hear the back door open, through the soft, dynamic sounds of her own voice.

Lilliana

Nathan was twenty-two and beautiful. Most girls would think so, and Lilli surely did. That's why she'd invited him in the first place: he was beautiful and twenty-two. That was really his whole allure in a nutshell.

She'd met him at Club REfuge downtown, and he'd been in her room later that night. And before that, in the bathroom stall.

She'd seen his blond beauty first. The strobes coloring him in snapshots of pink, blue, white. His face. *The eyes. His eyes are nice.* And he'd been easy. Very. And she'd been drunk, so all of her inhibitions had been lost, if she'd had any to begin with. And they'd danced and danced. And then he'd given her his number to keep. For times like these. It had made her feel special that she could have such a pretty man. One that other girls would be jealous of. Seeing her fingers laced in his like that. Smelling him on her in the morning. Stumbling into class, twenty minutes late, remnants of Nathan clinging firmly to her clothes.

I used to call him more. I guess. But I need it now. I do. He came in through the back door, and went up to her room.

"Hey. Fucking short notice you gave me, huh?"

"Yeah, look, I'm sorry about that."

"Well, I guess it's not a problem. I brought something to spice things up around here."

"So now you only like your girls drunk?"

"Only sometimes. Take the edge off you. You know, I haven't seen you in, like, a fucking long time. And I haven't seen this fucking pink room. At one time, I really got to know this place."

"I know."

"Do you still keep your pot in your tissue box?"

"Uh-huh."

"Getting on without me, huh?"

"Sort of . . . But well, obviously not tonight though. I guess."

"See, I knew that you'd call me sometime. You just know these things. You get . . . What the fuck's the word? Instincts. Instincts. Or intuition. Whatever. I knew you'd get sick of those fucking high-school boys."

"Sure. (silence) That's good shit."

"I only ever get good shit, you know. I don't drink crap. You'll see, once you turn twenty-one, your whole life changes. Like, all the stuff you thought was so special—all the stuff you work so hard for when you're a teenager—it's just right there. You're allowed to have it. Everything is just not the same. Like, where does the fun go?"

"Oh come on, Nathan, you know I can get whatever shit I want."

"And that's only because you get it from me. Are you feeling it yet?"

"Sort of. Are you?"

"Hell no. I have, like, the highest tolerance ever."

"Well, isn't the point so we're both drunk?"

"No, the point is so you're drunk. It's better if we aren't both trashed, you know. I gotta take the lead anyway. Besides, I had a few lines earlier, so I'm going pretty strong and all. Booze wouldn't do much for me at this point."

"Fine, whatever. Can we just get started already? There's no point in sitting around like this. I mean, I called you for a fuck, not for a cocktail party."

"Just drink some more, okay? This stuff isn't fucking free."

"Okay, okay. I'm sort of pressed for time. You have to be gone by five in the morning. Otherwise, my mom's gonna have the biggest shit fit ever. Like, you don't want to see her that way."

"I'm not scared of your mother."

"Neither am I; I just don't think you should stick around here. (silence) And I think it's best if we get down to business right now, so we can have the whole night. Don't you agree?"

"Yeah, Lisa, I agree. Of course."

"It's Lilli. My name is Lilli."

Harry

In short, her voice had felt like hell.

He was surprised at this. First of all, he was married to this woman. And second, he'd never before realized that her voice was not soothing, or comforting, or even demanding. It was just hellish to listen to. Too hellish for him to even think of deciphering what she was saying.

It was the morning, and her voice had rung through his head all night. Ricocheting off the walls and cavities and taking all of the empty spaces and filling them up with her unwanted presence.

It had disturbed his dreams; his dreams from which he'd wished to salvage himself had now become the salvation that he sought. Bea's voice, a voice he had called on purely for medicinal purposes, for redemption, had done the opposite. It had done the complete opposite. He had no idea how he could bear to hear her ever again! He didn't even think he could say her name without it evoking feelings of something like remorse, and a seed of pure hatred that was so hot inside him that he grew afraid. Germinating and feeding off the newness.

This is not normal.

Harry picked himself up and went downstairs to a greasy breakfast buffet, where food was kept warm under heat lamps and disinterested servers stood behind large tins of hash browns or sickly looking waffles. Of course, he realized that his appetite was nonexistent. So he sat at his table alone, and drank unsweetened iced tea, and wanted to tear his hair out every second, because he could hardly stand the persistent thoughts, the new hatred, the new sounds. Two voices. Singing. One grows loud, and the other speeds up. One grows warm, and the other grows cold. One stays steady, and the other grows bright, louder, brighter, and . . .

He closed his eyes for a moment. And then Bea's voice faded and blurred until the heat was just a dull glowing warmth in the distance, and then eventually it faded to an icy coolness, which meant that she was gone. And the woman, the frigid woman, burning in her own insulated, self-absorbed passion, held a warmth that he knew only she and her lovers had ever felt. And he wanted to feel her warmth. He wanted to feel the skin and lips that radiated such frigid drafts, but held such a temperate climate, dormant within the confines of her exterior.

He wanted to discover this climate. This temperate paradise. Walk in it. Swim in it. Dig his feet into her sands. He could, and he would. And if she had been there, he would've lost his inhibitions, taken her in his arms, and ripped away her icy outer layer. Right there in the dining room. He would've loved her, declared his love to her, forgotten all of his troubles . . . But when he opened his eyes, all the warmth that met him was that of a greasy hotel pastry. And three empty seats, and a cup of iced tea, unsweetened.

Beatrice

She wondered how many mornings like this could go by; how many mornings like this she could stand. Last night's dishes were still dirty in the sink; she hadn't even had enough energy to put them in the dishwasher. She used to love washing dishes, cleaning things, neatening up, scrubbing, polishing. And the only reason she liked doing any of these things was to make Harry proud.

It was always about making sure he was happy. And she didn't mind. Her life had no direction without him as a target. She looked over at the sink wistfully.

Only Lilliana had been coming to dinner lately. She hadn't really worried about her other daughter's whereabouts, because she was the responsible one who never went anywhere other than the library or a lab partner's house. She'd never suspected that her daughter's three sequential absences from the dinner table had been due to anything other than a late-night study session. And most of all, she was sure that her elder daughter, who would never do anything rash or out of the ordinary, would pick up a healthy meal on her way home so as not to ask anything more of her mother than was necessary.

And then she realized that she hated talking to them. Her daughters. Harry's daughters.

She didn't really hate *talking* per se—it was the confrontational talking that she despised. She had never liked getting the girls together and lecturing them or asking them what was the matter. It wasn't because she didn't care, and it wasn't because it didn't matter to her; it was because she couldn't stand the reactions that were bound to occur after the initial questions had been posed.

She remembered talking to the girls when they were very young, about reproduction. She'd been in a sweat over it for weeks, and finally, the time came when she couldn't hold out any longer. She'd sat the girls down on the couch, and told them the facts. Straight facts with no stories of love or folktales about storks and wishes. But she had, in some way, managed to take all of the romance out of sex, and turn it into some sort of mechanical deed that even she was surprised by.

The book had told her that they would laugh. The book had said they might be disgusted. But they were neither disgusted nor giddy. Not even curious, intrigued, suspicious. *They were completely silent.* The two girls sat there and looked at Bea as if she were the most awkward, sickening human being alive. *They didn't say one word.*

She'd tried to diffuse the situation. She'd even laughed herself. But seeing the two sets of eyes on her, the two sets of frozen eyes, had gotten to her ever since.

She had been scarred forever.

She was sure she would not get this reaction now if she asked her daughters of their troubles, or confronted them with the facts of life. No, this wouldn't happen. Lilli would give one-word answers until Bea would get so fed up that it would escalate into a screaming match, while Viv would quietly give vague reasons why, or else she would hardly act surprised.

I can't ask Vivi why she hasn't been coming to dinner. I just, well . . . I don't know. I just can't. She wondered why she was so worried. Did she not want to hear the real reasons? Was she afraid Vivian would lie? *Lie? Vivian would never lie. She would never tell a lie. She's a good girl. I wish Lilli were more like her. Much more.*

But it wasn't urgent. She could wait until tomorrow. It could wait.

"Harry," she whispered as the air hit her pursed lips. "Please, just help me. Just tell me what to do. . . ."

And just as she got up to close the kitchen door, she saw a girl whom she hardly recognized. This girl was her daughter; this girl was Vivian.

"Oh my goodness, Vivian!"

"Um, Mom, what's the . . ."

"Your . . . you look like . . . I just don't know what to say! I just—"

"I thought I needed a change. Just something a little bit different."

"A little bit different? Now that is a gross understatement. Look at you! What are you wearing? And your hair!"

"I . . . well, I like this color."

"It's purple!"

"It is not purple. It's red. Just calm down, okay? It's not such a big deal."

"It is a big deal. My only daughter . . ."

"I am not your only daughter! You have two daughters. Lilli is your daughter too."

"I meant my only good daughter. You knew that I meant that. The only daughter who listened to me. Who heard what I said."

"I had to grow up sometime. I'm almost eighteen."

"Oh God! And Vivi, your skirt, it's—"

"I bought it myself. With my own money."

"You can almost see your underwear."

"You can not."

"It's practically see-through."

"No, it's not!"

"And what are those shoes?"

"They're just . . ."

"Your hair is not permanent, right? It washes out? One of those twenty-day wash things?"

"It is permanent, and I don't know what you're talking about."

"Oh God! Why? Can you just tell me why? You couldn't ask me first? You look like a whore."

"I told you, I needed a change. So I made it. And I don't think it really matters that much. Plus, I don't have to ask you for permission to change my looks. It's me we're talking about, not you, and I'm surprised that all you were interested in was how I looked, rather than how I acted."

"This *is* an action, Vivian! Dyeing your hair *is* an action, and actions speak louder than words. And this . . . this mess you've made. This mess of yourself! This is an action that is worthy of—"

"Mom, just chill out. This cliché bullshit that you're rattling off is ridiculous! I don't understand this favoritism thing you have going here. And I don't really understand why, as a seventeen-year-old girl, I can't have some freedom. I can't have some freedom to decide how I want to look. I deserve to have some say in—"

"It's just that I—"

"Mom, can you please not get so upset? There's no reason to be upset about it. I don't see why you're crying."

"But there is a reason! There is! You used to be so compassionate. You were the good girl. You were the one who was the role model. For Lilli."

"I never thought that I was much of a role model for her anyway. We're completely different."

"I know, I know. But I cannot, and will not, have my daughter walking around with her hair purple, and her skirt up to *there*. Forget it! One rebel is bad enough, and I don't need another one on my hands. Go back upstairs, and put on something more acceptable. And tonight, we'll dye it back. We'll pick a shade like your old one. It was so pretty, just like . . ."

"*I've had enough of this!* I am *not* a baby anymore. I'll dress how I like, I'll wear my hair how I like, and I'll do what I like. And if you think I am going to agree to any of your manipulative bullshit, I'm not. It's over. Done. I'm finished with taking this parental crap! And if you dye it back, then I'll come back with hair like you've never seen. I've always wanted to get it cut, you know."

"Do not even think of threatening me, young lady. And it's your own head that you're butchering."

"Haha! I love how you say that: I'm late already. Thanks a lot, Mom, for ruining my entire morning. And what is all of this food in here? You're cooking like Dad's home."

Lilliana

The day had seemed to go on forever, and now she was home. Faced with an unmade bed, dirty sheets, and the empty bottle from the night before lying uncapped on the carpet.

She felt no better.

The purpose of his visit had been to help her overcome her guilt, not to make her feel worse, not to exacerbate the situation. It had been bad enough before. She never used to feel anything but pleasure. She'd never felt remorse or disgust or dirtiness before. *Accomplishment. Why can't I feel accomplishment? I should feel accomplished. I got what I wanted. I called, and I got what I asked for.* She'd felt bad enough already, and now it had been two guys, only a few days apart, and she felt even worse.

Fucking whore. Maybe I really am one. Well, at least we used a condom. Right? We did, and it didn't break. I won't get pregnant or anything at least. I think I should go on the pill. I can go to one of those clinic places. I can get it without Mom ever finding out, and then I'll never have to worry. Or at least almost never.

She hated feeling this way. She hated feeling dirty.

It never used to be like this. She never even used to think twice about it. *Bitch.* She never even used to care. It used to be fun. Like exercise. Like a workout. There were cheerleaders, there were track stars, and there were people who were *skilled*. She was one of those people. *Motherfucker.* It never even mattered before. And now, for some reason, it did.

She looked at the sheets, twisted and curled, almost tied in knots. The room smelled faintly of Nathan, his cologne, too strong, that was stuck in the minds and bedrooms of so many girls. She was sure of this, and she wasn't the only one who was thinking of him right then. There were probably ten, maybe twenty, other girls, just like her, who were letting dreams of Nathan intoxicate them. Though she was far from intoxicated, and she was not dreaming.

Why the hell do you feel like this? What's with this guilt trip? So what? It never mattered before, and now it just made things worse. Why can't I just be carefree? Remember when I used to not care? It just didn't matter? Just as long as the guy was hot. That's what used to matter. Why can't things be like they used to be? Just hot bodies and hot guys and me. Us. Together. Just like it used to be.

She wanted to be like her old self. Somebody who didn't care, who'd say *fuck you* to anybody. Make people angry, shock them, snarl at them, flirt with and smile at them, stealing other people's boyfriends. *Only the bitches who deserved it.* Ruining things. People had called her selfish. *But they liked it.* No emotion had ever factored into the act, and she had always had complete control, absolute power. Selfish in it. Swimming in it. People were afraid. *But it was a good kind of fear.* She had been in charge, and she had liked it. And it had just been something meaningless. Less than nothing. A base pleasure.

But this was not the case anymore.

And she wondered why she was thinking of Paul.

Harry

The evening had draped itself over the city as he viewed it from his hotel window. He watched as dusk turned slowly into darkness, the streetlights turned on, the neon signs became more vibrant. Time to meet Steve.

Fucking bastard. Sick stupid fucking Steve fucking Verchon.

It all depended on how you looked at it.

He did up his tie, and finished buttoning his shirt absentmindedly. He mechanically rehearsed what he would say. What his client might say in return. He took his briefcase in case Steve might ask to see the plans, and he combed his hair, brushed his teeth, walked out the door, and watched as it clicked shut and locked automatically behind him.

It was a restaurant across town. Nicely decorated, with mediocre food, a good wine list. He waited a while by himself, and then Steve arrived, red-faced (he'd obviously been walking briskly), and brashly apologetic for his tardiness. He said he'd been "tied up."

Harry wondered how he could have such a dull job. He met with customers at mediocre restaurants, made small talk. He didn't really do much of anything. He just sort of sat there, and made excuses, and dined on the company account, and smiled, and laughed at the appropriate times. *Like a computer. I just do the same thing every time. I have the same reaction to everything. "That's nice, Steve." "Oh, sure Steve, we can work it out." "That's great!" Stupid fuck!*

But I can't be sick of it now. I've dealt with it for years. I've dealt with it, and now that I have the chance I'm getting fucking sick of it? This is stupid. Ridiculous. He closed his eyes for a moment. Let her image come into view, and then his eyes were jolted open by Steve's prying questions.

I have to have her.

"Harry? Helloooo?"

"Uh, yeah, sorry."

"You looked like you were about to doze off there."

"I'm sorry."

"You tired?"

"No, I'm not . . . really."

"Traveling makes it pretty difficult to get that shut-eye, right? I need at least ten hours per night in order to be at my peak. Of course, that rarely happens—"

"Yeah."

" . . . due to the various activities that I engage in during the night, y'know."

"Yeah."

"So, before we get started on this deal talk, I've got a little problem. Well, haha, it's actually more of a question. You know, truthfully, I hate talking about deals. I hate making them because I always feel like I'm making a mistake, and I hate making mistakes! We all hate making damned mistakes. But I know you wouldn't let me down because you're trustworthy and not a low bastard like myself."

"Okay, I—"

"You know, I like you. I like working with you, but you always seem so down! Might be all of that booze you drink, but what the hell are you so down about? I mean, a minute ago your head was practically in your plate, Harry. You're not fooling anybody. You're here in Cleveland on the company's tab. Why don't you just loosen the fuck up?"

"I try."

"At our meeting the other day, you stayed in the bathroom for over fifteen minutes! Hey, buddy, I don't know. That's just not normal."

"I know, I'm sorry. I got a phone call, actually."

"You AA or something?"

"No, no."

"Well, I was in AA for a while, to tell you the truth. I was! But let me tell you, it didn't work for me because I hate talking about myself. They make you do it, seriously. They do. It didn't help me a bit though . . . My AA buddies and I used to go get plastered before the meetings. I mean, *plastered*! Just throw back pints until six o'clock when the damned thing would start. And if you're a quiet drunk they just think you're really withdrawn. Thank God they don't test your piss 'cause Lord knows what they'd find . . . Anyway, yeah, I know, you've got the family at home. You've got your little wife and your little house and that's all nice. Don't you ever just let go though? You know? Go a little crazy, get a little messed up on something? You seem so damned straitlaced, I want to pry my hands into your fucking head sometimes. I mean, you're here, in Cleveland! Don't you want to just lose it a little?"

"Well . . . uh, not up until now."

"You drink, Harry. I know you like it . . . So tell me, Harry, do you like the snow?"

"The snow?"

"Yes, the *snow*."

"I don't really understand what you're talking about."

"You know, coke . . . cocaine, blow, whatever the hell you'd like to call it."

"Oh, no, I'm . . . not interested in that really."

"See, that's my own little present to myself. I look at myself, and I say, 'Hey, Steve, you're doing good. You deserve to feel good too.' So I throw myself a little party when I want to. That was a major problem in my relationships, because the bitches were always finding out and flipping the hell out and finding my stashes and flushing them down the damned toilet. But now the wife and I can get blazed together if we want, and she doesn't really give a shit. You know? She's looser and more easygoing, and it keeps the weight off her. Lord knows I hate fat women. It's better this way, if two people are into the same thing . . . Well, marriage, it . . . Well, fuck it . . . I can set you up with a dealer if you're . . . We could do a little partnership deal on the side, huh?"

"No, I'm really not interested in that . . . cocaine stuff. I don't like illegal—"

"Harry, buddy, you gotta trust me on this."

"Seriously, I can't."

"Or what about a girl? . . . Harry, it's all about release. Release your damned stress! You've got to be stressed. Look at your damned eyes, they're so . . . damned disinterested."

"But I'm interested. I am interested."

"Yeah, and I'm George fucking Washington."

"I am. I'm just—"

"I've got a number you can call. Any type of girl you want, twenty-four hours a day, open all the time. Wouldn't you like that, buddy?"

"Oh?"

"You interested, Harry? I see a little glint in your eyes now . . . I see what you really want. You wanna fuck some chick! You want some random good old bangin' in your hotel room. You want some pussy, Harry. And I don't blame you. I mean, I myself am known to—"

"Hey, I—"

"So you want some pussy. I should've known! I'm so stupid sometimes; it was staring me in the face."

"But Steve . . ."

"Hey, everyone gets tired of their woman sometimes. It's the way we're made. It's damned human nature for you. See, we're making a deal. And a deal is about a partnership, and I'm going to make a lot of money off of this, so you should at least get a little something else out of it too besides your little commission. I just want to help you, Harry."

"Why do you want to help me?"

" 'Cause partners help each other out. And we're partners. And I wanna see you being alert and happy to be alive on this damned earth from now on, 'cause we aren't here for long. And I want you to do the best you fuckin' can."

"But, Steve . . . it's not . . . Let's just start on the real business now. I've got a deadline to—"

"I've got a number. Here, take this card. Real good guy named Sergeant, and the girls are pretty clean. Do whatever you want, and you get to pick your type. You'd like them, and he's a fine bastard. Well, myself, I'm particularly fond of a little redhead named Velvet. Isn't that such a pretty name? Of course, it's a stage name because what bitch would really name her kid fuckin' Velvet? Right? Real petite girl though, and the wife never knows. Now that's one thing she wouldn't like. You know, she's all good about the drugs, but if she'd find me in bed with my little gal, she'd probably strangle me. Or she'd try. But Velvet, you know, she's just good for a blow job or two . . . or six, haha. You're welcome to use her if you'd like . . . After all, she isn't even mine to start with. It's like library books, videos; you just check 'em out and move on, 'cause if you wanted them forever, you'd just buy them . . . You just move on. . . ."

Vivian

She couldn't believe how she'd stood up for herself. It was already nighttime, and she had skipped dinner again. But she couldn't stop thinking about her triumph, her raised voice, her strength, her victory.

It was all hers.

Soon I'll be skinny, and beautiful, and colorful. It's time that I grew up. I showed her. She deserved it. Bitch.

It was new. Liberating. Life-altering. Beautiful. Different. Bittersweet. And there were only two things left to do. *I need to get new friends. And I think I should get my belly button pierced. Yeah. That would be hot.* She pinched the skin above the inward dip in the center of her stomach, and smiled, thinking of the tight flat abdominals and taut skin adorned with a tiny loop of surgical steel. *It won't hurt that badly. And it shouldn't cost too much. I can do it downtown, and I can go tomorrow. It shouldn't take long. Then afterward maybe I'll get a tattoo.*

She smiled at the prospects. The ideas, the lovely procedures that could shape and change her identity. That were permanent. That were painful. And whoever would've thought that she would go through with it? She, the girl who cried at the doctor's office, the girl who had no pain tolerance whatsoever, the girl who was allergic to bee stings. That girl had gone away, and here in her place was a new, good-looking, fearless girl who was willing to do something that would last forever, regardless of the means by which she had to achieve it.

Yes, she would go tomorrow, and smile at the blood and the sharp pain. Tomorrow she would be new. Tomorrow she would be a girl with artificial red hair, and good clothes, and a nice little ring through the center of her body. And she'd put on a sexual grin and lick her lips and pray that some man, any man, would notice.

And maybe then, I'll be better than Lilli.

Or at least more interesting.

Because she had gone through more. She had eaten less. She had tried harder. She had spent money. She had paid attention. She had become someone worth being. Someone with a life worth living. And maybe, for the first time, she would get some credit. She would be better. She would be first, not in her mother's eyes, but in everyone else's eyes. And maybe she'd be first in her own eyes too.

Beatrice

My only good daughter! The only one! Gone. Finished. Changed. Oh God! What did I ever do to deserve two rebels? What did I ever do? I've never hurt anyone or said anything mean. I've never stolen, or forgotten someone's birthday, or forgotten about school functions. I've never done anything to anybody, and look what I get in return. I get two impossible daughters. Harry? Harry! If you were here, it would be all right. If you were here, they'd listen. They'd respect us. They would be respectful, and understand how hard it is to be a parent.

And she wished that Harry were there, because if he had been, it all would've been fixed immediately.

Fixed.

She liked fixing things that were broken, things that were malfunctioning in some way. She wasn't the best at fixing things, but she did try. She tried like she tried to do everything else, but Harry was the best. He could fix anything mechanical, and he seemed to have a way of getting the girls to listen, or be quiet, or do what he wanted them to do, without the tedious arguments that were now becoming daily affairs.

Well, maybe this rebel thing is just temporary. She'll realize that it makes no sense to go around looking that way, and she'll go back. She'll become the girl she used to be.

She looked over at the counter.

She'd bought the dye in the afternoon, while the girls were still at school. *Just in case.* Just in case Vivian suddenly realized that she'd made a mistake and that her hair looked terrible, and that she wanted to change back to her old, average-looking self.

This seemed perfectly reasonable to her.

Bea wished she could tell Lilli that she had to respect herself, that she could get sick, or get hurt, or pregnant. That men don't like to date loose girls or, better yet, marry them. She wished she could tell Viv that she was turning out the wrong way. That she used to be such a good, nice girl. That she should come to dinner because she'd already missed three nights. That she shouldn't change. That she didn't have to change, because she could turn out so well. It wasn't too late. She could teach her daughters so much. She could show them how. Help them.

But she just couldn't do it.

She couldn't even talk to her own daughters. She couldn't even talk to them, let alone give them advice.

Lilliana

She had no interest in doing schoolwork. It was evening, she had two tests the next morning, and she had no interest in studying, thinking, or even acknowledging that she had any mandatory tasks to do whatsoever.

She'd bought condoms on her way home from school, just in case. *Just in case.* She used to use enough of them so no pack got too old. This was not so anymore. She wanted her old self back. She wanted the old girl, who could be used, and stretched, and accommodating, and malleable, and left on the street afterward, and not feel a thing. *And now I'm made of fucking nothing.*

And now she felt something. And it felt like guilt. Or at least what she expected guilt to feel like.

At least I'm not like my mother. Stupid pathetic shit.

She thought about Viv.

What's happening with her? What's happening to her? First her hair, and then her clothes. What next? A tattoo? She'll probably come back pierced and tattooed tomorrow. And then, Mom will really freak out.

She looked at her phone.

Maybe I should call Paul. Because Paul would know what to say, and know what to think. I could just talk to him about it, and I could just say things, and we could have a normal conversation, and I wouldn't have any pressure. But there was pressure. She wondered why her heart was beating so rapidly when she dialed the number that was scribbled on the back of a receipt.

"Hello?"

"Hi, Paul. It's Lilli."

"Oh, hey, Lil, what's going on?"

"Uh, I dunno. I just need to, you know, talk to someone."

"Well, it doesn't sound like anything good. What about?"

"Well . . . it's sort of confusing. God, I dunno, my mom and my sister are both going a little crazy lately."

"How so?"

"Um, my sister, Vivian . . ."

"The good one?"

"Yeah, the good one. Well, she's becoming Little Miss Rebel now."

"What do you mean?"

"Well, she's doing, like, the whole rebellion thing. She dyed her hair, and she's dressing like . . . I dunno, like me . . . but more fucked up, more pop culture. I think she wants to be a slut or something, but a very cliché one."

"Is that so bad? I like how you dress."

"You do?"

"Sure."

"But, I mean, it's a little weird. I don't feel like having her steal my stuff, and use my makeup, and—"

"Do you really think your sister would do that?"

"I . . . she—"

"I mean, has she ever stolen anything from you?"

"Well, no. I mean, not yet."

"So wait until it happens to get all riled up about it."

"Okay, I guess you're right."

"She couldn't be so different from you, could she?"

"She's completely different. She's my opposite."

"In what way?"

"Well, for starters, before this whole, like, metamorphosis of hers, she was a pretty conservative dresser, and a great, great student. And she didn't really date."

"What do you mean by 'date'? It's really a broad subject these days."

"I mean, no sex. And she may have gone out with a few guys once, but no one reputable or anything."

"And she's older than you?"

"A year older."

"Well, that only makes her what? Eighteen?"

"Seventeen. I'm sixteen, Paul! You thought I was older?"

"Yeah, I thought you were seventeen."

"And you're . . ."

"Almost twenty."

"Older guys are so much more . . . mature. I really prefer them to guys my age, you know. I mean, like, most of my guy friends are at least twenty or nineteen, and—"

"It's true. Same goes for older girls."

"You like older women?"

"Not older older. I mean, you know, you've at least got to be legal." (silence)

"Um, Paul, can I ask you something?"

"Okay."

"Do you sell?"

"Pot?"

"Yeah."

"No, not really."

"Yeah, well, neither do I; it was for my friend. She wanted an in."

"Uh, maybe my friend Barry at the store. Tell her to ask for him."

"Right, I will . . . So, how's college?"

"You know. It's all that I thought it would be. Really."

"That's cool."

"Yeah, cool. I switched my major."

"Oh you did? To what?"

"Philosophy."

"Oh! I always wanted to learn philosophy."

"It's really engaging. Very interesting. If you're interested in it, you might like to read a few of my books."

"That sounds great. Oh! I saw a flyer for your band."

"Yeah, we're playing Harvey's *in a few weeks.*"

"Wow, *I'll be there.*"

"Yeah, great. Well, I gotta go. My roommate has to use the phone. But I'll see you tomorrow at the store, okay?"

"Okay, thanks so much! I'll be by tomorrow. Bye!"

Vivian

She didn't have class until noon because she was a senior. Therefore, in high-school terms, she (and all the rest of the graduating class) was special. She had decided to go over to the mall as soon as it opened, and get pierced.

She returned home afterward, dazed, with a faint, dull, throbbing pain in her abdomen, and a nice surgical steel hoop with a blue cubic-zirconia "sapphire" screw on the end. The hole itself was also nice and red, and she thought that it was possibly one of the greatest things she had ever done.

She flounced onto her bed; her new clothes, and new shoes, and new face and new hair all landed on her mattress. She looked like a person now. A complete person. She yanked off her shirt. And stared at the beautiful piece of jewelry that adorned her flesh. *Soon my stomach will be really skinny and toned, like those models' stomachs. And then the piercing will look really good. And tomorrow I'll wear a really short shirt, and really low jeans, and then people will see it, and they'll realize that I'm not the girl I used to be.*

And this time, I won't show it to Lilli like some nerd. I'll let her see it herself. She'll see it, and she'll wish that she looked like me. You'll see.

Her stomach *hurt.*

But she liked the jewelry. She liked knowing it was there.

And she sat there in her new lace bra, her new metal-infused abdomen throbbing with pain and puss, and she laughed. She laughed as if she'd never experienced anything so wonderful, so funny, so exhilarating in her entire life. It was as if she were laughing for the first time—and it was as if she were laughing for the last time.

She twisted the knob on the bathroom door. To look at herself. In the light.

It was daytime and the sun was shining, but still her room seemed so dim. Too forgiving and lacking in truth. The mirror on her wall would not suffice for her self-examination. Her face. The bright lights of the bathroom would serve to magnify every flaw. *I want to see the truth.* She wanted to see the flaws. There were things that she had to see so they could be fixed. Things that her eyes didn't want to see on their own. But as she flipped on the light, she realized that the other door in the bathroom was carelessly unlatched.

A slice of Lilli's room was plainly visible. And Lilli was out and unaware. And the room was quiet.

Vivian walked across the cool tiles. Leaned her head out the door. Surveyed the space.

She still had her sister's underwear in her room. It had been worn now, and she would have to wash it by hand in order to prevent it from being returned to its rightful place. She was still curious though. *Shouldn't sisters know each other?* But her eyes caught the black stain on the floor, still uncovered. She saw an empty bottle of liquor lying uncapped on the carpet. She saw fresh blood on Lilli's bedsheets. She saw a box of condoms unopened.

She slowly returned to her place in the bathroom, under the magnifying mirror. She closed the door that led to Lilli's room, listening to the comforting click of the latch. *But I don't want her to know me either. I don't want her to judge me. I don't need any help. I don't want to lose my own identity.*

Harry

He'd decided to take a walk. The hotel room was stifling. Too cold. Too dry. Windy because the air vents pointed directly at his bed. Stuffy because it was small. Always something wrong with it—and the temptation! The minibar. *Make me fat and drunk.* He'd never though of himself as a man who liked alcohol. He hadn't drunk heavily since high school. He'd never even taken the "edge off" in the evenings after work. There had been no desire for it. He'd needed no escape, no release. He'd just dealt with things. He'd never needed any aid.

Now he did. He really did. Because he didn't feel like knowing himself anymore. Even Steve had seen it.

Harry liked the dullness. The blur. Confusion, confession. *Maybe it can bring out the truth. Maybe that's what realism is. Maybe I need to be drunk to speculate.*

Maybe I need to stop being so damned predictable. I don't like it when people can read me.

Functionality. He knew it well. Knew what he had to do at home to get through the day, the night, the half an hour spent at the dinner table, the time spent in front of the television, the time spent in bed. He knew the script and the stage directions and the cues and even what to do if one of the actors failed. Messed up. How to recover and conceal it and make believe it never happened. How to convince the audience that this is indeed what would happen every night. Every single night, things like this would happen. He knew the basic themes and the certainties and the uncertainties. *Where's the unpredictability? Where's the variation?*

What's the point of even being alive if there's no guessing involved? *If it's all fucking reflexes? There isn't any thought.*

Maybe there's not supposed to be thought. Maybe humans really are creatures of habit.

But now I have something else. There was something else to which he did not quite know how to react. *And she is perfect.* Beautiful and forbidden and everything and nothing all at once. And fantasies were new. New phenomena. A dangerous new land of dreams: a boundless universe of possibilities, lacking the disappointing practicality of probabilities.

He turned a corner.

Just once. If I could have a woman like that just once . . . maybe going back to Bea wouldn't seem so bad.

But as of now, he didn't want to turn around. He didn't want to move backward and worry and start up again. He was fine with the present. He liked walking alone in Cleveland. He liked to drink. And he liked women. *The* woman. And he wasn't so sure about anything else anymore.

And he could feel the presence of the card in his pocket.

He could make anything a reality. He could try.

He could try and forget, revel in the fact that he was by himself. At least for the time being.

He was theoretically alone, but he wasn't really. He still had a wife. He had two kids. He had responsibility. He had people who counted on him. His salary went to buy food, school clothes, and gas for the family car. It went to charities and other such functions. Insurance on two cars, the renovation, and putting this much here and there for this and that. Pointless, wasteful things. Wasteful people. It really wasn't *his* money. He just earned it. He just earned it, and *they* spent it.

He was chained by marriage. He was chained by fatherhood. And he wished he could be free, because he couldn't remember the last time he had been. He couldn't remember the last time someone hadn't run his life.

But even if he didn't have a family, even if he had opted for the life of a bachelor, he wouldn't be completely free. He would be governed by law. By rule. He would have obligations. He would have taxes, and bills, and insurance payments. He would never ever live a life free of worry, free of stress, free of commitment.

He wasn't free, because the *woman* had taken charge. She had taken his mind and turned it into her personal breeding ground. "You're very greedy."

And he didn't know whether he was talking to her, or talking to himself.

Beatrice

She couldn't cook. The kitchen that used to be the antidote for all her troubles, now seemed to be the problem itself. She had always taken joy and pride in her cleanly scrubbed kitchen with its white wooden cabinets and smooth countertops. Whenever she lost her place in the world, she always found it in the kitchen. She could provide for her family, for herself, and reassure herself that she was indeed needed.

If I weren't here cooking and cleaning, nobody would do it. That's why I'm important.

That's what she usually thought.

But tonight, Bea didn't seem to care who cooked what, or how messy the sink got, or how much grease was caked on the stove. She didn't feel like chopping and washing, and clanging and banging around. She was finished. Done. She would not do it. It was the last straw.

She was going to order Chinese food.

Nice and easy. Chinese food. Tofu for Lilli. Chicken for Vivi. Egg rolls for me. And pork for Harry. And we can have those dumplings that everybody likes. She swung around to the chair at the table. "Harry? Is that all right with you? Do you mind if we have Chinese food? I'm a bit too tired to cook tonight." She smiled at the response that was only audible to her.

When the food arrived nearly an hour later, she set out four place settings, and called the girls down for dinner.

Then she called again.

And again.

But no one came.

She looked at the greasy food, all in the same sauce, all deep-fried or deeply sautéed. And she wondered why no one came to dinner anymore. They wouldn't listen. They wouldn't come when she called.

They probably wouldn't even come if I were choking, or dying. They wouldn't even come downstairs. They're just too busy with their own little lives and social events and boyfriends and clothing. They're too busy for dinner. Too busy for a goddamn fifty-dollar Chinese dinner! A fifty-dollar Chinese dinner!

"Harry? Why can't you make them listen? They don't listen to me anymore.

But they listen to you. They always did. I need your help. I can't do this alone."
She paused again, and sat down in front of her plate.

"They always used to love Chinese dinners. It was special. They would get excited. They would be happy about it. Remember that? You do remember it, don't you, Harry?"

The silence stung her ears. Though somehow she was able to weave his response out of the whir of the ceiling fan, the hum of the air conditioner, the distant sound of a lawn mower far down the block.

Lilliana

She'd heard her. She'd heard her mother call their names four and a half times. (She'd stopped midsentence on the last call, as if her frustration was too much to bear. *As if her breath had been too precious to waste.*) Lilli just didn't feel like seeing her mother again that evening. *I can't fucking stand that woman. When I get out of this house, I swear I'm never going to visit.*

Lilli was still happy from her conversation with Paul, and she didn't feel like ruining it so soon afterward. *I'll go down later. I'll go down after she puts the food in the fridge and goes upstairs. Then I'll go and get it. I like it better cold anyway.*

Paul hadn't even said he was interested in her. He hadn't even *invited* her to see the band.

Suddenly, her mood turned sour. *He barely even complimented me. Sure, he likes the way I dress. But that doesn't mean anything. He should've said he liked the way I looked. That would've meant something. Fuck. He could like the way Madonna dresses for all I care, and it wouldn't mean a thing. He hardly even . . .* "Fuck, you are such a loser." She whispered it under her breath. "You bitch."

It was time to find something sharp. Something that caused a nice amount of pain, a nice clean break in the skin. She frantically rummaged through her desk drawers, turning down the promising offers of pencil points (danger of graphite getting stuck in the wound) and bypassing paper clips (too weak). And then, she found it. In the bathroom, still wet from her last shower, was her razor. Slick with water and smelling of floral shaving gel. There were still bubbles on the metal.

She wasn't going to cut her wrists. *I couldn't ever do that. I don't really want to die yet.* But she admired how the three blades when scraped across the skin at a certain angle would cut three times as much. *A time-saver too. Why didn't I ever think of this before? It was right here all this time. Screw belt buckles. And scissors. This is perfect.*

The tile of the bathroom floor was icy against her skin as she slid all the way down into a comfortable position. She moved the bath mat out of the way with her foot. *I have to be more careful now. I have to do it on the tiles so it won't stain, and I can just wipe it up. Vivi is onto me. She knew what it was the last time.* She stretched out her leg and put her foot against the door leading to Vivian's room.

The double-doored bathroom had never been a problem until recently. In the last couple of years, the girls had become more conscious of their own territories, and privacy was essential at nearly all times. They hadn't even had locks before, when they'd first moved in. They hadn't needed them. They'd been young, and it wouldn't be the end of the world if Lilliana walked in on Vivian when she was on the toilet, or if Vivian walked in on her when she was in the shower.

It just wasn't a big deal.

But eventually, random walk-ins became grounds for verbal battles that occasionally escalated to the point of hysteria, and that could even become physical on days when the girls were particularly on edge.

They became resourceful. They wedged towels under the door, they dragged in desk chairs while they were taking showers and propped them under the doorknob. They stretched long rubber bands from the doorknob to the sink handles, wrapping them around each piece of apparatus several times.

And it did help, although arguments were not prevented by these attempts. If anything, they simply prevented arguments *in* the bathroom itself. But if someone was careless, tired, frazzled, late, rushed—intrusion was nearly inevitable.

But, the funny thing was, they hadn't fought in a while. Yes, they'd had confrontations, but they hadn't *had it out.*

In fact they hadn't really talked in while, and even a turbulent screaming match would've sufficed as some communication. They'd never been close though. Even as kids, they'd always competed, always fought, bragged, told each other's secrets, spoiled each other's fun. Just two jealous girls, jealous and competitive and spiteful. Outwardly so, not even attempting to hide their contempt.

It was nothing new though, so it didn't really matter at all.

And suddenly, she felt so much better. Prettier, nicer, more competent. Perfect.

She looked at the three symmetrical lines that boiled over with newly oxygenated blood that rushed hurriedly to the surface. *Oh God! This is so much better. It feels so much better. It makes me forget things. A high. Almost like being drunk. But better.* And when it started to run down her arm onto the tiles, she smiled at the ruby redness against the porcelain white. Her foot pushed firmly against the door. Her toes curled with the effort.

Her forearm started to throb, and the cuts were not scabbing. They hadn't even stopped bubbling over with the new blood that was always so nice to see at the start. The relief began to subside, but the blood did not. *Maybe it's a little deeper than I planned. No big deal. I'll just sit here for a little bit longer, and I'll just wait it out. It always stops after a while anyway. It's special. More special. I should be happy. Appreciative.*

She didn't realize why she was worrying in the first place. She was always so sad when the blood stopped flowing and the darkness of a new scab appeared in its place. Why was she worried then? Why wasn't this time the same as all the other times? *This is just like always. I've never had an accident.* But it just wouldn't stop.

And the floor, which had looked so nice, shining with splashes of crimson and occasionally larger round puddles of it, had now gone above and beyond what she'd expected. It had become excessive. Too much of a good thing.

The little pools of liquid had now expanded beyond safe parameters, blending together to become a shapeless mass of red. *Oh my God. I must be losing a shitload of blood now. Just breathe, don't worry, don't worry. It'll all be okay. It'll stop.* She yanked a piece of toilet paper off the roll to hold onto the wound, and she'd hardly even touched her skin when the paper was already completely stained. She threw it in the toilet.

Shit shit shit shit shit! Now what? I can't use a towel, Mom will catch me, or Vivi. I can't throw a fucking bloody towel in the laundry! She grabbed more paper frantically, as it soaked up color and was thrown away.

The puddle had grown larger, the toilet was full of bloodstained paper, and the wound had not begun to heal. She was feeling light-headed. Her hands were dripping with red. Her eyes were beginning to flutter closed; her vision had blurred. *I don't know if I want to bleed to death here. I don't think I want to die on this bathroom floor. I haven't gotten married yet, or even had a guilt-free fuck in a while . . . I just . . . I . . . I'm just gonna take it then.* And she grabbed a bath mat, and pressed it squarely over her forearm.

Vivian

It was funny how the world had evolved so much in less than two hundred years. In the eighteen hundreds it was a sin for a woman to reveal her anklebones. Bathing suits and pants were for men only, along with comfortable shoes and jobs in places other than factories. Up until the nineteen twenties, womens' waists were compressed by the oppressive corset, and their torsos were not freed until the womens' rights movement. With voting rights and world wars, dress codes became more lax and geared toward comfort and work rather than social stature. And until recently, anything even remotely sexual in the family entertainment industry was prohibited, all of it replaced with chaste, closed mouthed kisses and twin beds in master bedrooms. Slowly we evolved from the tulle skirts of the fifties, to the mod geometric colors of the sixties, the shimmering glamour of the seventies, the drug-infused club life and cutoff dance wear of the eighties, the colorless nineties, and the millennium, which so far had lasted only long enough to be characterized as either a plastic pop culture or a rebellious transitional phase.

Vivian decided that she would rather shape her generation's classification than embarrass her future offspring.

Thus, by classifying herself as a 'rebel', she had made it completely acceptable, even normal, to get a body piercing. She was part of her generation, and this was what they did. *This is what we do. My generation and me.* She had mapped the entire argument out in her head, and was almost positive that she could both justify her decision and confuse her mother with a few deft words of teenage wisdom.

The same argument could apply to her self-declared dress code.

She was still awestruck by the nice piece of metal impaled through her skin.

I can't believe that I did it. I actually fucking did it! And I'm not even thinking of taking her shit anymore. Fuck her! Wow, it feels so good to be me right now.

Vivian was thinner now too. At least thinner than she had been.

There weren't any scales in the house, because when Bea had started gaining weight, she grew depressed by the gradually but steadily increasing numbers that never failed to ruin her evenings. The only answer was to get rid of the cause of the problem altogether. Thus, the scale was promptly disposed of. Leaving all family members to determine their weight loss or gain by the fit of their jeans.

Bea wore "comfort waist" pants, with pieces of elastic on either side of the waistband, so she wouldn't be burdened with the struggle of buttoning herself into her gradually tightening pants every morning.

Problem solved.

Bea preferred dresses anyway. Dresses because they were just so feminine and pretty.

But Vivian knew. She knew because it wasn't only the waist of her formerly skintight jeans that no longer seemed to grab her the same way—it was the leg too. And when the leg felt loose on just-washed jeans—they always shrunk because Bea dried them on the hottest setting—Vivian was sure her skipped meals had paid off.

This was a strategy. There was a master plan.

She now ate half an apple for breakfast, the other half and a cup of tea for lunch, and two saltines for dinner. *This is how all of them eat. This is how the models eat. This is how the girls who get all of the guys eat. This is how Katerina eats. And if I ever want to look remotely good, if I ever want to be friends with her, I have to do more than pierce my belly button and dye my hair. I have to get skinny. You know. Really.*

And tomorrow, I'll go to the school nurse and get weighed on a scale, for real.

Tomorrow, tomorrow. She was falling in love with herself. What else could she change? She'd changed all outward things. She'd fixed her unruly hair, she'd elongated her unnoticeable lashes, she'd begun to show off her legs in tiny skirts and her toned arms in skimpy tank tops. She'd stopped shopping for practical reasons. She'd bought lingerie in patterns, fabrics, and colors other than white cotton. She'd pierced her belly button. And yet there was something else. There was something else missing from the near completeness of it all. She just wasn't sure what it was yet.

Harry

He looked at the glass of vodka that sat on his night table. Perfectly translucent, the curvature of the glass warped his view. He'd never quite understood why he'd chosen vodka as his "poison." It was a sexy drink. Something pure and mystifying and sane-looking all at once, harboring a perfect hidden potency that stung his lips like venom. Deceptive in its clarity. Especially when his parents had been around. *Goes down easier than water.* Even if it did bring tears to his eyes sometimes.

He stared at the business card.

Sergeant. Jesus. That was all it said: "Sergeant," with a phone number on it. The card was black though; the writing was white print.

"I can't; I just can't."

But he still wanted something else. He wanted it so badly. Clutching his drink, he stared at the wall. But her form kept coming into view. He closed his eyes. In his mind she danced. She danced and spun, whispering something, beckoning. Come closer, Harry! You know you want to. Reaching out her arms. "I *don't* want to!"

He wished he didn't want to.

I have to keep things going. I can't lose it. I can't! There was too much on the line. Too much that was resting on him. There was money involved; there were people involved . . . He was so close to landing something with Steve, things were falling into place, he had the girls, and there was Bea . . . *I can tolerate it. I can . . . What would happen if I just stopped?*

"You don't know what will happen if you go."

And the rewards for his work would surpass any small encounter he could possibly have. A promotion! A better life, something great and new and extravagant. But he'd been so disgusted, sick, tired of it. Tired of taking crap and being normal and having things always work out. *Things don't always have to work as planned.* It's okay if things get fucked up a little bit.

Because his life was full of handshakes and winks and nods and smiles and agreements and practical reasons *why.*

Maybe, if he let himself, just once, *she*'d go away. Maybe if he could get her, she would expel herself from his system. Possibly, if he just spoke to her . . .

just had a conversation with her, it would leave him. A phase. *Adults can go through phases. Just like teenagers.* Maybe he would realize that she wasn't what he thought she would be. That no one could be *that woman.*

But he was not intoxicated enough to gather up the courage to make a decision, or actually call the number on the card and speak to the mystical Sergeant. Even if he did want a girl to screw, it was the *woman* that he wanted. He was not looking for a whore; he was looking for a person to fill a void. But looking for her had been so difficult . . . *I'm not sure what's real anymore. Did I even see her? Did I even leave home? Where am I? Sometimes I open my eyes, and I don't know where I am.* He'd been trying though. He'd been asking around. He'd called the restaurant for her name . . . *I'm going to call again.* But there was little hope. He took another sip. He ordered another drink.

He *tried* to make himself smile at the thought of Bea. But he couldn't.

"*Fuck you*, Bea! It's your fault that I'm in this position. It's your own fucking fault. If you were just more stable . . . If you hadn't said some of those things just to make me feel that way . . . if you could be on your own . . . things would be different. I would've gotten used to this by now."

But her body! Her face! Her demeanor! It all made him think, *what a fucking mistake.*

He wanted to think of home as a place to which he could return and feel satisfied.

Because he'd left so much behind. And he'd seen things and heard things and known things that he'd had no intention of knowing. And he knew there was so much more. He knew that the people in his family needed his aid. *They need me.* He knew they would falter without him there. Stumbling and slipping and selfishly stating points with eyes and ears shut tightly against one another. He was not disinterested; he was just afraid. Too intelligent maybe. He liked how the alcohol dulled his perception. He'd never been a drunken philosopher.

He pinched the card between his fingers. The paper was thin, cheap. Almost as if the heat of his hand could dissolve it into a missed chance.

He didn't want to admit that it was his fault too.

He ordered another drink.

Beatrice

She had lost all power over anything and anyone.

The girls did not listen to her, or care, much less praise her effort and her daily duties of cleaning, making beds, and providing dinner every night without fail. That was Harry's job. Harry's job was to give her praise, so she could be sure that she was doing an okay job.

Okay is good enough. It's all I need. As long as I'm on the right track. I can always improve.

"Harry? Doesn't the carpet look cleaner to you?" "Oh . . . yes. It looks nice." "Nice? Do you really think it looks nice?" "Yes, it looks very nice." It was those typical everyday conversations that she missed, those pleas for praise, those probing questions that could only be answered with empty compliments lacking any enthusiasm whatsoever.

More than anything or anyone.

They kept her going.

Literally.

They reinforced her desire to do good, because "doing good" meant making Harry happy. And that was all that really mattered. And nothing really mattered now that he was gone.

My husband is in Cleveland, Vivian has turned into a nightmare, and Lilliana has taken every opportunity she could to fornicate under this roof when I happened to be out. Bea sighed. And got into bed.

She couldn't do anything.

They'll never change anyway. I'm not . . . I mean, I can't approach them. I know it will just drive them on to worse things. I'll just leave it be. I'll just let it be, and let things run their course and sort themselves out. There's no use trying to fix things that . . .

Her mind froze for a moment. And she realized she had not spoken to Harry in a while. She hadn't spoken to him, and she hadn't tortured herself about it, and she felt unexplainably guilty. *I'm so bad . . . I . . . How can I forgive myself?* She flipped off the light. "Harry," she whispered slowly. "Just listen. No! Listen to me. I'm so sorry; I was too focused on other things to worry about . . . You don't understand. You're not listening to me! Just let me speak.

Okay? Okay. I love you, and you know it, and I need you. More than ever. I love you more and more with every year, with every day, with every anniversary, and every glimpse of you. Things have only improved since we married. I've found you, and you're the one. I knew it from the first time I saw you at the party. I knew it from the moment you touched my shoulder, and I knew it from the moment I turned around. I always knew it, and you knew it too. See how perfect we are? I always thought we were perfect together. You make us perfect. You're the perfect husband. The best, most faithful, most perfect, most wonderful husband in the whole entire world. In our own entire world. You are the world."

Lilliana

She'd sat in her room nearly all night, clasping the bloodstained bath mat to her forearm and praying that she wouldn't pass out. She gasped for air; every breath was hopeful. *It's okay, it's okay. Shhhh. There's no reason to be afraid. You can just put a couple of bandages on it.*

When she removed the towel, she looked at the exhausted wounds. They still harbored blood and pain, discomfort, and death, but they had ceased bleeding, and simply sat as dormant crevices that dug deep into her flesh.

She ran her arm under cold water and then used six bandages to dress her wounds.

"Oh God." She wondered how she could've cut so deeply with a simple razor. A household item. An item she used so often, with caution, but with fearlessness. But it could cut so deeply; it could kill so fast, so painfully fast.

Guns are household items these days too. Yeah, people have fucking rifles. So, duh, razor blades can be sharp. It's not a big thing. But still, the fact that something so familiar could cause so much self-inflicted damage to her perfect, slender, and smooth arms, seemed to catch her off guard.

She looked over at the bloody mat.

Shit. SHITTTT! She grabbed it, and examined it. *Jesus Christ, I must've lost a lot of blood.* She held the mat up vertically, and realized that only a few small portions still retained their pristinely bleached clarity. *I have to do something. I have to wash it or bleach it before anyone notices. I'm dead if someone does. There's almost no excuse for this one.*

She hurried down to the laundry room in the basement, and looked at the bath mat one final time before she threw it in the machine. Then she thoroughly scrubbed her bloody hands. Why was she feeling guilt *now?* It was her blood that was swirling away down the drain, and her blood that would be covered and strategically concealed with that burning whiteness. She was no criminal.

She dumped in three cups of bleach, turned on the machine, and ran out of the room.

She thought of Paul all the way back upstairs, and in her room, and on her bed. She thought of Paul in his room. She thought of the compliments that he never gave her. The compliments that he should've given her. *There's something else about him. Something different. But he's a friend. I don't even know why I like talking to him so much anyway. Usually I fuck off my troubles. Oh well, it doesn't really matter. Nothing really matters, I hope. I think.* And she slowly peeled at the bandages until her artful mess glared up at her angrily. She was filled with newfound pride.

Vivian

She tried to sleep but couldn't. Her sister had been clanking around downstairs for a while, and Vivian couldn't stop touching the jewel in her stomach. The day had replayed in her mind, repeating and rewinding to those beautiful moments of perfection and bravery.

She looked down at her underwear.

It was crimson lace and she was in bed. It was a thong and she was in bed. It didn't really make sense to wear fancy underwear to bed alone, and she most certainly was. Alone. It wasn't comfortable. No one could see it. No one cared what was underneath it. She was alone. Sleeping in her fancy underwear, and praising herself in a way.

But no one could share her triumph. No one could share her needs, her wants, her feelings. Nobody could talk to her anymore, and she couldn't talk to anybody anyway. At least not there. She had no boyfriend. No one to share anything with. No one to share herself with. She couldn't talk to her sister, who was constantly outdoing her in all areas in which she wished to succeed. No one to praise her, or punish her. She realized that no one had any power over her anymore.

I'm practically eighteen, and this is how it should be. I guess I should stop relying on people. I guess that loneliness is just something you get when you're an adult. You just learn to deal with it.

I wish I had a sister I could talk to.

Stupid, stupid fanciful girl. You don't.

The past was full of broken promises. Lilli's pretty smile and shining eyes just aching to break Vivian's soul. And they did. Of course, she got away with it.

Maybe not a sister. Just a best friend.

She could hardly remember how her old undergarments used to feel. Clean bleached cotton against her clean white skin. It was as if she had buried all memories of the time when she had conformed. When she had willingly become the girl who stood alone. And now she wanted friends. Because she wanted friends and boyfriends and best friends and to be liked, loved, emulated, taken advantage of, and hated by those who just didn't have enough power.

She didn't know what comfort meant.

Beatrice

She had never before felt that she couldn't get out of bed.

It was as if her legs refused to move, her eyes refused to open, and her mind refused to let go of her beautiful dreams of Harry, paralyzing her in bed.

She'd heard the alarm ringing for nearly four minutes, and still she couldn't get up. She couldn't remember the last time that she had let it ring more than a few seconds before rushing to shut it off so as not to wake him. And then, she would tiptoe downstairs and feel happy that she could make her husband happy with a smile and a plate of warm food.

I have to get up. Come on, Bea, get up now. Get up now . . . She sighed. Reached over and shut the alarm off, revealing the silence that had been hiding behind it so slyly in its grace. She could almost hear his breathing.

She knew his breathing like she knew the exact shade of the kitchen tiles; she knew it like she used to know how many pairs of underwear each of her daughters owned, and exactly what time they had each been fed when they were babies.

She could listen to him breathing all day. She could be happy doing just that.

She went downstairs again. The kitchen. Her real home. The place where she was at her best all of the time. She thought of the full plate of food that she had disposed of for so many mornings now, but couldn't bring herself not to cook it.

Most women would think of this as a vacation. Most women would sleep late. They would be relieved. But not Bea; she would provide for him. And he would provide for her. As usual.

"Harry?" She turned to the silence. "I have only one egg today . . . I didn't go marketing yesterday. I'm sorry; I was busy with the gardening. It's still enough for French toast if you want that though . . . I know you would've preferred an omelet, but . . . I only have one egg."

She held the egg in her hand.

She looked down at it. And then she walked over to the mixing bowl. "I already said I had only one. I already said I was sorry."

And when it was ready, she set the full plate in front of his seat, and waited.

She waited in silence. It heaved, and breathed, and let her in. And then it spoke: "Glad you like it."

Harry

He had missed his meeting. Been asleep far into the late morning, and the sun now slanted in a perfect wedge-shaped beam through the large space in the undrawn curtains. He could only remember drinking something, and falling asleep right afterward. . . .

Everything hurt. His eyes. His legs. He smelled. He was in his suit. On top of the already turned down hotel bed.

He saw six glasses. An assortment of beer bottles as well, resting on every surface available. Even on the back of the toilet.

Jesus Christ, am I hungover. His tie. His good tie was stained with last night's potent substance, and he could tell he'd hit his head on the headboard from the tender wound that hissed at him with pain. *Christ . . .*

And he'd stood up Steve! He'd stood up a client at a breakfast meeting. An important meeting that had been scheduled weeks in advance. He'd written it down in his Filofax. It lay there on the page, blatantly glaring back, encircled in red. He had reminded himself yesterday not to miss it.

He imagined Steve—loudmouthed, self-absorbed Steve—arriving in the hotel restaurant, sitting at a table. Then he would wait awhile. Check his expensive watch impatiently. A waiter would ask would he like some coffee? No, he would decline. He'd say he was waiting for someone who should be arriving any minute. He'd check his watch again. Admire the rose gold bezel and the shiny leather strap. The waiter would come over again. Would he like some coffee? No, thank you. And then he would wait ten more minutes. He would think that Harry forgot. Steve would go to the front desk and ask could they please ring him up? Surely. No answer. Try again. No answer. Try once more. No answer. We keep getting voice mail.

He would go back to the dining room, signal the waiter. How about that coffee? He'd drink a cup. He'd drink another. Leave a generous tip and walk away. Then he would look at his expensive watch.

Finally, they were giving Harry his own opportunities, and he was throwing them away. Finally, a chance! To become better. *But what is better?* Really, though, it had been Harry's own fault for turning down opportunities that had been presented to him before. They'd told him that they'd wanted to promote him, but in order to do that he had to go to Cleveland. Tie things up and get acquainted with a few clients and the Cleveland office. *But NO! Bea fucking said no. Wouldn't let me go!*

But he had eventually convinced her. *Why couldn't I have done that earlier? Why was I weak until now?*

"I'm so fucked now." *What am I going to do?*

He didn't want to disappoint Steve, but his hatred for him was growing. Slowly expanding as if it had been soaking up water and dilating and sucking in fuel. Stories of misogynism, multiple wives, prostitutes, hard drugs . . . *it's just disgusting*. And it wasn't fair! It wasn't fair that an asshole like Steve could get everything and be catered to in the process. And have his ass kissed and be rewarded for it, and be loud and obnoxious and *just disgusting!* It wasn't fair that he could snort coke and have his dick sucked *simultaneously*.

"I'm a fucking failure." Yes, Harry was failing to cater to the rich assholes of the world. *He* wanted to be catered to. He wanted someone else to really love him.

He knew that he should call Steve. *But what would I say?*

He knew that he should set up another meeting. He knew it. Wouldn't do it though. He sat in his own filth. *I bet she wouldn't like me this way. No one would like me this way. I don't blame them.*

Lilliana

She skipped her last two classes so she could go to the music store and stay a little while longer, without her mother going crazy when she came home three hours later. *I get A's in bio, and I have gym last period. What a waste of time. Running around with those dykes blowing their whistles and getting off when they look at us in our uniforms.*

The walk was long; Lilli didn't have a car, and she had outgrown her Rollerblades. It didn't seem to matter though. She would rather be walking than running in circles or dissecting animals. She would rather be walking to the store than be anywhere else.

And when she got there, it seemed, for some strange reason, that she was the happiest girl on earth.

Pictures gleamed back at her. Old rock and roll screamed in the background. Posters adorned all empty wall spaces. She ran her fingers up and down the plastic spines of CDs, the glossy photographs of stars. She wondered why they were so expensive. So similar. Such a waste. She leafed through bins of vinyls. She tried so hard to remember the snippets of conversations that she'd heard Paul having with other music enthusiasts. She wanted to impress him.

There were always some rarities. Things that brought a smile to Paul's face when he looked at them.

She wondered what it took to be a musician. What it took to be marketed, sold, stocked, and restocked on shelves in stores like this one.

Selling a piece of yourself to *everyone*.

At least anyone who could pay.

And she looked up, and suddenly smiled at someone across the room as her heart seemed to hold its breath inside her.

"Hey, Paul!"

"Hi, Lilli. Isn't it a little early for high-school girls to be done with classes?"

"Yeah, well . . . Everyone cuts the last few anyway."

"They start to see it. You should watch it."

"Yeah, I probably should. . . . (silence) Okay. So I . . . I didn't know it was your shift now."

"Yeah, well, I'm always here at this time, I mean."

"Right, you are here . . . always."

"Hey, are you looking for anything in particular?"

"Well, I was sort of just browsing . . ."

"Because my band . . . we came out with this beautiful new demo . . ."

"You did?"

"Yeah. We produced it ourselves and everything. I've been working here so I could chip in my share. It's sort of eclectic. I guess it's kind of Stones-esque, but we have synth in there and a more dancy beat, so I'd say it's a fusion of The Stones and Joy Division and maybe The Cure or something. But don't quote me on that. It's hard to describe."

"Oh, it sounds awesome!"

"Here, check it out."

"Oh, you play guitar?"

"Bass. I do guitar also, but bass in the band."

"Oh, that's awesome. I always wanted to learn guitar."

"Yeah, girls who play the guitar are definitely special. There just aren't that many of them who are, you know, really good."

"I know! That's why I want to learn!"

"Well, I guess maybe I could teach you a couple of chords and stuff. I'm not exactly the greatest teacher, but I guess I . . ."

"Great! I mean, I've been meaning to ask you if you would teach me."

"Gladly."

"Okay! So, when is . . ."

"Uh . . . How's tomorrow night at eight?"

"Eight. Tomorrow. Perfect!"

"And your address is . . ."

"Here, got a pen?"

"Yeah."

"Okay, that's not even that far off . . . I'll be there."

"I'm psyched! I don't have a guitar though."

"No prob, I'll bring an extra. Hope you don't mind acoustic though."

"Oh no, of course not. Acoustic is . . . perfect."

"Good. Here, take the demo, and give it a listen. I want you to hear my band. I think you'd like some of the songs."

"I will. Thanks, Paul. Thanks so much! I know I'll like them."

"Great. I'll see you tomorrow."

Vivian

And that was the day when Vivian found out that Fiona, her former best friend—the girl whom she spent every available minute with in junior high, and spent countless hours on the phone with in eighth grade, and told *all* of her secrets to, her crushes to, her fucking fears to—had lost her virginity.

It shouldn't seem like such a big deal. Lilli lost hers about a billion years ago. . . .

But it *was* a big deal. It was a big deal, because suddenly her childhood had been swept away, ruined, popped, and broken. Bleeding like a paper cut on a fingertip.

And it wasn't even her virginity to begin with!

Remember, you don't even talk to her anymore. You hardly even see her. But when she'd heard it in the cafeteria, whispered in her ear by someone whose name seemed so insignificant in comparison to the news itself, it seemed that Vivian felt something inside her break. Not only in half. It shattered.

And then she noticed that they were laughing. Not at her. At the news. And she had erupted in fit of laborious giggles. To blend in. She had tried not to notice the pain in her chest, the disbelief that seemed trapped in her throat and that was tickling its way up unsuccessfully.

"And, it was in his hot tub, at his huge house."

"And he's twenty-five"

"And he's, like, a genius. He's got this fucking ridiculous IQ."

"And he graduated from Harvard."

"And they're, like, in *love*."

"And he is sooo fucking *HOT!*"

"And *I want* him."

"And you'll *get* him. If I don't get him first!"

"She's cute, but she's not that cute. You could so get him. Either one of you."

I shouldn't have to pretend anymore. This is fucking high school for Christ sake. This stuff is so old. This concealing of one's inner self. This constrained emotion. This farce. This travesty.

She had said something to which someone had replied, "Yeah, so? Just because you wouldn't get on a dick for a million bucks doesn't mean you have to criticize the people who actually do get action." And someone else had chimed in, "Yeah, get down off your mighty prude throne. Who the hell do you think you are? You can't say that about her." And the finale: "You know you're just *jealous* anyway. Of Fiona and her hot piece-of-ass boyfriend."

Vivian couldn't bear to feel the hot water run out of her penciled eyes. The eyes that she worked so hard for. The ones that had been encased in darkness and brightness so meticulously that morning. Shadows and sunlight strategically placed just so.

"And I *want* him."

She hadn't wanted to make a scene. She hadn't wanted people to look. To stare. She was too old for this sort of humiliation. *Cafeteria humiliation.* Too old. *I'm too old for this SHIT! And I am not me anymore. I'm new. I'm hot too. I could . . .*

But it had been too late.

The hot black tears had begun to run, and had left hot black lines in their wake. Crisscrossing, and staining, and twisting like lightning bolts, like a jigsaw puzzle. And the more she wiped her darkened face, the darker it seemed to get. The tears came faster. And she realized that this was a different kind of humiliation.

It was different because they hadn't noticed at all. Before, they would've noticed. Now, they just skipped over it. An internal mother, shielding them from pain. From emotion.

I wonder if I'd be any good at giving head.

Harry

"Hello? . . . Yes, I was at your bar the other night . . . Yep. Right . . . It was under my client's name; uh, try Verchon . . . You don't? Try Steve . . . Right, that was us . . . No, I didn't leave anything, but I have a question . . . Well, I saw a woman there . . . a woman wearing red and black. Tall. Very beautiful . . . No, no, I was wondering if you knew her name . . . What do you mean you're reluctant to give out clients' names? . . . Yes, I understand . . . No, of course I'm not a stalker . . . Yes, I know. You already said that. Right. You couldn't give it to me? Could you just check? Do you remember her? . . . You're sure you don't? She's hard to forget . . . Couldn't you just check one more time, for me. Please . . . Oh, come on! I didn't see a single celebrity at your goddamned bar! And I'm not a . . . Yes, you already said that . . . I know, it's against your policy! But you could make a fucking exception for a . . . Well, thanks a *lot* for your help, Mr. Linden. I'm sure that you've never been crazy about any woman after taking it up the ass so many times, you bastard!"

Lilliana

The excitement almost hurt. Like a new, deep, constant pain reminding her that she was proud. And happy. Because she didn't recognize happiness without pain. *What if I forget?*

She'd never really wanted to play the guitar. She'd never really considered it. She hadn't wanted short nails and callused fingertips. She wondered why she'd said yes. So fast. So easy.

"I've always wanted to learn guitar."

What a convincing liar I am!

She'd never so much as held a pick. She'd never banged out a few chords. She'd never even cared about playing *anything*. Instrumentally, that is.

So why had she lied?

Why? I want to be around him so much that I would take up guitar in order to do that? I don't even get this. He's not hot! In fact, he's kinda plain. Sort of below average even. I've had much hotter men. Of course I have. Nathan is hotter.

Nathan.

When she thought of him, said his name to herself, it struck some sort of sharpness in her. A pain that was new, stronger still. A pain that had at first been so subtle that it almost felt good, it kept her alive. Kept her aware and *feeling* alive. And it slowly increased until it felt like someone was jabbing her repeatedly with dull scissors in the pit of her stomach.

And what is with me?

She looked in the mirror to see what had changed. Why couldn't she be young again? She felt so old. Old! At sixteen! Why couldn't she be free? Where had her freedom gone? Why did her body want to stop, yet she, herself, did not understand why?

Or how.

How does a person lose desire in a matter of moments? And when it is lost, how does a person know it is gone? And how do they get it back? Maybe it is irreplaceable. Maybe that's the catch. And maybe it was gone for a reason that was too difficult to conceive of. And maybe it was gone because of someone. Something.

And she wanted it back.

She missed the days before. The days when *she* had been in charge. When *she* had needed a little perk. A little jolt. Like a sip of caffeine, it had fueled her. Like Coca-Cola in the morning. A whole can swallowed in thirty seconds flat before an exam. Propelled her onward. Reminded her that no matter how awful everything else was, she was always able. Able and loved, even for that moment, in the arms of another. It didn't matter whose arms they were.

But even that was gone. The security. The sanctuary. The connection had been lost.

The scabs, still new and dark against her pale skin, showed like an empty victory, a battle won, a war lost.

Beatrice

"Harry, baby . . . I have a little surprise for you!" She snuck into the dining room, crept slowly around the table, through the kitchen, into the living room, and upstairs to the bedroom. "Just take a look at this! On sale! Can you believe it? One hundred percent cashmere. Oh! It's so beautiful. And *you* would look beautiful in it!" She smiled and laid it down on his side of the bed. "I mean *handsome*. Manly." The big, empty bed. The bed where Bea had slept alone for days.

She checked the answering machine. A message from Mrs. Laur. A message from their insurance agent. A message from the bank. A message from her sister.

And no messages from Harry.

Bea frantically played through the messages again, hoping that the machine had skipped. *They do skip, don't they? Answering machines can skip. Can't they?* But there was nothing wrong with the machine. The machine was not at fault.

Oh! Why can't he call? Why is he so busy? "Harry, don't you understand, I *need* help with these girls! They're impossible." And she sat on the bed with a sigh. "Impossible! Lilli is being ridiculous, and Vivian is making a turn for the worse . . . and I just *can't do it* anymore. I can't. I need you to talk to them. Just to say a few things to them. Just to set them straight." She smiled awkwardly at the ceiling. "We need a *man* in this house. That's what we need. A man of the house."

She reached over and touched his sweater. Felt his heaving chest through the soft knit. Felt his breathing, the beating of his heart.

And then she kissed the garment.

"Oh Harry! You look so *handsome* in your new sweater!"

Then she kissed the cashmere again, lightly, letting it leave a soft fuzz behind that stuck to her lipstick like snowflakes. And she encased the sweater in her arms, and felt like a girl again. Harry in her arms, Harry's lips on hers. Hushing her, silencing her internal pleas.

Vivian

It was infected. The ring that had looked so pretty and erotic and dangerous only a few days before now seemed to itch constantly, showing an angry red patch of inflamed skin that had formed from her scratching, as well as some allergy to the steel that sat dormant within her body.

But I won't take it out. No way. Then she'd win. Mom would win; even though she hasn't seen it yet, she would win.

She had lost two and a half pounds.

She had snuck into the nurse's office and weighed herself there, carefully sliding out of her shoes and removing her sweater to get the most accurate measurement. And she had smiled. Smiled, and commended herself. For her success. Her strength.

She had begun to salvage old clothes from her closet; hacking off hems of skirts, altering tee-shirts, sewing patchwork onto her jeans, and dragging sharp scissors across the denim. *Look at me! Look at this! This is me. Me?* Whoever would've thought?

Whoever would've dreamed of this? Whoever would've dreamed that she, the ugly, smart, frizzy, ordinary, brunette, would become such a bombshell over the course of a few fateful days? A little pain. A little bit of change. A lot of change. Permanent change.

But Vivian thought of the day. And she realized she had not changed completely. Not yet.

Look at me. I'm still a fucking nerd. Still no respect. Still a virgin. Still a person that no one notices.

She remembered the hot tears. Hot and black. Staining her cheeks like a child drawing with a permanent marker. And no one had cared. *And no one had cared.*

I'm too old for this. Too old for any of this. *Someday they'll see that I've really changed. I have! I'm different. I'm not the same anymore. I'm really not.* She rested her chin in her hand, closed her eyes. *No one had even cared.*

But she had to *work.* Work for respect. You can't just fucking *sit there. Let them look away.* You have to go for it. You have to go for them. Go after them. *Stupid lazy lazy lazy bitch . . . Jesus. Nothing is ever going to change if you don't make it change.*

She needed friends in high places.

She needed the respect of . . . Katerina.

What Vivian didn't realize was that people like herself—weak people—kept people like Katerina where they stood. Their willingness to submit themselves to Katerina's cruel regimes, their regard of her as an icon, their willingness to emulate her. Katerina. She was just a girl. A bitch. But to cultivate a relationship with her, this was something valuable. Because Katerina wasn't stupid. She wasn't naive. And Vivian was . . . Katerina's subjects were; they all were.

Lilliana

She had told Paul to go up the back. She had said so. Deliberately. He'd said okay, but he hadn't remembered it. He came and rang the bell in the front, and she had run to answer the door, saying that it was a salesman. *Mom is such an oblivious idiot. Seriously. I could get by on complete lies if I wanted.*

She'd never even held a guitar before. She'd never felt the neck in her hand, slid her fingers up and down the squeaky, wire-coated strings. She'd never tuned one, strummed one; she'd never made music before.

Her room. She was embarrassed. *Such a little-girl room! Such a baby room. Just look at it. Just look at the carpet. Give me a break. He must think I'm, like, two years old. Even Nathan has said that before.*

Paul had smiled when he walked in. A smile of pity. A smile of disbelief. The girl seemed so mature. So grown up! And here it was. A little suburban baby room. He could see that she'd tried to change it though. Tried her best. Even if the basic amenities were the same, she'd done things like hang hippie beads over the doorway to her closet.

She had tried to make it seem less prissy, more adult, or at least college dorm–like. Her posters were a lame attempt; she had done her best to cover the pink bows on the wallpaper; Christmas lights adorned the perimeter of her room where the ceiling met the walls. She'd taped magazine clippings to her headboard and all over her desk. Stickers had been randomly slapped on furniture. There were pillows on the carpet. Candles lining her windowsill. Her bed was unmade. The door shut. The window open. There was a strange, dark stain on the floor by her bed.

He's looking at it as if I'm the lamest person alive. Jesus. No other guy has ever looked at it this way. They all treat it like a sanctuary.

"Oh, sorry it's messy in here . . ."

"Don't worry about it."

"It's pretty childish, I know. The wallpaper and stuff. I'm getting it redone soon. In a month or so, I think."

"I like it. Helps you stay young."

"It's okay. I guess."

"So, let's get started. Have you ever fooled around on a guitar?"

"Uh . . . no, I haven't, uh . . . fooled around on a guitar. Yet."

"Okay, that's fine. We'll just start you off with some basic stuff. Here's a G, right here."

"Okay, a G."

"And this is a C chord."

"Okay, like this?"

"Uh, almost. More like this."

"Oh, okay."

"So you could just go back and forth. We can start slowly. Here, just . . . that's right, put your hand right there, and those fingers on each one of those strings. Yep. That's the right position. Press down a little harder. Now, just take the pick, the pointy side . . . Strum it downward. . . ."

"Like this?"

"A little softer. The touch shouldn't be that tough, and give it a little more pressure up there."

"Okay."

"There, that's better."

"So now, move your fingers to the other chord position. Like this . . ."

"Here?"

"No . . . there. Perfect. Now strum again."

"I like this."

"Good. Now go back and forth between chords. Okay, one, two, one, two . . . now switch. Right there. Good, now strum again; three, four. . . ."

"Paul, is it supposed to be killing my fingers?"

"Yep, you know you're doing it right then."

"Good! So, before we move on, do you want to lie down for a minute on the bed or something? I'm so . . . tired. I'm just, like, exhausted."

"Um, no thanks, I'm okay right now."

"Yeah, you just look a little wiped out. And I'm . . ."

"Haha, I am."

"Then maybe . . ."

"The thing is, I have rehersal at nine-fifteen tonight, so we can't really afford to waste time."

"Right. Of course, Paul."

"Have you listened to my demo yet?"

Harry

"Hey there, Harry, I thought we were buds . . . What's with standing me up today? Did you enjoy the girl? I hope you were at least having some fun with yourself since you are responsible for wasting about an hour of my time. Hey, what can I say, it's better than jacking off. Time is money, Harry. I'm expecting your call."

Harry erased the message right away. He was sorry. *I'm sorry! I'm sorry that I've messed up. But . . . I'm realizing things. I'm realizing that old mistakes are new mistakes too, and that it's not all my fault. Because it's Bea's fucking fault too. It's her fault that I'm like this right now. It's her fault that I want to . . . that I want this girl and that my priorities are getting all mixed up.*

Why can't I just make it? Why can't I just make myself do the stuff that I have to do?

But he'd never been good at forcing himself to do anything. He'd done the routine. No pain had been involved. The whole thing had been too painless, in fact. Devoid of feeling, he'd trudged through days, years. Time had passed in milestones. He'd learned to disregard things that had been disruptive, and minor events slowly blurred and softened and turned into a colorless haze. With little pieces, like fireworks, streaming out. People had become silhouettes, conversations had become sentences, a day had become nothing unless something groundbreaking happened within its span. Vagueness permeated everything. Bea had taught him that. To close his eyes. Turn around. Close doors against things that made him afraid, or threatened to throw things off. *Taught me how to ignore. How to fucking ignore things. People and things.* Even when he'd walked in when Lilli had been doing something to herself with some sharp-looking thing and bleeding, he'd just closed the door and walked back down the hall. Sheepish in his apologies.

Of course, Lilli had just gone off rambling about privacy and things. "Don't you *ever* fucking come into my room again without knocking on the fucking door! That is disgusting, Dad! I'm a girl; you *can't* do that. I'm not, like, six anymore. Leave me *alone.* Just leave. Get out of here."

So he had. Muttering things like, "I'm so sorry."

But he'd thought about it. A whole lot. He was wondering why she would hurt herself that way. He kept trying to figure out whether what she was doing could've been accidental. *Perhaps she'd been picking up some sharp thing and it cut her by accident?* Confrontation, though, was too much. Besides, this was a recent occurrence. Maybe only a month or so had passed. And he had put it off and put it off and pushed it out of mind because that's what he'd learned to do. He'd learned to take care of himself that way. But just because it was learned, it didn't mean that it was correct. *I was worried about her. I was! I should've said something then.*

"I'm so sorry."

He didn't feel like feeling sorry though. *All I do is feel sorry. I feel sorry about everything. I regret everything. I regret every fucking thing I've done, starting with Bea. I regret how I've dealt with things and avoided things. I fucking regret it! And I regret not waking up today. I should've gone. I don't have to be his friend. I just need to make the deal—even if that does involve hearing about his goddamned sick life. Because it's not about* me. *It's not about how I feel. It's about obligations.*

But all that his mind's eye could see were two long legs—long, feminine legs. Bending, twisting, shimmering. And he could feel the business card still inside his jacket, the thin paper pressing on his body with a thousand times its weight. He could succumb to it, if he'd only let himself.

I can't mess up. There's too much riding on this. I'm the one who's responsible. For everything and everyone . . .

Beatrice

She'd never dreamt a dream without Harry in it in some way, shape, or form. If it wasn't Harry himself who made an appearance, she would analyze what she remembered of her scattered sleep-ridden thoughts, and prove that Harry had been depicted as a cat, or a television, or even as one of her daughters, when she was extremely desperate. Because dreams meant love. And she needed proof. Even more than the feeling.

She dreamt of refuge. Of perfection. Of things she had, but was afraid of losing.

But he hasn't called. The phone did not ring. It had not rung. And it would not ring. She was a girl again. A teenager. Sitting by the phone. Praying for her crush of the week to dial her fateful number, and speak to her in a low, movie-star, husky voice. A pubescent voice that was capable of such ranges when exploited to its full capabilities. She hadn't heard one of those voices in so long. *Where* is *he? He's busy. Of course. Harry is busy. Harry, you're busy, right? Occupied. You have things to do. Keeping us all alive.*

Or maybe he *had* called. After all, he had been at breakfast that very morning, just like all other mornings. Mornings past and mornings to come.

Vivian

It seemed the morning had come much too soon, and she had slid into one of her newly hemmed skirts and a cutoff shirt that exposed her belly button. Boots that hugged her calves with black skin, and her mask. Painted-on beauty.

I feel more whole. More like one person. Not like a shattered mess full of other people's parts. I've found me. I've found an identity.

But there was a pang of emptiness inside her.

She tried to figure out what it was that she needed to do. Her hair? Was it her face? Something about the lipstick she had just bought? Yes? No? Was it her clothing? The color of the ring in her stomach? It was none of these things.

Today I'm going to fucking suck it up. Suck in that stomach, bitch. No one wants to be friends with a girl whose belly-button ring is looped through flab. No one. And I have to talk to Katerina. I have to say the perfect thing. I can't fuck it up. I have to say the one perfect thing in the perfect way. We have to be friends. She would be my connection to everything . . . guys and parties and everything. We have to hang out. We have to chill.

Katerina: she *was the* cliché. Beautiful.

Vivian could hear her mother clanking in the kitchen downstairs. She could smell the sizzling bacon on the skillet. She could almost taste it. Disgusting. *Who could just voluntarily eat fat?* The most repulsive thing on earth: fat.

She had lost three pounds.

She descended the stairs, wincing at the weight of her muffled footsteps on the carpet.

"Vivian? Is that you?"

"Yeah, Mom, I'm a little late now, I really have to—"

"I know you have to go, but I made bacon. Your favorite. Why don't you come in here and take a piece? You can eat it on the way."

"No, thank you. I'm fine. I'll get something at school."

"Here, I'll bring it out to you."

"No . . . Mom, I said no . . ."

"Okay, here it . . . That is not real, is it? Vivian, tell me that that piece of steel in your belly button is not real."

"Oh, just forget about it; it's not really important."

"I didn't ask if it was important; I asked if it was real. Because I *hope* that it's not. What are you thinking? I wouldn't even expect your sister to do something like this! Haven't you heard of hepatitis? And that skirt! You look like a hooker. Vivian, what have you done? What do you think you're doing? What happened to the nice sweaters I bought you?"

"You know, I'm late."

"Do not walk out on me. I'm trying to—"

"Yeah, lecture me later if you'd like. I have a chem test. And I'm not starting my morning like this. What's done is done."

"Do not walk out on me. . . . Please."

Lilliana

He'd let her keep it so she could practice. He'd said she could keep it for the week if she took care of it. She had not touched it. Had not felt the worn, bent wood that had lost its polish with years of Paul's rugged touch. Mostly because she was afraid. Didn't want to ruin it.

She wondered what Paul's bedroom looked like. . . .

She expected a chilly dorm room, a bed with flannel sheets, a CD player. *It would do. For him. I guess I wouldn't really care about the furniture.*

What had he thought of my room? I know it's juvenile, but still . . . Had he seen the bra I left on the floor by the bed? Had he seen the box of condoms on my dresser? Had he . . . wanted me? It hadn't seemed like it.

And why the fuck do I care anyway? I don't like that type of guy. I don't go for that type. The smart, scruffy, creative type. Bet you he's not even good . . . bet you he's not. Bet you he doesn't even like sex.

She looked wistfully over at her phone. *There's no point in waiting for Paul to call. There's no reason for him to. Why had I even tried to get him? And I don't like him! I don't even want to fuck him. I swear. I don't.*

How could he make her feel so small? Why did she feel so awkward? So ordinary? Not at all up to par. She was just another average girl to him. She had never been average before. He was in college. He was studying philosophy, for God's sake! He was intelligent. He had respect for the future. For what was to come. Not just the moment. But what was to come.

She'd never felt so unattractive in front of anyone before. *Ugly.* "You ugly bitch."

She'd never been turned down when she invited someone to lie on her bed. What an honor! To lay on Lilliana's bed. To lay on an icon's bed.

So many boys would love to lie next to me. Slide in between the sheets and touch me. And smell me. Smell my sheets. Smell my hair. My perfume. But he sat so far away.

She glanced down at the three symmetrical, perfectly executed scabs on her arm. Gave them a little kiss. Felt their ruggedness, their danger, against her lips, which had been pressed against so many things. Things of her own. Things she hated. Guys she hated. Guys she knew she'd never see again, and guys she knew she would have to face in school every day. And these things. These scars were *hers.* By choice. By nature.

And she liked that.

I could have someone. I don't even care about Paul. He's just another stupid guy. He probably goes for the smart prudes in college anyway. Whatever, I can have fun if I want. I can have anyone I want. I can. I will. Tonight.

Anything to avoid turning out like my mother. Anything.

The point on her tweezers made a nice fine line. Not too shallow, not too deep. Just perfect.

Harry

He had an intense desire to do nothing. Maybe to let his mind wander and to let himself dream undisturbed. *To have no obligations. No fucking obligations.*

But that wasn't reality. And he did have to be somewhere. *Can't I ever just fucking sit down? For more than five minutes? Can't I ever do anything for myself?*

What would happen if I just stayed here? If I just stayed and . . .

"I can't. I can't!"

The aggression, unrest. Churning within him. Bubbling, burning, threatening to erupt. It would soil everything: expensive things, things that couldn't be dirtied. He couldn't afford to have them cleaned. Fragile things. Staining everything with tears the color of ink and burning things into nothing but worthless dust. Stuff that you would throw out without thinking twice. Ashes.

To be a kid. To not worry all of the goddamned time. No guilt, no remorse. Isn't that what it is to be a kid?

But when he thought of his own childhood he could not really remember a distinct time when he had been worry-free. He'd never been a belligerent kid. He'd just wanted to have friends and to partake in some slightly rebellious activities just for fun. *I was stupid, and I put the pressure on myself though.* He'd smoked pot only a few times, and he had never experienced the supposedly euphoric dullness that seemed to intrigue his friends and be the focal point of countless social gatherings. *Just the fucking paranoia all the time. Every time.* But he'd felt guilty nonetheless, always under surveillance. Always returning home with an expression on his face that screamed, "I did it! I smoked a joint with three of my friends, and it was damned good. And I wanna do it again tomorrow." Even though less than half of that statement had been true. So he'd gotten found out. He'd had the smell all over his clothes, and he'd been looking afraid, disoriented, disheveled. He remembered how his father had grabbed his chin, staring into his bloodshot eyes. And the whole time Harry had been thinking, "You hate me, everybody hates me, the whole world hates me. It's the world against me, and it's my responsibility to keep everything working and in place." He'd been forbidden to hang out with the three friends, he had been grounded for a month, and his father had threatened to call the police. *The fucking police!* "They arrest kids for doing that stuff! Kids like *you*." And he had pointed a finger down at Harry.

What would I do if I caught the girls smoking pot? He didn't really know.

I would've rather caught Lilli smoking than chopping herself up like that. . . .

Being the self-proclaimed "functional, self-sufficient" parent in the house, he should've been the one to talk to her. *I should've said something.* He squeezed his eyes closed and tried to think of something that didn't lead him back home. *Why can't I just pretend to be alone? I mean, really really alone.*

Maybe I should call Lilli.

But no, then Bea would get involved, and Vivian would feel left out, and . . . no.

His conscience was stifling. Because he wasn't doing anything productive and because he was alone and because he had thoughts and desires like any human would. *Like any other man who's alive and who has needs that aren't being met. I'm allowed to have needs, and nobody can stop me. Not even Bea. Because she's fucking selfish and spineless, and now that I'm gone she's letting everything go. I know it! But it's not only* my *job! It's her job too, and*

I'm not there, and I can make the choice to break some rules if I want.

He'd never liked pot. He'd just smoked it because it was the hippie thing to do. After the experience with his father, Harry used to go to the liquor cabinet to steal some booze to spike his own orange juice. He eventually began taking entire bottles that he knew his parents wouldn't miss. Taking long swigs of vodka in the darkness of his room, he'd dreamed of a future that was fanciful and far from the present in which he was living.

He'd had a nifty collection of almost twenty empty bottles of assorted types of expensive alcohol lined up in four neat rows of five bottles each under his bed.

Bea never drank alcohol. *Not even at our wedding.* She'd been a virgin in every way when they'd met. He'd still failed to break her completely. *Sex with Bea is like fucking a virgin because she just lies there and lets me have my way. Cold and motionless in the bed. Noiseless fucking. Just me and the bedsprings going up and down, and Bea, the corpse. Face contorting, but no sound.* Harry always used to try to get some drinks in her to loosen her up. But Bea would just shake her head. Wouldn't even part her lips into a smile ("Harry, you know I don't drink. . . . Just tell me what to do. Just tell me. What is it that you want exactly?") He couldn't tell her. And so nothing ever changed. It wasn't possible, because the parts had been learned and the relationship had been set and the dynamics had been decided upon. And so nothing had changed at all for almost twenty years. He could try and try, but it would never ever change.

Beatrice

She awoke with arms outstretched, but empty. Her skin stung with the emptiness. Her body. Cold.

Her lips cold. Her feet. She missed Harry's heat. The heat he radiated. She remembered when she'd first slept with Harry. He was so *warm!* So warm to her! She was so young then. She thought it was special. Something that made Harry special. Because he was warm. Because she was cold.

And she still believed that this was important.

She'd never slept with anyone else.

She'd hardly kissed a boy when she'd met him. And he had seemed so manly. So much older and smarter than she had been. She had been so naive and pliable. She believed every word that sprang forth from Harry's sacred lips. She believed every truth, and untruth. *I've never doubted you, Harry. I never would. I never could.*

How could anyone not trust her husband? How could any woman survive with anyone other than Harry?

Their wedding had been small. In a room in a nice hotel in the city. And she had looked so beautiful! Even Harry had said so. *He hardly ever says I'm beautiful. Unless I ask. Then he'll say it. He doesn't even have to though. I know he thinks so anyway.* And she had worn her mother's dress. Her hair (it was longer then) was pinned up and styled. Her eyes shaded with pale blue. Her lips pink. Her cheeks rosy. Her eyelashes, cloaked in mascara for the very first time. *I had felt so new. Like a new person.*

And she remembered the bed in their hotel room. How she had been broken at will that night. How she had winced at the pain, and then smiled when she saw Harry's eyes light up with pride. And when she had woken that morning, she had felt his warm chest. His warm hands. There had been a draft in the room.

But she had not heard from him. This husband who loved her so much. Whom she loved so much.

Her body shivered beneath the sheets. "I love you, Harry. I feel like I don't even need to say it anymore. We say it silently. Every day." And she felt the warmth recede over her. A temperate climate in a frigid room. She melted under his silent response.

Vivian

It seemed the first time in ages that anyone had noticed her. But today it had happened. She had counted: three sly glances from okay-looking boys, one catcall on her walk home, two whistles from older men. *Possibilities!*

What would it be like to kiss an older man? Not just a little older. A lot older. Like thirty, thirty-five. Would it feel different?

Now you're being juvenile. See? Didn't you see today? You are attractive. You can be loved, if you try. And the jewels in her stomach caught the gleam of the lamplight in her room.

School seemed less important. Less of her main focus. *Before, it was all I had. Now I have so much more.* She seemed not to care about papers and tests. She strolled into class late, doting on a stare from any of the nondescript males who dared to turn her way. *It's almost like I can see their hard-ons through their pants. Just seeing them look at me when I walk in there.*

And she had used school to her advantage. She *needed* things. She had needs. She needed to be friends with Katerina. Katerina needed a subordinate, and Vivian needed a leader. Thus, it could be a perfect match. Katerina knew guys, and Vivian wanted to know guys. Katerina was strong, and Vivian was spineless. She was intelligent, but her mind was pliable. She was tall, but she was dwarfed by Katerina's presence. Vivian was willing to listen. *I don't care what I have to do. I have to have the right friends. I need a new friend.*

Yeah, it was perfect. It could be disgustingly perfect.

BecauseKaterinahadalreadybrokenupwithVincentbecausehe'dgotten headfromthisotherbitchnamedDarienneandKaterinawaslikesoooupset,like,you don'tevenknowhowupsetandDarienneusedtobeKaterina'sbestfriendlikeBFFand shetotallyfuckedheroverandwhocaresifitwasbecauseDariennewassupposedly drunkorwhat,right?Yeah,like,whatabitchandshewasall,like,"Weweredrunk"but whatever,Imean,Katerinawassolikedisgustedwithbothofthem . . . shedealt withitinthesickestway,shewasjust,like,"Whatever,fuckbothofyou,"youknow? Itwassoawesomeonherpartbecauseweneedpeoplewithfuckingbackbones thesedays.Besides,Vincentislikehotandallbuthe'snotashotasRickanywayso whatever,butshe'sstillnotoverhimyet,like,notoveroveratleast.

And, if Vivian bent over backward in just the right way, maybe she would have the privilege of filling that position. *It's important.*

There was a party that weekend. A party! Finally invited. A place where she could dress up. Show off her thin thighs, her glossy calves, her taut stomach, her smoky eyes. A place where sex was casual. Meaningless almost. Where someone would fall in love with her body and actually *want* her. At least for an hour or so.

She'd always hated those parties. Never went. Was never invited, but always told herself she was better off at home anyway.

I was so stupid! I missed out on so much! I could have someone if I wanted. I could be like Lilli. Guys in my bed. Between my sheets. Inside my thighs. Used condoms on my floor. Haha! Maybe not yet. But I could do it. If I wanted to. Because it's not such a big deal . . . sex maybe, but all that other stuff? Who really cares? Who really gives a fuck?

Lilliana

She'd gone to the club on a weeknight. When the real diehards went. When the real music lovers went, the druggies, the ones who discreetly popped pills in dark corners, and couldn't get up in the morning without some sort of stimulant. She wondered what type *he* was. The evening's piece of fun. The new thing to occupy her time, space, etc.

Smashing, bumping, thumping against the walls.

Ruining everything.

He had been drunk as hell. Dressed nicely. Unabashedly, bearing his rippling abs. Stroking her shoulders, her neck. They had only met, what, ten minutes before? And ten minutes later . . .

She could still feel the cool metal of the stall pressing against her back. The bottom hems of her pants were wet from the leaky pipes.

She was panting. Drunk herself. But not enough so she could forget. Just enough to make it stick longer. Like a splinter in her mind that refused to pry itself free. *At least he was beautiful.*

He *was* beautiful. And he had been beautiful. He said something about modeling. Something about some agency, some campaign. Some tour. Some ad in some magazine. And she had said yes to everything. *Everything.*

She remembered that there were couples in the stalls on either side of them. She remembered thinking it was funny.

I . . . At least, I got . . . some. Action. Her legs felt heavy. Her head spun. *That's all I wanted. Action . . . from anyone with a . . .* And that's what she had gotten. Nothing more. And nothing less.

Suddenly, she felt so tall. Not like a little girl at all.

Her bed had shrunken. So had the pictures, the dresser, and the mirror. It all seemed so disproportionate. So overused. Abused. *I never liked pink. Like wallpaper, I never . . .* and she sat on the bed . . . *I never wanted pink fucking wallpaper. I never asked . . .* Her eyes glazed over with steam. His smell stuck to her; a reminder. She couldn't stand to breathe it. To inhale this smell. To be a part of *him.*

Lilli began to laugh again. This time harder. More forced. As if she were desperately trying to stay intoxicated. Not to let the feeling go.

And that's when she saw it. The CD laying on the floor by her bed. Paul's demo.

The words blurred, changed, linked, and collided into one another. They swung around. They multiplied. They seemed foreign. She tried to read the titles. Something that started with a *W?* Oh no, an *M.* Or a *V? Help.*

And finally, the music, Paul's music. The lead singer's whiny vocals. The strong base. The pulsing drumming. Classic rock derivatives. And then she heard the words. As if they were the first lyrics that ever made sense.

And the song was called "Make Me."

Beatrice

She had heard Lilli come in late. On a school night. Last night's dinner dishes, heaped with food, rested silently on the table. She smelled the heavy smoke on her daughter's clothes. In her hair. She smelled alcohol on her breath. And, of course, something else. Something sweaty and strange. Something she couldn't recognize.

Bea had always meant to tell her daughters not to smoke. Or drink. Or have sex until marriage. She had always meant to talk to them about moral issues.

She just never had. After the reproduction talk, she never could.

Is she smoking because of me? Is it all my fault? Because I never said it? Bea sighed. *No. No. Bad girls will be bad. Good girls will be good. My mother never told me not to do anything.* But that wasn't true. It's funny how memories become skewed over time.

If Harry were here, everything would be right. Everything would be perfect. He would have control.

What a gift! To control the uncontrollable. To be loved. To own love. To own a love.

But she didn't own a love. Her love owned her.

"Harry, if you were here . . . you could make everything right. You could! I have faith . . ."

She looked over at the dripping faucet, the dirty dishes. The food that had gone to waste. The dirty tablecloth. The chairs that were pulled out and turned in different directions. The empty food containers. The garbage that was beginning to spill over the top of the bin.

This isn't right. I'm letting myself go. I'm letting the house go! I must speak to Harry. I have got to talk to him. Now.

She ran over to the telephone. Searching. Looking for the insignificant piece of paper on which she had hurriedly scribbled the number of his hotel.

"Hello? Yes. Room 347 please. Yes, thank you. Harry? Hello? Oh, I see. Well, could you please tell him to call his wife, Beatrice? At home. Right when he comes in . . . Yes. Thank you. All right. . . . You wouldn't know, would you? I didn't think so. That's all right. I'll just wait for him to call. Or call again myself. Whichever happens first. Okay . . . yes. Thank you for your time, Miss."

It's okay for him to be out. There's no reason to worry. He just hasn't called in a while because he's busy. He's tied up! Tied up in business. He's okay. I know it. I know it because we love each other. Because we're so in love.

Harry

"I hate that bitch. It's all her fucking fault."

More messages. Steve. Bea. Steve. Bea. Bea.

Five messages! None of them from people whom he valued. *It would be nice if I could value my wife. It would be nice if I could miss her. But I can't!* People should value their spouses.

He paced rapidly around the room. *She's doing this to me. She's the one who fucks everything up. With her goddamned insecurity and her fucking needy bullshit. Everything. She needs me for everything! She makes me feel guilty.*

What did I ever see in her?

Maybe he had been desperate. He had never been a heartthrob. Wasn't ever the one who the girls stared at or carried on about in their diaries. He'd had girlfriends though. He'd lost his virginity the summer of his sixteenth birthday. *You'll never get it back. That feeling. That pride.* He remembered Saturday nights in his parents' dark basement. In his room. In his bed. But they had all been mediocre girls. The ones that no one else really wanted. He'd never had to push them. He'd always been polite.

But none of them had been perfect. There had always been a prominent flaw that took too much energy to ignore. Big nose, flat chest, hairy legs, braces, acne. But they'd always won in the end. Always left him for something better. Got out of the car and walked away. He'd wanted someone who would see him as the best. That nobody could be better than Harry.

And so he had chosen Bea. *I guess she used to be remotely attractive. She seemed like a nice girl. A naive girl, but I liked it. Because I wanted to affect her. But I didn't know her then. I didn't know how we would grow together, how she'd grow on me.* He hadn't known! It had been a mistake. An eighteen-year-old marriage that had taken him eighteen years of unconscious drowning to realize that it had been a mistake. It wasn't fair.

Nothing's fair.

"This is stupid, Harry. No one's here with you. No one can hear you."

He reached into his pocket to remove his address book so he could search for Steve's number. *I have to call him. He's getting impatient. This isn't fair to anybody.* But in his jacket he could still feel the thin film of Sergeant's card. The white numbers throbbing against his body.

And he remembered the airport, when he'd first realized his mistake.

I have new priorities now. He'd searched and searched, and he'd tried.

It felt good to surrender. Fly his white flag and succumb to new arms. The silence was invigorating. The fluorescent flashes of color that emanated from the television seemed to transport him to someplace new and different. Finally, his body was overriding his mind. His physical needs had surpassed any small flashes of electricity that his brain could produce to say otherwise.

The sounds of the phone were hardly sharp. Because he was ready. Because he'd accepted his destiny and . . .

"Hello?"

"Harry? Harry!"

"Bea . . ."

"Oh Harry, I'd been trying you. I'd tried you a few times yesterday, and you weren't in. They said you weren't in your room, so I left a message but you never called back. I supposed that you never got it, so I—"

"Just slow down, Bea."

". . . so I called you early, because I thought that you'd be in at this hour, and here you are!"

"Right."

"So, tell me all about Cleveland!"

"It's just a little city. Nothing to get excited about or—"

"Have you gotten to know it well?"

"Well enough."

"Maybe we could take a vacation there. To Cleveland. Wouldn't that be fun? How about next summer? When the girls are away?"

"We'll see. It's not much fun here. Next summer is a long way away. And things change."

"But you know it there. And nothing's changing."

"But still . . ."

"Still what?"

"Never mind."

"So, where have you been all of this time? You were out a lot. Very often, you know."

"Business. And I need to—"

"They really are working you! Aren't they?"

"Sure. I'm just doing my job."

"Is something wrong?"

"What?"

"I mean, is something the matter? Did something happen?"

"No . . . nothing. I sort of have to—"

"I know that work is difficult. But just think. You'll be home in a few days, and we'll see each other again. You and I, Harry! You know, I miss you. I miss you so much!"

"Please, Bea, I have to go."

"I understand. Just one more thing. The girls these days. They're just awful."

"Are they?"

"Yes. Lilli is just as bad as usual. But Vivian! You won't believe this . . . She got one of those belly-button piercings. It's just disgusting. Dirty."

"What? *Vivian?*"

"Yes."

"She's a teenager. Don't worry about her. I have to go. I'm hanging up."

"Okay, are you sure nothing is wrong? I know you must be a little depressed. It's hard to be without your spouse for a long period of—"

It was a done deal. He'd had the power then, and she had not been able to take it away. It had transcended him. *New priorities. New hatred. New love! I know new things now. I am no longer naive.*

Vivian

"*I'm so sorry about your* misfortune. Yeah, Katerina, I heard; I'm sorry. They're both assholes. They had no right to do that to you . . .*"

But I can't say words like "misfortune." Don't you see how fucking arrogant that sounds? It's like saying, "I'm smart and you're not." It makes me so inaccessible.

"Hey, I heard about what that bitch Darienne did. She deserves to fucking, like, rot in hell for that. Does she think she can actually do that to her friend? I mean, like, what the hell?"

Katerina had eyes that seemed as if they could never cry. She had lips that seemed as if they were created for giving head. Permanently slicked with gloss and shining, pursed as if she were waiting to blow someone a kiss. Gripping a cigarette during her lunch break. Pink or red or clear and sparkling. She spent time on them. She had the body of an anorexic pop star. She had a nose that was frequently numbed and slightly red around the nostrils. And before her she saw some girl named Veronica or something? Trying to be her friend with all of her might. *I just really need this to work.*

Vivian's determination was visible. Her statement had been rehearsed.

Katerina had seen Vivian's lunch tray, upon which rested nothing but a small packet of crackers. She knew this girl from somewhere . . . but where? This girl, this girl was pathetic. But Katerina could use someone for, you know, a couple of weeks. *This has to work.* Maybe until the whole Darienne thing blew over. It was after all, really embarrassing. Technically—very technically— Katerina had been *rejected.*

But most of all, Katerina was sick of buying her own cigarettes. She was sick of paying for her own drinks, and she could use a lackey. A *temporary* lackey. And Katerina wanted Rick. And this girl—this Vivian—could help her get him. She could be useful.

As long as she had cigarettes on her. Pot would be even better. Coke would be the best, but Katerina already had someone for that.

Katerina wanted to know if this girl would buy her pot. Would she run errands for her? Would she listen to her? Would she be okay with giving this girl the satisfaction of befriending her? But most importantly, would she buy her pot? Did she have pot on her? And Marlboro reds.

I hope this works. Please let this fucking work.

"Got any weed?" (Vivian had thought of this beforehand.)

And . . . I'm in.

Lilliana

There was blood on the bedsheets. The carpet. Her pillowcase that had seemed so pristine before. The wound had scabbed. It had bled in the night. She had grabbed a towel again. *I could've died in the night. I guess. If I hadn't woken up.*

But the pocketknife had seemed so sharp, so inviting. As if the pain it promised was too much to bear, and too much to resist all at once. It was his pocketknife. It had fallen on his way out.

And what pain it had delivered! What a sharp resilient pain. What a high. What a trip. But she had overdosed on this pleasure that she loved so much. Loved and loathed all at once.

The scars had begun to become more noticeable. She started to cover them in sleeves, hide them beneath sweaters. She no longer wore the tank tops that showed her colorful bra straps. She no longer wore the skirts that revealed the vulnerable scars on her legs. She could no longer say that she'd had an "accident." *So? I like pants. I swear. I do.*

She still *hurt.*

Everything about her. Her ass and her crotch. Her arms. Her head. The hangover was still with her. Persistent in its penetration. Soaking into every orifice of her body, bringing a throbbing numbness to each pore. Making her skin cold and clammy. *Like a sick baby's skin. A cold sick baby.*

What if she had a cold, sick baby of her own?

I guess I could get pregnant. And I wouldn't know who the father was. I'd have to wonder. But I'm not. I haven't missed a single period. I haven't even been a day late in a while.

But she felt worse than she had ever remembered. So bad that even a baby would seem small, insignificant.

Beatrice

The girls as babies. So difficult! So easy.

She had looked at the albums. When Lilli had been fair-haired, though disagreeable for such a young age. And when Vivian had smiled and sang to herself in her stroller. When the girls would throw their food around the kitchen. When Lilli wasn't a vegetarian. When they had worn diapers. Cried unabashedly, and aloud. When they'd needed her. Holding her skirts and crying at her departure.

But they don't need me anymore. Not really.

When she had been thin. Running around the house. Stealing kisses with Harry when the girls were asleep. His hands around her waist. His eyes glistening. And she was happy. And they were happy. And the world was happy.

But now, she couldn't even bear to step into her daughters' rooms.

So different! Her two girls. And so alike. She couldn't even wash their sheets anymore. They did it themselves. She didn't even wash their towels. *Little rebels. Little adults.*

I wish I'd had more babies. I wish Harry and I had had more babies. Baby boys.
But that was almost impossible now. It wasn't rational to think of that. *Harry is just too tired for sex these days. I understand. His job is very taxing. Very tough. Too tough to have sex when he comes home. He hardly even speaks in the evenings! Why should he want to waste his energy? Right?*

But it's not too late for a baby. We could have a boy if we really tried.

He'd never been much of a talker. He hadn't. Not even when they had met. He preferred actions to words. He preferred to sit around. To live simply. Peacefully. *We never fight, and we never argue. That's what I love. I'd much rather have silence than an argument.*

Her parents used to fight. Big, loud, screaming arguments that had vibrated through their small house. That had embarrassed her. That had been so loud that the neighbors had heard *everything*. She was sure of it.

And Bea had vowed that she would never, ever have a turbulent marriage. She would never hurt her children, embarrass them, embarrass herself.

Why should she embarrass herself? Why should there be arguments when silence seemed to sort out everything on its own?

Vivian

So she went to Katerina's house after school.

Katerina smoked up. Then she left the room for a minute and came back in. Then she went out of the room a second time and returned with a tiny bottle of prescription pills and took one.

"I have this rule: I never drink during the week." The smoke curled through the air. She swallowed the pill effortlessly.

How can she be so pretty?

And as she had watched Katerina's eyes glaze over, opening and shutting in slow motion . . . blood shot, weeping, tripping over her words.

Why don't any guys want me?

Vivian had danced that weekend. She had practiced in the mirror beforehand. She had applied self-tanner meticulously to her exposed flesh. She had been an orange, sparkling, glowing redhead. She had looked willing. She'd made eye contact. She had danced, yes. Danced and danced for them, danced until she was sweating . . . could hardly stop.

It had been her first party with Katerina. So why hadn't it been fun?

So what if I was getting her drinks? So what? We're friends now. Friends get each other drinks.

But why doesn't anyone want me? Why am I so . . . alone? She had danced that night. She had given them what they had asked for. Worn the red thong that caught the light in the best way. Let them smile. Was seductive in her gazes. Watched their eyes go wide. Wider. *Is it because I'm untouchable? Too much?*

What does Lilli have that I fucking don't? What does Katerina have?

I thought I had more. I thought I could do it better. She had it! She did. She had the underwear, the hair, the legs, the ass, the makeup. What she didn't have was the resumé. The raw appeal. The animalism. She didn't have something that said, "Take me instead."

"Shit! What's your name again? Yeah, you have to . . . just, like, if you want guys . . . to like you or whatever . . . just be like . . . Do you have any . . . blow? They like . . . fucking, like, exchanging favors."

But this advice was important. *This is important. This advice.*

I should be thinner. I could wear skimpier stuff if I didn't have this fat on me. This useless fat. The fat that made up the person she saw. *This useless person.*

Harry

"Uh, hello?"

"Wasup man?"

"Is this Sergeant?"

"Yes, and who the hell is this?"

"Uh, I, uh, was given your card by a friend of mine who—"

"Who's your friend?"

"Steve, uh, Verchon. He—"

"Oh yeah?"

"Yeah."

"Steve. Good fuckin' customer."

"Um—"

"So, then who the hell are you?"

"I'm Harry."

"Harry, so I'm expecting that Steve told you about my girls?"

"Well, just a little bit . . . I mean, I'm not that kind of guy. I don't want—"

"Sure you aren't. This is my business. You called because you want a girl."

"I—"

"When do you want her for?"

"Uh, I—"

"Yes?"

"What about later . . . tonight, I guess."

"Tonight?"

"Can . . . can I specify a type?"

"If you want, Harry."

"Dark hair, please."

"Latino?"

"No, Caucasian if that's okay . . ."

"Whatever. You're the one who's payin', not me."

"And uh, really nice legs, and well . . . pretty. Really attractive. And thin."

"Pretty and thin? Hah."

"Is there something wrong with—"

"Are you married, Harry?"

"Isn't that personal . . . information?"

"That's just the impression I get, that's all."

"No, I'm . . . I'm just in town and—"

"Sure, sure, that's what they all say."

"I—"

"So, Steve's your friend?"

"Well, he's my client so—"

"Yeah, you don't fuckin' sound like him at all. He's a confident bastard; you just sound fuckin' scared."

"Oh, no . . . Well, we're very different."

"Yeah, you guys are really different. It's fucked up how different you are."

"I guess you could—"

"So, just have the cash ready."

"I will."

"If you have any questions and shit about what's what, ask her. Like about payment and shit like that. So it's five hundred an hour flat. Anything 'extra' will cost you. As I said, ask the bitch what's what."

"Well, that's a little steep . . ."

"Well, all I can say is: you don't get better fucking girls than mine. You get what you pay for, and you're paying for prime ass. My clients are some notable bastards. Really notable."

"What's her name?"

"Chloé."

"Can she be here at eight? Tell her I don't want her to introduce herself. Tell her to come in and that I . . . Tell her I want her to . . ."

His heart was racing as the wind burned his face. He was still wearing dirty clothes; he was unshaven. But he didn't mind. He was in a hurry.

The department store.

He pushed past fussy ladies, and slow old women, and salesclerks and displays. He bolted up the escalator. *The women's department.*

It seemed as if he had never been to the women's section of a department store. He and Bea had never gone shopping together, and he was not the kind of man who bought his wife clothes or lingerie as a gift. *Because she'd look awful in it.* Even for the girls, he'd never been to the woman's department. He was always waiting downstairs in the car. Always.

He'd never seen such a high concentration of feminine things anyplace: clothing brands, perfume bottles, satin shoes with four inch heels, pictures of models, all in one well-lit space in the middle of Cleveland. And the women! Walking hurriedly, holding up garments, looking in mirrors, conversing with one another. Laughing! Having fun! *I bet you Bea never liked going to these places.* The women, encircling him, saleswomen offering to help him. Women like animals, eyeing him. *For once, I'm a fucking minority!*

"Can I help you? Sir, please may I help you?"

Yeah, help me figure out who I am. Help me figure out what I'm doing. Help me figure out what's going on.

He made his way over to the lingerie section. The women around him either glared or smiled sweetly. *I know they're thinking I'm a dirty fuck. A dirty bastard who's hiring a whore for the night.* He didn't want them to think that. But he liked it, the women watching as he held up tiny sheer panties and bras with ribbon closures and opalescent rhinestones adorning their straps. *All I want to do is talk to her. I just want to hold her. Touch her to know she's real.*

He walked toward the clothing section. Lingerie still in hand, he endured more dirty looks. Digging into him. Was it because he smelled of booze? Because he was unshaven? Wearing a creased suit? He heard some girl whisper to her friend, "Now *that's* just disgusting. Look at that guy."

And the friend agreed. "Well, I feel sorry for him. He probably buys this stuff just for fun. Look, he's, like, still drunk from last night or something."

Fuck you! You don't know me. You don't know about my life, or why I'm buying this, or why I haven't shaved yet. You don't know me!

He was holding a red silk blouse and a black miniskirt. *Thin. My girl is going to be thin and beautiful. Not like Bea at all.* And he walked over to the counter.

"Is this for your wife, sir?"

No. Harry discreetly slipped his left hand into his coat pocket and wrestled his ring off his finger with his thumb. He felt the weight of the gold thud against the fabric. A heavy ring. A ring that held burden and memories of a time within it that he wanted to melt into nothing but liquid and sell as a hardened chunk to a jeweler for cash.

"No, it's not. My wife recently passed away."

He saw the saleswoman's face grow solemn. *I'm so sorry.*

"We're all sorry."

The ring's ghost still clung to his finger.

He hurried back to the hotel. He hadn't thought about his daughters for days. He'd been so happy to rid himself of the responsibility at first. *What are they doing right now? What are they doing living there with HER?*

I really love them. I love them both, I swear.

The two girls. So different. So alike.

Haven't talked to them in a while. They're just busy. Too busy to talk to me. I don't blame them. Lilli with her boyfriends, and Vivian with her schoolwork. What do they need to bog themselves down for? So young. So little pressure!

He imagined them at school. He saw them as children again. The two giggling little girls whom he had loved so much. Still loved so much. He had wanted boys. He used to say it. He *had* before he'd had the girls. So different!

His coworkers had boys. What pains in the ass they were! The boys! But he had *girls*. And his coworkers envied him. They envied him because his girls were so good, and their boys were *so* bad.

Or at least that's how he interpreted it.

And he wasn't about to convince them otherwise.

Lilliana

Paul had called. He was coming over again. He'd left his sweater there, and he could spend a half hour with her on the guitar.

Lilli sat and held that sweater. The stupid olive green sweater that was *fifty-percent acrylic, fifty-percent cotton*. And so nice. It smelled just like him, and probably felt somewhat like him too. She imagined feeling his arms through the fabric. Two strong arms that were connected to two strong hands with five guitar-playing fingers on each. And his chest, how she could just hold on to the sweater and feel it.

But why should Lilli have to hold on to sweaters and pretend? She could have as much of the real thing as she wanted. As many boys and men with sweaters or without. With muscular arms and all.

And her heart was throbbing in her chest. Like a wound that had taken on a life of its own. Not even self-inflicted.

What should I wear for this? Something casual. Something tight. So I can show off my boobs, with the silky bra. . . .

But why? *Why are you trying to impress him? Why?*

She was confused as usual. *I'll change my sheets. Put on fresh ones. You can't have any sort of guy up to your room with bloody sheets on the bed.*

The stain was almost black. The cuts on her arm pulsed with the feverish, uncontrollable beating of her heart. *I didn't know that my blood was so . . . dark. Evil almost.* And the carpet! Black too. Black and dry. A part of herself, removed. A black part.

What would Paul say if he saw my blood?

The thin kind of blood. The kind that seeped from freshly severed veins, and flowed quickly. The kind that released itself so well, so smoothly, that you could fall asleep to it like music. And awaken to find too much of it stolen by nature.

The fresh sheets smelled too clean. Unslept-in. She lay down. Mussed the sheets up with her hands. And she closed her eyes for a moment. Rolled around. Smashed in the pillows. Kicked the covers to her ankles.

She got up and pulled a rug over the stain on her carpet.

I don't understand why I want to impress him. The guy I fucked a couple of days ago was a million times hotter. This is stupid. Just really stupid. Paul's a fucking college nerd! It doesn't matter. Why do you act like such a dork around him then? It's like . . . what? Every guy you see you have to jump into bed with?

She put on a black lace bra. A tank top. A thong that just peeked over the top of her jeans. Lipstick the color of the life that was freed with her quest for sanctuary, for true pain.

Beatrice

To hear his voice! The sound of his voice. It's probably the best sound I could ever imagine. Better than when her daughters had been born. Better than hearing her mother's laugh as a little girl. Better than hearing bacon sizzling on the stove for Harry. It was *his voice!*

The resonance.

The hidden tenderness she knew he harbored.

He was never one to be overly affectionate. Who could expect a husband to be affectionate at all? Who could ever have a husband who runs a house? *That doesn't exist. But Harry does run this house. He's the backbone for all of us.*

She could never imagine *divorce.*

How could I break up my family? The girls rely on us so much. They look up to us. They depend on us. And we're just supposed to desert them? They need us.

His voice had seduced her all over again. The depth. The strength. The words didn't matter. *It doesn't matter what he says; it's how he says it.*

The day he'd asked her for her phone number at the party where she'd worn her cornflower blue dress. *That dress! It's still in the back of my closet somewhere. A beautiful dress. I wish Lilli would wear that dress.* When she'd smiled, and swooned at the manliness that sprang forth from his lips. Watching his tongue flicking up and down behind his teeth, forming the consonants. His lips, curving, shaping the words that were so painfully beautiful to her. "It would be such an honor to get your phone number. . . ."

An honor. To get my phone number.

And she had laughed like a girl that night. Spread her own ruby lips into a toothy smile for him, and complied. *How could I say no to such a beautiful man?* To a man of few words. *He didn't need words. But when they were there, how beautiful they were.*

Vivian

Somewhere it was real for her. It was real for the people who saw her but didn't know her. It was real for the people who had never looked at her before, but looked now. It was real for the people who had scoffed at her old, drab, frizziness. Her grotesqueness. Those who smiled at her now.

I should get a tattoo. I should.

A tattoo. A tattoo to show what? Endurance? Pain? Lack of feeling? Stupidity? Disease? Danger? Popularity? Peace? Love? Happiness? Hatred? Disgust. Stupidity. Ugliness.

Tattoos aren't feminine. They're butch. They're white trash. And they're expensive. She didn't have fifty bucks of her own to hand out to a tattoo artist. She didn't even know what it should say. Or look like. Or mean. *Are you supposed to decide what you want a tattoo of before you go? Or are you supposed to pick one out when you get there?* What was the point?

She'd talked to people who'd been tattooed. "You have to like pain, hon." She'd smiled at this. *I have to like pain.*

But who can really like pain? What kind of person really likes pain at all?

Her belly button had been different. She'd winced at the pain. She'd forced back the tears that pressed themselves to the front of her eyes, and threatened to run down her cheeks, leaving long, snaky trails of makeup behind. *But who likes pain? How can anyone actually like to get hurt?*

But Katerina has a tattoo. Yes. Katerina. She had a tattoo: Kat+Darienne with a heart around it. It was on her wrist. Maybe their hiatus wasn't going to be so permanent after all.

Lilliana

Paul's footsteps on the carpet. How he opened the door. The slight smile on his face, showing just a peek of the pearlescent sheen of his slightly crooked teeth. *Not perfect. Perfect teeth, they're so, well, everyone has them.* His perfect lips. How he formed his words.

How he held the guitar.

How he held her hand. Put his hand on hers.

The way he strummed the strings. *The ridge between his eyebrows. The birthmark on his neck.* Songs he played so well. *The songs that I love. His songs.* How his hair was slightly rumpled. His shirt, slightly creased. *His hands.* His smell.

I've never felt this way. Ever.

Looking at Paul's hands as if they were a god's hands. Looking at the little things. *The little things about him. I never looked so closely before. I never had the time.* Always rushing.

How many faces have I forgotten?

But she would never forget his. The little things that made it special. Because it was not the prettiest face. His was not the perfect portrait. And hers was weathered by the eyes of men. Sixteen and *old.*

But he was oblivious. Oblivious to her silent pleas.

Wrapped up in his music. He closed his eyes while he played. Tight. And she looked on, at the darkness of his lashes; the strength of his forearms; the way his Adam's apple moved up and down with the words, with the music; and the way he didn't care. About anything. At all.

Harry

I resent everything. I resent marrying her. I resent our lives together. I re-sent our life together.

Dim the lights.

The clothes were spread on the bed. There was a bottle of champagne in an ice bucket.

And all I have to do is wait. "Just sit here and wait."

The clock said 8:03. *Three minutes late.* But it was a comforting lateness. There was anticipation. Bea would've been early.

For a moment, he worried that Sergeant would send some woman who would look exactly like Bea. Some woman who would remind him too much of her. *I don't want to have sex with her; I just want to talk. Is that so bad?* Just for a few hours of Harry's life, he wanted to talk to someone to whom he was physically attracted. *I don't want to fuck her. What's so bad about that?*

I'll have to make this quick because I have to call Steve. Steve Verchon. Door opener. Gateway to so many new things, new emotions, burning passions, and hatred all at once. *A passionate hatred.*

Waiting.

Anticipating.

Finally, a variable. Finally, there was a new breath of air in the room: a breath of life. The windows were not open, but air flowed freely. He was start-ing to forget. He didn't need to think about Bea. He didn't need it. *Why should I think about her? It just fucking pisses me off.* And he didn't need to think of the girls then. No family ties straining his limbs. He could still love his daughters; he just didn't want them to own him.

It's better if I don't think about her. Bea, killer of passion. Killer of love. Killer of moments.

It was 8:07, and he liked it.

Beatrice

Clean house. Dirty house. Weighing the two alternatives in her hands, feeling them. Clean house. Dirty house. Touching them almost. *This is a dirty house. And dirty houses are no good. Unkempt women keep unkempt rooms, and I am not unkempt. I am not dirty. And Harry would never be satisfied with an unsatisfactory house.*

She turned the faucet. Let the water run over the filthy dishes. Poured in the soap. Let them soak. Let the dishes disappear in a sea of iridescent bubbles. It was her favorite smell.

Bea. Standing there, inhaling the smell of detergent with her eyes closed. In her suburban kitchen. Alone.

She remembered bathing her daughters in such warm soapy water when they were babies. How they'd loved it.

And then she thought of her daughters in the present. Lilli, free, uninhibited, smart, curt. Vivian, a rebel, coming into her own. Smoking now. Drinking now. *Are both of them having sex now? Are both of my babies having sex?*

But the thought was too painful. Too strong. Detergent undiluted by faucet water.

She pushed it out of her mind. Banishing it to a far-off corner where she could forget. Where she could return to her world of pretty bubbles. Cleanliness. Simple beauty. Something that just didn't really have to change.

But the images were hard to keep locked away. Stowed in the closet like winter clothes. Raw and unsightly. Her daughters. Her daughters growing up. Making decisions of their own. Decisions in which she had no part. No influence at all. *But it's so hard to influence headstrong teenagers. There's no use hoping for something that just won't happen. They'll do what they want. And Harry will straighten things out when he comes home. He'll fix everything.* What an antidote.

Lilliana

In ecstasy in between her bedsheets. She watched her favorite plaything, the Swiss Army knife, flicker in the light as she brought it down to her skin and pressed the point in. *Deeper. Harder. Faster.* And then comes the relief. A journey to her sanctuary.

Climaxing. A moan.

Mine. They're so mine. This is mine. This is all mine. This blood is mine.

And she dragged the point up, over, and around the lovely unmarked flesh. *These are my tattoos. They say so much more.* There was nothing to read. There were no pictures. No bright colors. But there was experience. There was emotion. There was depth. Fear. Truth. There was blood. It said it all. It was all there. *Who needs words, when life is here? Written on my arms is my life story.*

Dribbling down the front of her tank top like melted ice cream. Lilli laughed as it trickled down and around, and then sat frozen and woven into the fabric. And it was so *personal.* What a way to be.

To have something all your own.

And she thought of Paul. Again. How she had looked at him. Seen him differently. As a different person. As someone who felt and saw and lived. As someone who meant something else. *But what else is he supposed to mean? If I like someone, I want to fuck them, and if I don't, then I don't. If someone's hot, if someone's older. You know. But not Paul. I tried. He doesn't play my game. He doesn't fall into my traps.* Smarter; a smarter animal. Different tactics would have to be employed.

And she dragged her index finger through the tiny pool of blood on her arm. *It's like artwork. It's beauty. It's truth. This is reality. This is my epicenter.*

Vivian

She doted on the idea of a small Chinese symbol on her pelvis which meant "peace." But she didn't speak Chinese, so it didn't seem that worthwhile. *To have a tattoo in a language that I don't know. It's supposed to be about* me! *It's supposed to be mine. Chinese isn't mine.*

A tattoo with writing in English seemed too cliché—even though Katerina had one. The tattoo had been a mistake on her part; an armful of bracelets was all that she could do to cover up the blatant message. Everyone knew it was there anyway, though. But a stream of Chinese characters wouldn't exactly be unique either. *Because it's not really mine if everyone understands. It's supposed to be semiprivate. Semipublic.* French? There was nothing that could please her. Maybe no language that existed on earth.

And what else did she have?

Besides a ring in her belly, and self-restraint?

Her grades had begun to slip. Studying became the last priority. *I only study if I have time. Sometimes you have to prioritize. An autobiography on my metamorphosis alone, in conjunction with great SAT scores, should get me into all of the Ivys anyway. All of the very best. And I won't even have to try. FUCK tests. Fuck everything. I HAVE THIS. I have friends. I have places to go after school.*

She ripped off her skirt, her top. Stood there in her shoes. Staring. *Who would've imagined that good girl Vivian would diet? And get thin. And hot. And be pretty. And who would've imagined that I would shake my ass, and they would love it. See, you have to show a little to get a lot in return.*

Stardom and respect do not fit into the same category.

She didn't really care about respect at this point. Notoriety was the important thing. And she looked good next to Katerina at school. They complimented one another through their apparent contrasts. It was clear that one of them was trying very hard, while the other wasn't trying at all. *But that's okay. Because I'm going to get a boyfriend soon. I have to.*

This was an honor. Katerina hugging her good-bye before class. Her infamous lips tugging on Vivian's cigarettes. She never used to buy them before. *It's okay though. I don't mind.* Katerina's arm linked to hers. Her skinny thighs swishing beside her.

Harry

"Hey baby, this is a nice hotel room you've got here."

"Stop. Shhh . . ."

"What?"

"Just, uh, wait right there. Could you come in again?"

"Jesus, what is this bullshit? . . . So what's my name, Harry?"

"You, uh . . . you don't have one."

"Okay . . . And what do you want me to call you?"

"Just Harry."

"So, *Harry*, you really want me to go out and come back in here?"

"Will you, please?"

"Fine."

"Thanks."

"So, Harry, does this turn you on?"

"No, no, stop it. Don't do that."

"What about *this*?"

"I said *stop.*"

"Why are you so tense, Harry? Just calm down. You want me to—"

"Please just stop. I don't want you to do that."

"Jesus, what's your fucking problem? 'Cause if you're not going to pay me or if you're a fucking psychotic, then I'm just going to leave."

"No, don't leave. Don't ruin the mood. Please . . . Didn't Sergeant talk to you about what I asked?"

"Baby, Serg and I have a special relationship. He doesn't give me no directions. I do what I do best."

"But I asked . . . just wanted . . ."

"You wanted a brunette, and that's what you got. And I'm the best brunette that you're ever going to get. You just wait—"

"Will you put these on . . . please?"

"You want me to change right here? I didn't know you were into role-play, Harry. This should be fun. I'm a damn good actress."

"No, no, there's the bathroom."

"What the fuck . . . Isn't this what you're paying for? Isn't *this* what you're paying for?"

"I don't want to talk about money. You're my girl. Go into the bathroom like a classy woman."

"Sure, Harry. (silence) Is this what you wanted?"

"Ohh, uh, oh yes. You look—"

"Do you like my ass, Harry?"

"Don't *say* that. Don't talk to me that way. Just be quiet. Just walk over here, slowly."

"Okay, just most of my clients like it when—"

"Well, I don't . . . Listen to me. You are no longer yourself; you're a woman who lives here in Cleveland. You work. You're single. You're elegant. I don't want to hear any vulgar language come out of your mouth. I just want to talk to you . . . her. You as her."

"Okay, Harry, baby."

"Don't call me that. Just Harry. (silence) So, would you like some champagne?"

"Oh yes, that would be great."

"Here."

"Thanks."

"So . . . (silence) I mean, I saw you, and well, I just lost control of my—"

"Baby, does this turn you on?"

"Just sit there. All I want to do is look at you. That's all I want to do. Just to stare at you . . ."

"Jesus, you're not like most guys."

"And you're not like most girls. You're the most beautiful girl in the world. The most beautiful woman I've ever seen."

It was the next morning. She had been gone for hours.

The clothes were laid neatly on the bed. Almost as if they hadn't been worn at all.

He'd wished for something different, but it was the best he could get. "The best brunette that you're ever going to get."

But once she'd learned to stay quiet, once she'd learned how to stare back, things hadn't been so bad at all. Better than "not bad"; things had been good. *All I wanted to do was see her. That was it. No big deal.* He wasn't planning to call her again.

The best brunette.

According to Harry's logic, he should no longer have had to torture himself. *That was it. It's out of my system now. The whole thing is over. Stupid. Just a dumb, childish, impulsive thing, but nothing really happened, so I'm fine.* His needs hadn't been met though. He was trying to make himself believe that they had been, but they just hadn't.

But they could be, if he'd let them. *If only.*

But now that you've had your fun, it's time to call Steve and get back on track. Stupid fucking slacker. No diligence, no morals . . . Why does everything have to get fucked up now?

He tried to make himself forget it. There was guilt. About everything. Because he wanted to care and he wanted value and importance to be present in his life, and he wanted these properties to be assigned to the appropriate people and things. Just have them assigned, and that way he'd have to obey. That was a dreamworld though. *And that means it doesn't exist. It doesn't exist.*

Beatrice

She had not been in her daughters' rooms in so long. It was as if she could hardly remember the layouts of the two tiny bedrooms with the thin wall and the bathroom in between. The little rooms with juvenile wallpaper. Lilli's dirty little room, and Vivian's clean one.

She mounted the stairs carefully, one by one. Her hand sliding up the banister just like it had when they'd first looked at the house.

She had held Harry's hand. Linking her fingers in his like a child. And she had felt the polished mahogany slide through her own. *Our house. Together. I'd only ever lived with my parents. I'd never looked to buy a house of my own. Of our own.*

And Harry had given her the lightest kiss on the mouth at the top of the steps that first day. Her hand still clutching the banister for support.

I would give anything to have him kiss me now. Here. Just alone in our new house on the first day. Before the girls. Before anything. Before the world began.

She crept through the hallway. Slowly. Very slowly. Walking softly on the carpet. The dull thuds that were her footsteps. *Why am I walking so quietly? The girls aren't even here.* It was the middle of the school day. There was no reason for Bea to be cautious. Afraid.

But there was *something* there, it seemed.

And then she arrived. The two doors. Side by side. Separated by no more than a yard and a half of wall space. Identical doors. As if the girls were identical people in identical worlds. Two girls harbored in two rooms. Two separate worlds kept from clashing by no more than a yard and a half of wall space.

For a moment, Bea couldn't remember which room was which.

She placed her hand on the chilled brass knob. Locked her fingers around it. Felt a tingle in her palm, an intense beating in her heart. And then her hand grew limp. Loose.

As if something, somebody, doesn't want me to do it. I can't go in. Something won't let me do it.

She stood, gazing at the brass knob. In her house. Atop her stairs. Standing on her carpet. The knob would twist so easily. The door would swing open so effortlessly. And she would see all that she had wanted to. Not if the room was neat . . . but if the room had changed.

But she would not see any of this.

Standing at the two doors. Wanting to open them. But she couldn't.

She looked at her hand. The hand that had failed her. That wouldn't let her in. That was keeping her away. Holding her back.

She sat on the floor. On her clean carpet in her clean house. And let the tears stream into the creases of her palm. And permeate the steel surface that was her shield. Against everything that she didn't want to see. Everything that she didn't want to feel.

I can't even go into their rooms any longer. I can't even open the door.

Lilliana

Thinking of Paul while she looked at the nice stain on her carpet. There was a new stain. This one was on her comforter. And another on her white tee-shirt from bed. But she didn't want to wash it away. *It's nice to look at. Pieces of me all over everything. This is the way to personalize a room. To personalize anything, really.*

Lilli was wearing the tee-shirt. The bloody one.

Okay, I know I couldn't wear this out. I know. But, still, it's nice to wear right here. Alone. When it's just me. When no one else is around. Not even Paul.

She hardly cared about anything else anymore.

What would it be like to fuck Paul?

She thought it would be different for some reason. That it would feel different. That there would be something more that was there, and something that was a little more special. *I bet it would be like losing my virginity all over again. Bet that that's what it would be like.*

She closed her eyes. Imagined Paul's strong arms and his simple face and his rough hair against her. She'd never fucked a worthwhile man before. She'd never cared about her conquests.

It would be different, because with the others it was just movement. Like dancing.

Lilli had heard that her sister was doing quite a bit of dancing herself at parties. She had heard at school. She had passed the sister she hardly knew any longer in the hallway. Stared at her as if she were a stranger. With long, cran-grape hair, straightened meticulously so that all of the shine had been burned away. Lots of makeup. *As if she spends hours on herself.* Her legs had looked long, and she had looked taller and thinner; her pale skin had been smothered in bronzer, shimmering under the fluorescence. And her sister's midriff had been showing, and a little artificial blue stone had sparkled. Winking in the hallway light.

Her sister had not seen her.

And Lilli wished she had not seen her sister. At all.

She wished she hadn't seen Vivian trying so hard. *With her new friends. Friends? Yeah, right. Doesn't she know that all those people do is talk about her?*

Doesn't she know they make fun of her? Doesn't she know I fucking hear them doing it? That bitch, Katerina. Doesn't Vivian know how stupid she looks walking around with her? Everyone knows Katerina's just using her.

Well, of course not. How would Vivian know? Obviously, no one was telling her. Lilli sure wasn't going to.

Vivian

The room had been nice and dark. He had said that he thought she was hot. Complimented her. Not to her face. To her friend. And she had taken his hand and sat beside him. And then, yeah, he was all over her. *And I like it! I want to do it again! More!*

Would anyone believe that she'd never made out with a guy before? Games didn't count.

Now I know that guys want me. I'm sure.

Just like Lilli. When you know things. When you know that people want to do you.

She hadn't learned his name. He had been okay-looking. Kind of cute. Kind of handsome. Sort of tall. Sort of muscular. He sort of had a little acne. And he sort of had stubble. But none of that mattered. Because he was sort of all of these things, but he was surely her first step. *Her* first conquest. The commencement of the truth of her new life. Her new self. The one with the red hair and nice legs and abs. Tried to make everyone forget that anyone was hiding beneath the sheet. At that moment, at least.

But, of course, he hadn't been *that* great, because, if he had been, Katerina would have taken him herself. And he obviously wasn't hooked up in any valuable way, because she would have taken advantage of that. She had pointed and said, "You can have *him*." Almost in disgust. *Him. That one over there. That thing.*

"You could have that one over there." The one with the acne and the lack of connections. "You could *have him*. He would fuck you. Totally. If you wanted." Even if you didn't want him to . . . he would still fuck you. "Yeah, that one." You could have that second-class citizen because that's what *you* are. You're lucky to be friends with a girl like me. . . . Don't think you're not. And in exchange for your friendship, I get everything, and you get the runoff. Because you're lucky. To be. Friends. With such an Important Person.

And don't think you're not.

If you start thinking that way, it's better not to think at all.

Beatrice

She was back in her sanctuary—the kitchen. Smelling the smells. Creating something new. A nice enormous breakfast for Harry. *Fit for a Sunday morning.* "You're going to love this! I bought all of the eggs fresh yesterday, and I'll just poach them for you. And you can have the bacon, and the French toast . . ."

His response was perfect. Just what she needed to hear.

"Thank you! I completely agree." She ran around the kitchen. Beatrice running around the kitchen, spatula in hand. Flipping sizzling things. Beating eggs. Creating. For Harry.

"I know you're in a rush! It's coming! Just one more moment for the eggs."

Running, running.

"Okay! Here they are. And here's your tea. And your bacon and everything. Here."

She stood there, eager and waiting to be evaluated by Harry's waiting eyes and melancholy smile. "Glad you like it! Oh, I love you, Harry . . . so so much!"

But the door was open. There seemed to be nothing to hide any longer. Because this was just life. Just living. Just going on. Just moving forward. *Why move backward in order to progress? Life is so precious. So simple. I just say that we should all look ahead.*

Lilliana

She had woken from a dream. There had been two tall trees in a field. The house had been looming in the distance, and the sun had been setting, though too bright to watch. There had been a metal pole in between the two trees, stretched out and somehow secured to each side. It had been high off the ground, so high that when she looked down, she had grown dizzy and faint.

Someone had given her a joint and had ordered her to smoke it. She had refused. The person who had given it to her was Nathan. And he had said, Come on, take the fucking joint. And she had kept refusing, and he yelled at her for wasting it and told her that it was an order to smoke the entire fucking thing. She had been afraid, and had complied.

And then, after the effects had become apparent, Nathan had ordered Lilli to dance across the pole from the first tree to the second without stopping and without falling off. And he had pushed her out onto the pole that loomed high above the ground, and she had said, Nathan, please, please don't make me do this. I'm going to kill myself. And he had said, You don't know what you're saying. You don't know anything. And he had flipped a switch, and suddenly the air had been flooded with Paul's music screaming at her, "Make me, make me." And a wind had come and flung her off the pole and through the air, and just as she was about to hit the ground, her eyes sprung open and she woke up.

She didn't know whether it had been torturous or wonderful.

Beatrice

She had tried the hotel, but his phone had been disconnected. *It is strange, but Harry likes quiet. When he works, he wants quiet, and I have to respect that. There's no reason that I should bother him, or that he should be bothered by anyone at all. He shouldn't.*

She had done nothing but straighten up all day. There was nothing else to do. She had organized and reorganized the vases on the coffee table, trimmed the stems of the flowers. Fixed the small crystal figurines on her night table in her bedroom. She had straightened out the picture frames on the dresser. She had cleaned all of the toilets and showers (except in her daughters' bathroom). She had taken a few stains out of the carpet in her bedroom. But whenever she passed by her daughters' rooms, she could not even attempt to go in.

I don't know what it is, or why. I just can't. I just won't. They're big girls. They can have their own rooms with their own things in them. I'm sure that they're neat. The rooms have got to be livable. At least.

But she didn't know what to expect from her daughters anymore. *They're not the same girls anymore. I used to know them. I used to know what they liked. But I don't now. I don't at all.* She could hardly speak to them any longer.

But she would call her daughters down to dinner as always.

She would wish for them to come. The two girls she no longer knew.

Like sharing my table with two strangers. Harry and I share the table. And they probably won't even come. "You'll be there though." She smiled at his thoughtful face, at the pasted-on banal grin that was such a relief to her.

Vivian

Stupid fuck. It took so little to do so much. And being drunk felt good to her. Puking on the lawn had felt just fine. *Too fucked up to know.* Three screwdrivers and a few tequila shots. Just enough sickness to make her feel healthy. This was just the beginning. *This is just the beginning.*

As if no one's been drunk before? Fuck, yeah . . . But the feeling was gone. And now she was awake, awake and at home. Naked, hungover, awake and at home in the room upstairs with the thin walls.

Lilli wasn't even home yet. *Probably screwing someone's brains out right now. God . . .* Her palms were clammy against her hot forehead.

She'd hardly ever drank before. Hardly took a sip without thinking of the weight of engaging in illegal activities beforehand.

But it felt so good! It feels so good! So fun, so free, so deep.

But the feeling was gone. And in its place: emptiness.

Her body pulsed under the sheets. In need of a man. In need of new hands to do something more. To do something else she was incapable of. *It's no fun being alone. I'm ready. I'm seriously ready.*

She touched the ring, the stone in the middle. And thought of the tattoo that she just might get.

There were guys at the party . . . I could've had that guy if I'd tried. Katerina said I could have. I hadn't tried though. It's my fault. She hadn't realized that the drunkenness had come on fast. That her empty stomach had not held onto her sobriety. That her mind had wandered further than she'd expected. That her eyes had closed, and music had seeped into her being. Amplifying everything. And making her say no. Stiff under his searching hands, she had pushed him away. To everyone's dismay. Sick in the bathroom. Too sick to realize.

If I could do it over, I'd do it right. But I didn't like him . . . I didn't want to sleep with him. I hope Katerina's not mad at me or anything.

Harry

The picture in his wallet was taking up too much space, he'd decided. He was accumulating business cards, and the picture would have to go. He drew the shades, walked over to the trash can, removed the picture, and dropped it straight down into the bin.

It hardly made a sound: it had fluttered gently on the way down. Coming to rest finally in the bottom. It lay facedown. He wouldn't have to see the wife in the red dress anymore.

So heavy and yet so light. So easy to throw away.

Every time he opened his wallet, that picture had glared at him. And he needed new space, and he needed clarity, and he didn't need remorse. But he did stick Sergeant's card in its place. Bleak in its message.

He'd contemplated disposing of it. He'd walked it over to the trash with the family photo and was about to toss it in as well *just to start over, just to forget everything,* but something had made him stop. Because it had been a release, and *what if I need a release?*

It's not like we had sex. Just someone to talk to. And someone who held so little significance that she became the most significant thing to him.

I should be working right now. I should be better. I should call home and talk to the girls.

But he couldn't.

His mind was filled with dire messages. Painful images. Things he shouldn't have seen. Lilli, drawing her own blood, Pricking her own fingers and enjoying it. He couldn't return to that. *I can't.* He was reveling in the fact that he didn't have to return to it. And he wouldn't have to hold his breath as he passed her room. And he wouldn't have to read the teleprompter hanging over Bea's shoulder in every conversation, and he wouldn't have to deconstruct her pleasant sentences, her idiomatic phrases and looks, and even her blinking eyes in order to find out what was underneath. Unclothed, Bea seemed just as unreachable. Her face, washed with plain soap and stripped of all cosmetics, seemed just as covered. He was sick of looking for deeper meaning.

He would just take things at face value. A card was nothing more than a card. A name was nothing more than that. A whore was nothing more than someone with whom he could amuse himself. *But I just talked to her. We just talked!* "Bea? You're a fucking ugly cunt! Hear that? A fucking cunt." So he could amuse himself at will, and it would mean nothing more than . . . amusement. Right?

Lilliana

She had called Paul. Got his answering machine. She had hung up. She had wanted to talk but couldn't. The razor blade was second best.

Actions speak louder than words, after all.

Lilli had sat on the bathroom floor again, drawn the blade against the peachy skin on her thigh, lightly at first and then with increasing pressure. *Rubbing, rubbing until the blood squeezes through.* Gentle but rough. Calm but frantic. Euphoric but hellish.

She knew it would bleed a lot. *I guess a thigh must have a lot of blood in it;*

it's pretty wide. And it did. Running down to her underwear, and spreading out into a lake on the floor.

Filling in all the cracks. All the spaces that were available.

She didn't grab for the towel so quickly. She hadn't really wanted to do it in the first place. *I guess I would've rather talked to him . . . but I guess he doesn't wait for me. I guess I rely on Paul too much. I used to be so independent.* But blood was being lost, spreading, growing, increasing in size. Turning from a lake into an ocean.

She felt the intoxication and then . . .

She grabbed the bath towel, holding it against the open, deep wound. Letting it turn the white part crimson. Letting it contaminate the cleanliness it screamed.

And when it was done, she held a towel in her hand. She had used two this time. *I don't know . . . I can't bear to wash them right now.* Her eyelids were beginning to flutter closed. She slowly walked down to the laundry room, placed the blood-soaked towels in the machine with a dull thud, and left. *Besides, it's not like anyone notices anymore. It's not like anyone cares.* And went upstairs to bed.

Vivian

To win.

How many times have I lost? How many things?

She had been looking. Her eyes had been peeled. She'd searched around school. *The ones who stare . . . they're just good for the attention. But they're not anyone I would want for a boyfriend. They aren't anyone I would date or anything. Just boys. Just eyes.*

Just tongues.

Just dicks. "Vivian, it's just a *penis*; what the hell are you afraid of? It's not gonna, like, hurt you."

Just a pair of coveted new hands. "Vivian . . . it seriously, like . . . it doesn't matter or anything, you know? It doesn't matter. I'm sick of talking about you and your, like, neuroses."

She was still a virgin underneath though, underneath the makeup, the hair wax, the thong. She was still a virgin underneath the smile, the glances, the things that she had practiced, awaited, and loathed. The things she had lost.

She had bought condoms.

To be safe . . . just in case, I guess. She'd practiced. She'd practiced everything. She was ready for it. So she thought.

The face in the mirror said that she looked nice. More than nice. She had *achieved something.*

I never thought I could look this way. Never ever. With my new friends and the drinking on weekends. The parties. The fun. For once, I'm having fun! She was waiting for a chance to dance. To show off her taut skin, her curling tongue hidden behind her straight white teeth.

But look what I've gained.

Didn't she feel cool guarding the bathroom door for Kat? Didn't she feel cool buying weed? Cigarettes? Yeah, in fact, she did. She really really did. There was a reason *why* now. She understood it. *You can't just say no to something because people tell you to . . . you can't just be a follower. You can't judge something just because people tell you to judge it. If everyone did that, imagine how boring everything would be.*

Beatrice

She had heard someone's footsteps. Quietly shuffling upstairs, smoky, controlled, holding back. In the house. She had heard a daughter. A teenage girl. *I used to know them by their footsteps. I used to be able to tell so easily.* By the squeak of their sneakers, the click of their heels, the beat in their step. There was nothing now. None of it had meant anything. Just noise.

She had called them down for dinner again that night. But no one had come. They probably weren't even home.

But Harry was home, because he is always home for me.

"Isn't that right, Harry?" Of course, it's right. "Didn't we have a wonderful dinner tonight?"

But her bed was cold.

She could smell the dishes from downstairs. She could smell the food. The stale food that sat in the garbage. She had never taken out the garbage. *Harry always takes out the garbage.* "Harry, you ought to take it out. I know you're busy, but still . . ." Rancid, curdled. The smell of brisket and Chinese food. Eggs and French toast. Wafting up to Bea's room, into her nostrils.

She had the urge to clean, but could not.

I'm just so tired. And the girls might be awake.

Harry

Rolling the wedding ring across the desk. *How much could I get for this?* Rolling back and forth. He'd removed it from his pocket so as not to lose it . . . didn't want to forget it there. Solid gold. Eighteen-karat. *No! It's my wedding ring! My own fucking wedding ring!*

Why am I thinking like this? Why?

Why do I hate my wife? Why am I so scared of home . . . ?

But the gold looked promising . . . and it was just plain embarrassing to wear with his brunette. *But it's out of my system.*

He slid it back on, but it felt too tight. It made him itch, irritated his skin. He felt his finger turning red, his knuckle hurt from the pressure of the metal being forced over it. But it was his obligation as a married man. With duties and a purpose. *Married men wear rings and I have a ring and I'm married and I should wear it.* But what if he didn't want to be married anymore? What if he was liking this?

He couldn't like it. Too risky.

But so so nice. The brunette. Domineering brunette. The best he could ever get. So good that he'd have to pay for her. Take large stacks of twenty-dollar bills out of the ATM and slip them into her waiting palm. And she hadn't been easy, but that's what he'd liked. He'd liked that! Even though he'd wanted her to be someone else . . . the original girl. He was already bound to a submissive woman. *Submissive spineless pig of a woman.* And the brunette was not submissive.

Steve noticed at dinner . . . He noticed I wasn't wearing this . . . this thing.

Harry ordered a bottle of vodka from room service.

But look at the bright side. Steve likes me, the deal is working, and things are falling into place. And if this works . . . He grew distracted by the tight loop of metal gripping the flesh of his left finger. He slid it back over his knuckle, which only increased the pain. It was red and swollen afterward, but he *would take that over gold any day.*

Lilliana

She had stopped by the store again that day. She had stood at the cash register. Waited for Paul, who was on break.

He had said hi. They had talked briefly. He had been preoccupied. She'd asked him was anything was wrong? No, he had said. But he was going to come over tomorrow. *He's going to come up to my room. Sit on my floor again. Oh Jesus, I have no idea what the fuck is up with me. . . .*

I need to go clubbing again.

The music. That's what she needed. The attention. The glittery faces and the sweaty bodies. She needed to feel good. *Because I feel inferior when I'm with Paul. He's so . . . I don't know. His presence. It's special.*

She wondered, though, on the walk home. What had ever happened to her fun? Her power? *Even the fucks I've had recently—they haven't been THAT good. They're not like they used to be.* When she'd been the nymph. The powerful, manipulative Lolita who melted men with her glances. Who warmed them, and then pushed them onto the street and out of her mind. Who froze them with her stares, as if to say, "You're wrong. None of it even happened. You wish."

But it's not the same anymore. Now all I do is think about Paul. I've never been the type who just thinks about one guy all the fucking time. Such a waste of energy!

Paul. A guy who had brushed her off. Who had barely said hello. Who didn't faint at the prospect of coming up to her room. The one guy who wasn't afraid of her.

She ran to the bathroom, shut the door. Reached for the razor and controlled its descent toward her waiting calf. And then she heard the knob turn from the other side.

"Get out of here! Don't you knock?"

"I'm sorry; you usually lock it."

"We don't have fucking locks! I forgot to put a fucking chair in here."

"So don't yell at me then. You're the one who made the mistake."

"Get the fuck out!"

"What are you doing?"

"Nothing. I, had a . . . shaving accident."

"Oh . . . really?"

"Yes, really. Just leave! I'm trying to shave here."

"Looks pretty deep for a shaving cut—and your legs aren't even wet."

"I'll take care of it. It's not such a big deal. If you'd just leave me—"

"Fine, Lilli. You know what? I don't give a fuck anymore, okay?"

"Yeah? Well who the hell do you think you are? You bitch. You dye your fucking hair, and you pierce your fucking belly button, and you just think that you can start walking around like a fucking—"

"Fuck off, and lock the fucking door next time if you want to 'shave' in private. Maybe you should just relocate your little self-mutilation project elsewhere, because some people actually have to use the fucking toilet."

Beatrice

She'd woken in the night three times, and tiredly dragged herself down to the kitchen. The sun was still tucked behind the houses across the street. *I haven't seen a sunrise in so long. And when was the last time I saw the sun set?*

It had been with Harry. The morning after their wedding. They had awakened in the hotel bedroom. She had been sweating in his arms that clasped around her body so securely. She had been naked; ashamed of her nakedness in the morning. And she had been ashamed of his as well, but mystified nonetheless. She had never been naked in front of *anyone,* it seemed. Or seen a man, a real man, naked.

They had walked to the window, stood together. Two naked bodies. Bea, ashamed of her womanliness. Harry, proud to own the woman he held. And the sun had slid up over the buildings. *I'd shaded my eyes; it was so bright. So young.*

The sun had not changed.

Bea had changed.

She was no longer the young nude girl. Barely out of her teens. Barely experienced at anything. So willing. Willing to listen. To comply. To serve. To ask nothing of anyone except for herself. She was no longer a bride. No longer a prize to be won, no longer a conquered possession. No longer a great beauty. No longer of any real value. *Except to Harry.*

But Harry made me brave. And unashamed. He showed me beauty. He let me know what love is.

She had the urge to call him. Pick up the phone and dial his room.

He's asleep. It's barely six here. Barely. He has meetings. Business. He's busy now. Unlike you.

She dropped to her knees and scrubbed the floor. Carefully, meticulously finding the gleam that lay somewhere dormant within the worn tiles.

Vivian

A high . . .

One apple, one glass of water, three Altoids. *And abs. And definition. And muscularity. And beauty. Let's see them look at me now. No more fat Vivian. Hot Vivian, pretty Vivian. Skinny Vivian. Let's just see how they look now. This is how Katerina eats. And look how good she looks.*

She'd heard the girls at school talking. She'd heard what they'd said. The old friends had said that she was becoming a slut. Glaring at her from across the room. Staring at her in the hall by Katerina's side. "Whoever would've thought that anyone would *ever* like Vivian?" *I don't blame them. Whoever would've thought? And I don't care about the old friends. They're so . . . ugly. Ugly ugly ugly.* Those were the old friends. The old days. Back in the days when Vivian wasn't special.

But there were rumors.

"I heard Vivian was so high last weekend that she had a threesome in a gas station!" With who? "Oh, like, probably an attendant and some truck-driver guy or something."

"Did you hear Vivian was so drunk that she tried to blow Liz's boyfriend right in front of her?" Omigod! Are you serious? "Yeah, and Liz totally like bitch slapped that slut, and then she left and started like hysterically crying and shit. Oh God, it was so stupid of Vivian. Liz was so upset, and she was all 'I'm gonna make that bitch pay,' like, all weekend. It was really awful."

"She fucks well. That's all I have to say. Trust me on this one. You should try her out sometime. Seriously! I'll let you borrow her if you're nice. Yeah, you can borrow her or whatever, as long as you have some weed."

Is that so bad? So? My virginity has almost been lost for me. I don't really have to worry. At least Katerina doesn't know that I'm a virgin. She just thinks I'm shy. Good.

Was it better before? Being ugly?

But Vivian was not ugly any longer. She was a pretty mannequin now. One who had nice little womanly things in all the nice little womanly places. She was not ugly. No, no, no. Ugly was not even in her frame of mind.

Harry

"Baby, I knew you'd call . . . 'Cause we had so much fun last time."

"Yeah."

"You want me to put on the clothes again?"

"Yeah, that would be . . . um . . . great."

"You still want me to go into the bathroom?"

"Will you?"

"Whatever you want."

"You look . . . you look gorgeous."

"Yeah, where's the drinks?"

"Sit down . . . shhhh."

"Ugh, fine. (silence) So . . . you lonely baby?"

"Shhhhh. Let me just look at you."

"Harry? Don't you wanna—"

"You're so—"

". . . at least—"

". . . just so beautiful—"

". . . fuck me?"

"No! No! I just want to talk to you, that's—"

"You don't like it when I do this, Harry? This doesn't make you hot?"

"Please, just—"

"You don't like it when I—"

"Please, don't do—"

"You don't call girls like me just to talk, Harry."

"Stop! All I want to do is look at you. I just want to look at you, and that's it."

"I'm totally clean, baby. And, well, it's not like you're married, unless you are . . . But look what I brought . . . just for you—"

"No, she's actually . . . my wife; she—"

"You don't have to talk about it. I was just saying . . . you got a girlfriend?"

"No."

"So what's the problem, baby?"

"I—"

"You make me so hot—"

"Please—"

"Okay, well . . . fine, we'll just fucking *talk*."

"You don't understand."

"What?"

"I said you don't understand. I don't want to . . . I just want a beautiful girl, just to—"

"So make a fucking friend. Look, if you ain't got no girlfriend and your wife's dead or whatever, what the fuck is your problem? I got way bigger jobs that I could be doing right now. I got like three pages in the last hour . . . So pay me and I'm gonna go, 'cause this is just fucking stupid. I mean, like, I do role-play all the time, but you know, it's not like just to drink champagne with some random guy. And I get paid next to nothing to do that, so—"

"Please don't leave . . . It's so cold out. Don't you at least want a drink?"

"Well, I guess a free drink, fuck it."

"Yeah."

"So, tell me you don't think I'm hot."

"Please sit down. Remember? You're a classy woman."

"Classy women still have tits, Harry; they're just uptight about them."

"I know."

"So tell me that if I sit on your lap, you won't like it—"

"No—"

"Yes. And I bet you won't like this either—"

"No—"

"And this—"

"But . . . you—"

"Bet your wife didn't do it this good, huh?"

Sweating. And her smell was all over everything. Cheap and wasted and drunk and vomiting her smell out onto his clothes. *People will know.* But he hadn't had sex with her. No intercourse. He'd stopped her. But what had happened . . .

He could've gone through with it. He'd been ready and turned on, and she had been too. But thoughts of Bea, sitting at home, sleeping alone in the bed, silent next to him, cold and still as he fucked her, made him say, "Stop." And Chloé had gotten what she'd wanted. She'd gotten a bigger wad of cash than the last time, and he knew that if he invited her back she'd push and push until she'd get her way.

She'd make him miserable. Make it unbearable. Make him beg for her to finish the job. *Finish me off.*

He wondered if he really did make her hot. *Or maybe it was just one big fat act. Maybe she's right; she IS a good actress.*

I'm a despicable man. A horrible man for doing this. But what had he really done? Steve had proved to him that a man could have it all. Wives and cocaine and whores on the side, down on their knees, strange perfume clinging to *his* business suits when he would go home at night, and no blame would be placed upon him. Because it didn't have to be. *But I don't think I could get away with it. I don't have the ability. And now I'm no better than he is. I used to be better, and now I'm a fucking prick.* But there was no one to judge here. No one to in-spect him.

Did he really have to feel guilty? His needs weren't being met, so he was meeting them elsewhere—and nothing groundbreaking had occurred. Sex had been just within reach, but he had not taken the opportunity. *And I hadn't asked her for a . . . I hadn't. She'd just started, and I hadn't meant for it to be like that. A classy woman wouldn't have done it like that.* But no one had to know—and no one had to know what had triggered this in him. It could all be a big fat secret, and he could compress it and compose himself and squeeze it into an abandoned room and hope to forget. Lock the door against any who would dare to open it. Yes. If he wanted, he could return and turn this into the taboo that it should've been in the first place. He could turn away and shield his eyes against the sunlight. And put on a smile that was comparable to the one on the picture that he had disposed of so readily. Almost without a second thought. He had hardly felt the usual pang of guilt.

The past is not my fault.

It's not my fault. Something drove me to do what I've done. Why do I have to take the blame for everything? Bea is at fault. It's her fucking fault that I can't stand it and that our daughters have problems and that I don't like to think of home. I don't. I don't like to think of home.

Please don't make me go back.

Lilliana

Sitting on the bed, while Paul's strong, able arms cradled the guitar. She cannot play though. She has not practiced, and she cannot play what he asks of her. Has she finished the song he gave her? Well, not exactly. She needs more time. Fine. Can she get it done by Friday? Yes. She can. As long as he will come again. And again. She will never be fully ready.

I looked at him in that way. I gave him all of the hints. The signs. I did what I always do. Why doesn't it work? Have I lost it? Lost my touch? What I used to have?

She sat by him on the floor.

So melancholy when he plays. He has such a sad, innocent, unconventional face. She reached out a quivering hand and touched his neck gently. Her thin knuckle rubbing against the part that made his jaw strong. Her thin hand quivering against his skin, his skin warming her knuckles that were cold. The cold rings that wrapped themselves around her fingers.

He didn't move though.

The music had swallowed Paul, and Lilli sat on the border. *He didn't even look up. His expression didn't even change.* But he had closed his eyes and stayed inside.

She had grown scared. Scared of his nonexistent response. Afraid of the reason why. *Why? Why doesn't he like me at all? Just a single look. A glance. That's all I'd like. What the hell is wrong with me? I've lost all my fucking power.*

Lilli had wanted to touch her lips to that same place. She should have, could have. It had been done before. Flawless in its delivery. She had wanted to whisper something in his ear, but she didn't know what. She had wanted to, but couldn't.

She moved to the window.

Let the music finish, and let Paul leave. Unfazed. Still sure. Still strong. He hardly gave her a smile when he left the room.

Beatrice

She had been cleaning her closet that evening. Searching through rows and rows of old clothes that she would never wear. Tossing things away: things that she would never fit into, things that were too risqué. Things that she would've worn twenty years ago. She wasn't looking for anything in particular.

Tossing out all of the beautiful things. A red suit, a blue blouse, a black skirt, the red dress she had worn for the holidays years earlier . . . *God, all of these things. Taking up space, valuable space.* And then she saw it in the back. Covered in plastic. Hanging silently, solemnly in the darkness.

The cornflower blue dress.

She gently removed it, sliding the plastic wrap up and over it. Touching the fabric. The softness. Taffeta. *I'd felt so special in it. The taffeta dress. Taffeta!* And the smell of the party. The smell of the party that night. It had been in a beautiful room, a large room. A wedding? A dance? She had been in college.

And she had dropped out of college. For Harry.

So we could get married. Couldn't wait.

How he had asked her for her phone number that night. How he had smiled so nicely. How his eyes had glanced upon her from afar, lingered on her legs. She remembered this. Feeling self-conscious. How Harry had made her self-conscious.

And then our wedding. A small wedding. A perfect wedding.

Bea clutched the blue dress to her breast, feeling the taffeta brush against her skin. Feeling Harry. His hand on her shoulder. His warmth against her in bed. His nudity by the window. The fresh morning sunlight bathing the two new bodies that morning.

Vivian

She had come home drunk. She had not been afraid. She had not been like the other kids who snuck through the back door and brushed their teeth right away. Jumped in the shower. She was free. *Because no one notices; no one cares.*

Stumbling up the steps. Watching the world spin and spin. Spin again.

She'd never used to get drunk. She'd had a beer or two before with her old friends, and that had been all. She had even felt guilty then. *After one beer. What a loser I was!* She had thought that her parents would catch her, just like all of the other kids thought that their parents would catch them.

No one was ever caught. Ever.

And if they were, it was a one-off; a fluke in the system.

Still, she used to be a responsible drinker, interested in preserving her mind and integrity. She used to be the one to say, "No, thanks. I've had enough." No more. That was the old Vivian.

Shaking her head. *Stupid despicable girl.*

Maybe I should just get drunk and then get the tattoo.

Making Vivian's world tilt just enough. *Three screwdrivers . . . fuuuck me. God. And two Coronas, two tequila shots, and a whiskey sour. . . .* She had already vomited in the bathroom downstairs. And she had vomited at the party. She had vomited outside in the bushes in the yard.

And she felt *fine.*

"Whatever, Vivian, get up! Stand in front of the fucking door. Don't let anybody come in. Get the fuck up, Vivian! Hurry up! Stand up."

It didn't matter that her shoes were stained with her own puke. It didn't matter that she had forgotten her sweater, her ride home had been drunk, and she had had to go with someone else. Some strange man she had never met. It didn't matter that she had taken off her bra and danced freely. She felt good. She had guarded the bedroom door for Katerina and some man that night. Vivian felt important. She had watched Katerina emerge from the darkness, perfectly combed hair awry, a prominent stain on the front of her shirt. Vivian felt needed. Could she give Katerina *her* shirt? Because Katerina's had had a big ugly stain on the front that would confirm *everybody's* suspicions. The stain: it was the truth.

So whatever. Of course, Vivian had complied. She had taken the clean shirt off her back, and she had slipped the stained shirt on, sticky and warm. And she had felt its cheap material pulling against her skin, her skin barely breathing under the tightness of it. And she had felt the eyes on her body, moving down the shirt and fixating on it. *But it doesn't fucking matter. I can understand.* To them, though, there was no question. The evidence was right on Vivian's chest. No, there was no question; only an idiot would think twice about *that.*

Fucking whore. Coke whore. We all know who got it. We saw him zipping up his pants. Good one. A score for you Vivian! *I don't care.*

Her small room spun. The juvenile bed, the wallpaper, the carpet. So clean. Untouched by smoke, untouched by dirt and alcohol. Untouched by sex. All of the dust had been vacuumed away. She looked in the mirror again. She looked at her eyes, bloodshot; her stringy-straight red hair that had begun to curl up at the ends; her arms that had been bitten by the chill of the evening. She removed the stifling shirt, put it in the bathroom to wash it by hand in the sink for Katerina. She looked at her midriff, the gleam within it. Her lips, her thighs. Her tight skirt made of cheap fabric that glistened slightly in the lamplight. Her shaven calves dotted with razor burn. Her feet crammed into her boots, polished toenails and all. She could hardly remember her *old* self anymore. *What did she look like?*

She grabbed a hot straightening iron and yanked it over the ends of her hair. Perfectly straight, even just for bed. After the party's over, perfectly straight. No curls here. Not even for bed.

What did she look like? A fake?

Lilliana

She quietly sat on her bed, flipping through the address book. She'd always thought it funny how many names were in it. How many numbers she had never bothered to call. How many "I love you's" had been said? How many kisses had been stolen? By these men she hardly remembered.

I fucking have to get him out of my head. Paul.

But she could not think of him with anything but affection. She didn't know why though. She didn't understand. Why was she so attracted to someone like this? *Jesus, I'm losing my touch. I used to be so good. It was so easy. Have I changed? Am I not the same anymore?*

Flipping flipping flipping through the book.

She didn't know why she kept it exactly. She'd never actually called anyone but Nathan and a few others. She'd never actually looked through it before. A record. She had wanted to count before. She had wanted to look at their names. Play games. Try to match their faces to their handwriting and such. She never had.

Why am I even looking in here anyway? I can just call Nathan again. At least I know he's not some fucking psychopath. Sort of.

She glanced at the phone but couldn't bring herself to dial. She couldn't even think of Nathan for more than a moment without his face becoming Paul's. And even then, she was confused. *Fuck, why can't I decide what the hell I want?*

She quickly looked beside the phone. The razor blade glinted in the light.

She'd begun to keep it there. She had fallen asleep one night afterward, and she had just never put it back. But it was nice. To have an outlet. An easy way out, and *fast*.

She ran the tip of her finger over the three blades. *This is what I want. For now at least.*

Beatrice

Bea had not done the laundry in ages. *What am I thinking?* She had not realized that she was running low on socks and underwear, and she had surely not realized that the girls were running out of clean clothes as well.

She slowly descended the stairs. It wasn't even six in the morning. She had woken suddenly, shaken by a dream that she could not recall. *It's not even breakfast time yet. Harry's not even awake yet.*

She walked slowly, slowly. Hand sliding gently down the banister.

And down another flight of stairs past the kitchen. And then she was in the laundry room.

Bea had always loved the smell of clean laundry. She had always loved the damp darkness of that laundry room. She had reveled in it. Folding clean clothes, getting rid of messes. Blotting out stains and making all of that dirt just disappear. *Wonderful.*

She had always loved doing laundry. Even before cooking. She couldn't remember when she *hadn't* done it. Her siblings had always complained when it was their turn, but she had offered willingly. She was always compliant. Complacent and perfect. She hadn't minded touching the dirty things. She hadn't minded touching the underwear, the socks. As long as they came out clean.

They always came out clean.

She flipped on the light switch, closing her eyes for a moment, lingering in the doorway. She inhaled deeply. *The smell! Oh, I love it.* "Harry? Isn't it great down here? I really love it here. I know you think this is work, but it's not. I love the laundry room. And the kitchen. And you! Harry, I love *you!*"

Bea carried the heavy laundry basket as she drifted through the room and over to the machines. She sorted the lights from the darks. She measured her detergent. She nonchalantly opened the lid.

And in the machine were two towels, stained almost completely with blood.

At first she just stared at them. Foreign objects. They didn't belong in the laundry room, where things were clean and sanitary. Even dirty things weren't *that* dirty. This did not belong. *Oh my God . . . is this from the girls?* "Harry! Do you have any idea about this? Did *you* do this? Did you have an accident?"

"It must be the girls."

Did one of them have an accident? Did something happen?

But she suddenly grew at ease. Looking at the towels, dried, caked with blood. Thin blood. *One of them must've gotten her period. A heavy period. That's what it is.* "It's the girls, Harry. Never mind." She casually poured in a good dose of bleach.

Harry

He could ask *why* forever.

Why me?

But he wasn't going to because it wasn't going to do a thing.

He knew that it would just waste his time. And he didn't have time to waste. He had decisions to make. Consequences to face. Priorities. *I have to pick.* Things would suffer. There was weight to it.

How are my daughters? How is Lilli? Has she bled herself to death yet? How's Vivian? I don't know them. I really don't. He liked the memories better. The memories that were now nothing more than snapshots, nothing better than negatives even. Practically worthless, *but they're worth something to me.* Because he could never get it all back. Because it was gone. He missed their smiles. He missed the days when they had just bought the house. It had seemed so special then. Things had seemed so clear, and Bea hadn't troubled him then. She'd even seemed to enjoy spontaneity once in a while. Everything had been all right. Things had been looking as if they would only get better.

He used to wake up to the sunlight every morning.

But now things are just set. In cement.

The time before he had known who they would become. *Just babies then.* And he'd been astute, kept his eyes peeled. Looked for all of the problems they had told him to look for: short attention span, chronic bed-wetting, dizziness, hyperactivity, hypersensitivity. Ran through the checklist in his mind every day, and none of these conditions had been present. He'd made assumptions and had drawn conclusions; two things that led him to the letdown of the present. A letdown because he had felt so sure; so confident. Too comfortable. *I feel so stupid. Cheated.* Thinking everything was good, and nothing would hurt him or his family. Or anything within its armored facade.

And he knew his time in Cleveland was not forever. And so it would benefit him to forget that he had once assumed that he had produced two girls who would be individuals, nothing like Bea. He could find fault with his wife, but not with the girls. And when he was faced with things, obvious and red and aching, he shut them out. *It's time to live in the fucking present. Stop being like Bea! She's a bad influence. A terrible influence. She's delusional, crazy. I'm better than she is.*

He had asked her for head before.

Many times, but she had yielded only once. Not recently, but in the early days, before the girls. Finally, she'd complied. *After months! Months and months!* He'd worked on her. Worked it out of her. He'd been patient. He'd been willing to direct her, give her silly constructive criticism. He lay down on the bed slowly. He had been ready for his five-minute vacation. That was all that he'd needed! *Was it so much to ask?* She'd been wearing a nightgown with sleeves and all. With a high neck. *Like a fucking Puritan.*

He'd asked her if she would get undressed before the whole thing started. He'd begged her. Even tried to seduce her. Too shy to do that though. She hadn't been naked in the light since their wedding morning. Just darkness now. *Just groping around like fucking children in the fucking dark.* And once she'd started, the whole act had gone on for less than ten seconds when Bea sat back on her heels. "I'm sorry, Harry. I love you. I can't . . . I just can't."

Of course, he'd been angry! Of course, he'd wanted it! Of course, it was an awful letdown. And in the heat of the moment he'd just said, "Damn it," and then sat up. One big letdown. Just like everything else. And she'd apologized and apologized until he had no choice but to forgive her. And then she'd gone into the bathroom and vomited. And he had just jacked off and came all over his pants. Didn't even bother to aim or even grab Bea's handkerchief. He had soiled the bedspread, the top part, and just lay there, listening to her vomit because she was so disgusted with his body and listening to her sob because she was so disgusted with herself. Or at least he'd felt that way.

So maybe this whole new thing was well deserved?

Vivian

She had done it! The red blotch of sore skin, the small butterfly, the pain. It was all there! She had done it. She had gotten the tattoo.

She had gone alone. On a late afternoon devoid of a sunset. Katerina had said, "No, babe, I have plans. Sorry. Good luck and all."

Vivian had swallowed four tequila shots in an hour, and she had stumbled through the doorway.

The men had laughed. She had laughed too. They hadn't asked her for any ID. One of them had hit on her. She heard the buzz of the gun. Felt the sting of the needle, closed her eyes, and took two more shots by the end of the procedure. She paid. She left. It was done with.

She felt no guilt.

Look at me! Look at this! Her drunkenness had dulled down to a brief tingle, and the patch on her stomach hurt. The man had told her it would be sore for days, and to pile on sunscreen for the first month when she went out. *Still, it was worth it. Now I have a butterfly. A permanent butterfly, which makes me unique.*

But what did the butterfly mean to her?

She hadn't quite thought of that. She hadn't picked it for any specific reason. It had been spur of the moment. A need. She had been passing by. She had had enough money to pay. She had gone across the street and bought the bottle of tequila just like she said she would. It had dulled the pain some. It had dulled her memory some. She had felt somewhat better. But then again she had no basis for comparison.

Just wait until everyone sees. Just wait until the guys see it. My butterfly. And wait until my old friends see it. Wait until Katerina sees it. God, they'll all freak out. What the fuck though? Do I care? I don't.

She had the urge to walk through the house in a cropped shirt, prancing in front of her mother, her sister. But she didn't. *What's the point? They can't do anything about it. They don't care one way or another, really. Mom can rant and rave all she wants. It's permanent. There's nothing she can do.* Vivian was glad. "That bitch has nothing on me."

They'll probably never see it anyway.

At least not until she put on a bikini.

There was no point in it. If they were just going to make her feel sorry. It was the last thing she needed. She did not need to lose the nerve that she had worked so hard to gain.

She did not need to be made to feel sorry.

Lilliana

She had reached his voice mail. Told him to come as soon as possible. She had nearly been crying. Trying to hold back the tears, stabilize her voice. Trying to smile through it. "Hi . . . it's Lilli. Um . . . I just wanted to know if you could . . . come over. To my house. Use the back door. Come whenever. As soon as you can."

She was shaking now. She sat in bed alone. She glanced over at the guitar in the corner, but quickly looked away. She tried not to think of him. *Why the fuck do you think about him all the time? It's a waste. You could be having so much more fun.*

Her fingertips had hardly stopped bleeding. She had covered them with a Band-Aid, and she had gotten the stains out of her pillowcase with cold water. She sat, staring in the mirror on her closet door, waiting.

She wanted to be drunk—and fucking.

I will be. Don't worry. Nathan is coming. She prayed he had heard the frantic message. He would never turn her down. But there was nothing she could do but wait. There was nothing she could say. She couldn't leave another message. She had no other numbers to call. *Please let him come over. Please!*

I just really need someone now. I just really really do.
Two hours later, she heard his car in the driveway.

"Lilli, what's up? Twice in one week? Getting a little desperate?"

"I'm never desperate."

"Haha, it's great how you give me a call whenever you need a little 'help.' You know, like, whatever floats your boat though, right? It's not like I care, right? It's not, like, a drag or anything. For me, I mean."

"Sure. Right."

"Jesus, I'm getting to know this little-girl room of yours."

"Yeah."

"Have you been, like, crying or something?"

"N-n-no. No."

"Yeah, whatever."

"Let's just go, okay?"

"Okay, okay, hold on a sec. You really *are* desperate."

"I am not desperate, you fucking asshole! *Fuck you.* Just take off your fucking pants and let's go! It's a fucking honor to be in *my* room. To be called by *me*. To be fucked by me."

"Whoa, calm down."

"I *am* calm. . . ."

"Won't your parents hear you if you scream like that?"

"Who gives a fuck? My mom's probably down in the kitchen or something. My sister is probably drunk. It's not like they care what goes on up here! It's not like they have any fucking clue. Whatever. Who gives a shit. Just hurry the fuck up!"

"Okay. Okay, all right. Calm down."

"Let's go."

"What's the rush?"

"Just hurry up!"

"Lilli, um, why are you crying?"

"I'm not fucking crying. I'm just . . . stressed. Let's just go, okay?"

"Fine, okay."

"Do you have some booze?"

"No, sorry."

"Fuck! You brought it last time!"

"I . . . I just couldn't get it this time. I didn't have any extra cash, and I had to get gas."

"Do you have anything? Something? Any fucking thing?"

"Umm . . ."

"I'd do a fucking line right now! I need something! I know you're on something. You have got to be stoned right now. I'll pay you for it. I have a twenty right here."

"I seriously don't have anything right now."

"What are you on?"

"Just a little coke, that's all. I ran out right before I got here."

"You fucking ran out of coke? You're practically a junkie. You must have some sort of emergency stash."

"That was what this was. I'm going to my dealer after this."

"Fuck you, Nathan. Let's just go."

"I wish you'd stop crying first."

"Fuck you."

"And what's that weird-looking stain on your carpet?"

Beatrice

The blue dress was hung on the hook on their bedroom door. A reminder. A nice reminder of what was, what used to be. *The day we met. The day Harry and I met.* The day the two fated lovers met. The day the string of fated words had been uttered. The day life began and ended. The day that changed the world, took two small worlds and from them emerged a single, slightly larger world united by marriage three months later.

"I knew it was perfect. Didn't you?"

It was too good to be true. And now the too-small dress, stained with years of use, hung as a reminder of it all. She wished she could fit into it. *I know I used to be thinner. I know. But we all grow a little older. Gain a little more around the middle, in the hips. Harry has gained some in the belly.* "But I don't care! You're just fine for me!" Close enough.

The laundry was hung, and the rest of it had spun in the dryer and had been ironed meticulously.

The white things had gotten whiter. All of their little imperfections covered, blotted, lightened, erased. All of the colors had gotten cleaner. The lint, the small stains, gone. Laundry was magic. And pressed laundry was even better. When it was dry and immaculate and warm. When it was creaseless and flawless.

Bea had left the girls' things outside their doors. Stacks and stacks of neatly folded shirts and underwear. Bras. Socks. She had knelt down quickly, resting the piles there softly and hurriedly, but firmly. And she had stood there. Looked at the brass knobs that would not let her in. Looked at her hands, which had grasped those knobs so tightly. The hands that had failed her. And she had hurried away. Shut the door to her room—her room and Harry's— and stared at the dress for nearly the rest of the afternoon.

She examined the stitching, the stress in the fabric around the waistline. The delicate gathering and lace appliqué. The slight iridescence that had been nearly lost with age. A memento. A memento of things lost forever. Things found.

And she looked at her wedding ring, winking in the light.

She remembered when he had given her the icy diamond. He had not done it lavishly. In fact, he had done it over breakfast at some restaurant, and she had nearly fainted. *A proposal! Oh, I was so excited then!* As the years passed though, she thought that a ring was almost superficial in its beauty. She didn't need a diamond to express her love for Harry or her marital state. *Marriage is stronger than a ring; marriage is stronger than any diamond is.* She sometimes found herself looking upon the ring with a sort of scorn. It was too materialistic. It was too commercial. Her marriage could withstand anything. It could withstand births and deaths—and travel. It could uphold through the toils of daily life, and mortgages, and taxes. Her marriage was almighty enough. *It's necessary that they know though. That the world knows we're married. But it's not necessary for us. It's not necessary for me or for him. We know it. Our marriage goes beyond this.*

Harry

Don't make me do It again.

He looked at the dirty women's garments on his floor. He looked at his watch.

I don't know why anybody would want to be around me. All I do is let people down. He wasn't meeting anybody's expectations. All he wanted to do was abandon things. *It's instinctual.* He wanted to abandon his project. He wanted to abandon Steve. And Bea. Even the girls. If he hadn't had the girls . . .

You fucking asshole. You're a horrible man. Look at yourself. His left hand felt light without the ring. Lighter than air.

The ring told him who he was. Did he even know himself without it?

Consequences seemed inconsequential.

Maybe he could just decide to ruin things, and it wouldn't even seem like an accident. Because it wouldn't need to. *I don't want my family anymore, so I left them and hired a whore and moved to fucking Cleveland, and I'm going to lose my fucking job. Nice.* Nicer.

What had grabbed his attention in the first place? He remembered the taste of his first kiss with Bea. He could taste the inexperience on her lips. She had been confused and trembling, and he could feel her heart racing through the material of her blue dress. He could see the imprint of the lace on her bra. He'd wanted to take advantage of her. The zipper was just within his reach. He'd taken it between his two fingers to let it fall a moment later.

He'd felt sorry for her.

But in that brief moment there had been some mystery to her. He'd wondered just what she was thinking. He'd wondered how she liked him. He'd wondered what her last name was. He'd wondered what her room looked like. He'd wondered what she was majoring in. He'd wondered if she was smart. He'd wondered if she'd had any pets, what her mother's name was, if she'd had any siblings, collections, passions, hatreds. What he hadn't wondered was if she was a virgin or not. Because he could taste it all over her. And he'd wanted power. He'd wanted to dominate someone. For once.

He was over that. He was grown up now. *I was just a stupid college kid. I was ignorant. Fuck that. Fuck her!* "I don't know why I ever cared. Why I ever picked you." Stupid. *That's what happens when you marry a virgin. You don't know your mistake until your wedding night.*

Sergeant's card offered solace.

Vivian

She had showed it at school. The little butterfly that peeked above her jeans. She had newfound courage. She was fearless. She had flirted with her gym teacher. She had been terribly hung over. She had taken six Advil before noon. She had gotten three hours of sleep. She placed her hand unabashedly on boys' shoulders. Complemented them relentlessly. Brushed against them innocently, yet obviously, in the hallway. She had smoked half a joint at lunch with a bunch of boys and a few other girls out behind the bike racks. She had tossed her hair. She, the possessor of a butterfly tattoo.

Finally, I'm unique. Really unique, for once. Finally, I'm my own person.

But Katerina didn't think so. "Oh, a butterfly. It's cute, I guess. If that's what you're, like, going for. Lots of people have those."

Back pressed up against the brick wall by the bike racks.

This is so fuckin' cool.

She had gotten a few compliments. Some people had simply stared at her in amazement. She listened on. She smirked at these statements, these *compliments*. It didn't matter as long as she was the subject. Positive/negative, sexual/nonsexual. None of that mattered.

The point is, I'm chilling with Katerina, and I look fuckin' good. So they can all eat shit.

It's not even what they're saying; it's how they're saying it. They're saying it like they envy me, because I know that they do. It's obvious. These were, after all, the sort of things that used to be said about her sister. These rumors, these comments, ripping through the hallways like electricity between classes. The glances. The "Is *that* real?" exclamations. The unremitting stares. How could

she ever give this up? Revert back to her old self? Why not live this way forever?

She would look at the old friends sometimes. She would glance in their direction, pitying their lifeless bodies. *What kind of life is that? Reading, school.
It's all nice, but is that it? Is that really all there is? See, it's not true. There's more.
See, they think they're smart, but they're the naive ones. They don't know what
they're missing. Let's see who's going to get into the better schools anyway. Me.*
She looked at the group that she had once been so much a part of. She looked
at the old lunch table in the corner of the old, boring cafeteria. She saw them
chatting busily with one another, studying. Throwing their hearts, bodies,
minds, and souls fully into their academic pursuits. She didn't have to anymore. She was more knowledgeable than all of *them* combined. *Fucking straight-
A bullshit. It's not what anyone cares about anyway. I've done that. It's just a
waste of time.*

Look at them. *Do they have boyfriends?*

Do they have fun?

Do they even know how?

*So they study their asses off for chemistry. I used to do that. I've been there. I
get Bs now. So what? Am I any worse a person? Does it make me a worthless
slacker? No.* She would hurry by the old friends in the hallway, turning her
head, trying to look preoccupied. She would flip her hair. Quickly duck into
the nearest circle of new friends, grip Katerina's arm tightly, coil her fingers
around her new friends' wrists, and squeeze herself into a part of their conversation. *So it didn't matter. What did we ever do that was fun? Study?* It had not
been all that they had done though. They had gone to movies. They had gone
to the mall. She had had fun before. Even if she refused to admit it.

Nothing mattered though. Things had changed, and change is good.

Vivian smiled purely, demurely. She placed two ringed, polished fingers
atop her butterfly; she placed the palm of her other hand against the ring that
protruded from her stomach. *Like hell I'd ever feel sorry for anything.* Someone
smiled at her then. She couldn't help smiling back, even though it seemed to
evoke a dull, buzzing pain.

"Hey, Vivian, can we talk?"

"Sure, Kat, what's up?"

"Um, well, first of all, don't call me Kat. Vincent used to call me that. You know, bad memories. Haha."

"Oh, sorry."

"Anyway, I heard Rick—you know, the guy I like. . . . He was talking to his friends, and . . . shit, and like well . . . I have to, like, ask you something."

"Okay . . ."

"So, like, yah, there's this big thing, like, for a lot of money. It's stupid and all, but it's not like it's a big deal or anything. And, like, I need the money for stuff."

"Wait, I'm confused."

"Okay, well . . . basically, Rick's friend said he'd pay two hundred bucks to see you go down on me at this place tomorrow, and like, whatever, Rick's really into like lesbian stuff—not, like, real dykey lesbians, but you know how guys are—and this would probably, you know, make him go crazy or something so—"

"What?"

"I said, all you have to do is go down on me at this place."

"What do you mean?"

"What the fuck do you think I mean?"

"But we're just friends, Katerina. I don't really—"

"It doesn't fucking matter! Haven't you ever hooked up with a girl before?"

"Um . . ."

"It doesn't matter. It's not like we're real lesbians or whatever, we chill and shit, and like, it's just, like, two people who chill together doing shit together. It's not for fun or anything."

"But . . . you mean, like, people are going to be watching this?"

"Only Rick and his friend."

"Where?"

"In a room or something, I dunno."

"And they're paying us?"

"Well, I'd give you some of the money."

"Like how much?"

"I dunno, fifty bucks?"

"But they're giving you two hundred."

"If you don't want fifty bucks, I'll get somebody else to do it. Besides, we've been hanging out all week. What's the deal with you?"

"I know."

"I mean, I fuckin' hooked you up with that guy at the party over the weekend and, like, got you stuff. What the hell? I mean, if I hadn't been there, you never would've gotten that dude."

"I know."

"And you know how much I've been going for Rick, and it's like, it's like really bitchy of you to just be like, 'whatever' and not care about all the shit I've done for you. And I mean, it's just, like, nothing. Like it wouldn't even take that long, and I need the money and I know you want some too."

"But, I mean, I wouldn't even be any good at it."

"Whatever, I'll fake it."

"Don't you think this is a little—"

"What? I fake it all the time. I have it down by now."

"Don't you think this is a little much, just for Rick? I mean, if you think about it, this is basically prostitution."

"I really want him, so? And you're supposed to be helping me. I helped you, Vivian; the least you could possibly fucking do is this. This is not, like, a thing even. And how could you say that? It's not fucking prostitution. We *know* them. And I want to get with Rick, and this would totally get his fucking attention. I mean, he's, like, gorgeous . . ."

"It's just . . . I . . . I mean, we're being paid to do something, so that's technically—"

"Technically what? Fuck that. Make your choice, but friends do favors for one another, and I can't be friends with someone who won't like, go the extra mile or whatever. Don't you like hanging out together?"

"I know. Yeah, I do."

"You know, people do this shit all the time. It's not a big deal at all. No one's going to think you're a lesbian or whatever."

"Okay."

"If anything, it'll make you seem hotter, too."

"I guess."

"Well, yeah, it's up to you. I mean, I've been dealing with your shit all week, remember. Your weed isn't even that good."

"What's that supposed to mean?"

"Whatever."

"Okay, I'll do it."

"You will?"

"Yeah."

Lilliana

He had been afraid, but for the wrong reasons. She had scared him, but not correctly. The fear that she had instilled within him was not the adrenaline rush that improved performance; it was not the fear that made his heart beat twice as fast or that made his temples pulse with the fear of the unknown. No. He had been afraid. He had been afraid because she had been afraid.

The night had been a blur though. She could hardly remember half of it. Nathan had left right afterward. He hadn't even fallen asleep. He had run out like a frightened child, afraid of the monster he had never seen. *Is this who I really am? A neurotic, sick bitch? I wish Paul were here. Now.* She had felt Nathan's slick skin slide out from underneath her bare arm as she lay there. Heard him scramble in the darkness for his jeans. She had seen him go out the door quietly while she pretended to sleep. She had seen him wipe the sweat beads off his forehead, and she had seen the color drain from his face. She had felt no power. He had felt no power. If sex wasn't for power, then what was the point? If it wasn't with Paul, that is.

With Paul it would be different. I know it. It's intuition. It's instinctual.

Nathan had been distant. He had been quick. He had not restrained himself. He had been silent, and she had been crying, cursing through the whole thing. He had wondered if she had wanted her mother to catch them. *He was being silent because I was being so loud. He didn't want Mom to come in. He wanted her to think I was alone.* But it didn't matter what her mother thought, or where her mother was, or if her mother had heard anything. She wouldn't do anything about it anyway. And Lilli knew that.

God, what kind of life is that? What does she do? She cooks so much wasted food that it's like she's cooking for Dad too. She's stopped making my tofu. She

makes all this pig shit now, and she probably wonders why no one comes to din-
ner anymore.

Sitting there in bed, Lilli felt as if almost all of her emotion had been drained. Her tears, her blood. She was motionless, naked, cold.

But one thought prevailed, and that thought was of Paul. His majestic, foreign, melancholy beauty that she was sure was visible only to her. The power he possessed. Was this unknowing power? Did he understand how captivating he could be; how talented he was? How his music had changed her?

She got out of bed and turned on the CD player.

Paul's guitar music flooded the air. The lead vocalist's nasal words singing, moaning, screaming, "Make me, make me, ma-ake me-ee!" She still didn't understand where she'd heard that before. All she knew was that it felt like something wonderful. It felt like Paul's strong hands in hers, her head on his shoulder, and a small pin scarring her skin in all the right places.

Beatrice

She worked feverishly. *He'll be home any second now, and this kitchen is such a mess. The dinner isn't ready; the table isn't set. I'm so discombobulated. I'm so disorganized! How is he supposed to be proud of me if I can't even get his dinner on the table?*

She opened the refrigerator quickly, reaching for the meat that had been chilling. And then she saw them: the soybeans. *Lilli's soybeans. I would die happy if I never saw another soybean in my life.* She had stopped cooking tofu sometime around the middle of the week. She had stopped expecting the girls to show up for dinner. She set their places dutifully. She heaped their plates with food, just like she did with Harry's.

But no one came.

It's not MY fault that suddenly they want to starve themselves. I call them. They don't even come down. Maybe they don't hear me. They're probably out. Out with friends. Vivian may be studying, but I'm not sure what she's doing these days. And Lilli. Well, she's certainly up to no good. At least Harry comes to dinner. And he LIKES it.

She had heated the pans, and the meat sizzled on the stove.

Working working. Couldn't sit down.

Bea scrubbing, scouring, mopping the floors and counters. Vacuuming the carpet. She had set the table with her nice china. Her best tablecloth. "I thought you would like it on the good dishes, Harry. Good meat should be served on good dishes, don't you think?"

She smiled a slow, bashful smile. The smile of a person who was in the process of being showered with praise. "Well . . . I knew you'd agree. At least I hoped you would."

Cleaning the cushions on the kitchen chairs. Dusting with rags, with her hands.

And then she got to Harry's chair. The slow concave dip that still held onto his shape. Where he still sat. She had wanted to get the cushions re-covered, but she had always feared losing that indentation. She could not bear to do away with that piece of him. *Our wedding fabric. It matched our first kitchen in the smaller house. I could never get rid of them though. We had our first breakfast together on these chairs. How could I buy new cushions when these mean so much more?*

She knelt on the floor and gently leaned her head in that concave place. That beautiful, peaceful place. That sanctuary. Finally, a place where Bea felt safe.

Vivian

She had a paper due, but she did not have the will to start it. She had a test the next day, and she did not have the will to study for it. Her room was a mess, and she had never been messy. She did not have the will to clean it. There were a thousand things she should've been doing, but she just wasn't going to do them.

How could she, when her new self seemed so surreal?

Just stop thinking.

Don't you see how fucking juvenile you are? She's right; it's not a big deal. And I do want fifty bucks. And maybe his friend will be hot, and maybe he'll think I'm hot or something, too.

She was transfixed by her own reflection. She was awestruck. She had almost forgotten the homely girl of before. That girl was almost completely banished to the deep crevices of her mind. Locked in a box that she hoped to forget. Burned in hatred's fire. She had replaced the old photos that had once sat plainly on her dresser with new ones. Taken at parties. Vivian in motion. Vivian with a beer. Vivian laughing with three guys while gesturing lavishly with her hand. Vivian and Katerina. Arms linked. Smiles deceptively pure, lips suggestively glossy. She could not stop looking. A little over a week before, she had been looking at herself in this same way in disgust. *I could still manage to lose a few more pounds.*

Pinching the skin on her hips until she made two red marks.

Breakfast was water. Lunch was a small salad, no dressing. She had a snack only if she was exhausted. A few pretzels. Dinner was almost nonexistent. She would occasionally reach for a small piece of chicken, or more pretzels. More water.

But I'm not even hungry, so it doesn't matter. If I'm not hungry, then why should I eat? I don't want to, so I won't.

She saw how the old friends looked at her during lunch, when she sat with the new friends. Even Katerina ate more than she did. *But it doesn't matter. I have willpower.* "So you're dieting. Good. You're gonna look so cute in, like, two weeks." Staring at her protruding collarbones. Her cheeks that were beginning to grow sallow. What was the point though? What was the point of food when she could do just fine without it?

What's the point? Do I want to get stretch marks? Do I want a flabby stomach? My tattoo and my piercing wouldn't look good at all. There would be no point in any of it. Plus it's easier to get drunk at parties on an empty stomach anyway.

Vivian. The anorexic slut. The alcoholic. The lesbian?

It'll be okay; just stop fucking worrying. Stop.

I'm not a lesbian. We're just two friends hooking up to impress some guys. What is wrong with that? Obviously nothing. Kat wouldn't do it if it was wrong.

She'd overheard things. The old friends and the new were saying them. She tried not to mind though. Put it all in perspective. Would close her eyes and just pretend that things worked and that she could win. No consequences or setbacks or anything.

Harry

"Hey, baby."

"Hi."

"I knew you were gonna call again. I knew you'd like me 'cause of that thing I did to you last time."

"Yeah."

"That's why Serg hired me originally, because I'd, like, do it to him whenever he—"

"I bet."

"All I wanna know is why you wouldn't fucking let me do it the first time."

"It's . . . it's really nothing—"

"Have you fucked anyone since your wife?"

"What?"

"You said she's dead or something."

"She's—"

"Well, I was wondering—"

"That's none of your business."

"Whatever. You're kind of a jerk. I don't really get you."

"Hey, fuck you."

"I like it when you get angry, Harry."

"Shut up."

"You wanna chase me?"

"Just sit down."

"You're gonna have to make me."

"Just come here."

"You know why you called me. I shouldn't have to remind you."

"You don't. I know why I called you. You don't have to tell me!"

"So get over here, Harry. I'm so hot for you. I've been thinkin' about you. Our last time together—it was, like, amazing. I wanna make you so happy—"

"Be quiet."

"I just wanna make you feel real good; I want you to get off as many times as you fucking want to."

"Come here."

"No! you're going to have to come and get me."

"Get over here."

"No! You're going to have to chase me."

"Get the fuck over here!"

"Hahahahaha. You wanna fuck me now, Harry? You wanna make it?"

"I said—"

"You wanna fuck me? Last time I knew you did too. It was obvious. Say it. You wanna fuck me."

"I won't—"

"Fine, I'm going then."

"No, please . . . I want to fuck you. Okay? I do. That's why I asked you here this time. I want to. I'm such a stupid prick."

"Whatever. So take me."

"No. I want you to—"

"So your wife was a submissive. I should've known."

"Stop talking about my wife. I hate my wife!"

"She's not around anymore."

"She's . . . not around anymore. You're right."

Lilliana

She had stopped off at the store, but Paul was on a break. She waited around, weaving in and out of the aisles, and wondering. Wandering and wondering where he was. Did they know when he would be back? No. Sorry. *Shit.*

Where could he have been? He never stays away that long.

He had not come. She had waited for over an hour. She saw the people behind the counter smirking. A high-school girl. A sixteen-year-old baby waiting for Paul. Paul with his magical ways. With his presence. His music. *His eyes, his voice, his everything.* It was different. The whole entire thing.

What is this? I've never felt like this. She was at home, but it was as if only half of her were there. She was always thinking of him. Wanting to see him. Wondering when she would see him next. She practiced the guitar for him, even though she hated every second of it. She had begun to callus her fingers. She had cut her nails. She was changing. And none of it was for herself.

She couldn't stop thinking about her breakdown with Nathan.

I never act that way. What was that? Why am I so fucked up these days? I never used to be this way. I used to love fucking. Especially with Nathan because he's hot, and he's older. But why doesn't it feel the same anymore?

But she'd been asking herself this ever since her life had changed. She'd been asking herself, and she could not answer.

She wanted to call Paul, but something inside her was holding back. *Won't it seem desperate or something if I call?*

She looked at the nice long scar on her arm. She looked at a nice long scar on her leg. And three similar scars on her other arm. And three small parallel marks right near her elbow. Nice.

But she was in her room, so she didn't have to cover herself. She was wearing a tank top. Vulnerable, but secluded enough. Safe enough. She hated sweaters. She had been wearing them for some time since she had started. *Fuck sweaters. Maybe I should just wear my old shirts and be proud. Fuck everyone and what they think. I really don't care.*

She thought of the way Nathan had looked at the scars on her body. Silent. He had not said a word. She had seen his thoughts though. The fear. Even he could realize that something was out of place. He knew that girls shouldn't have to scar themselves to take the sting away. *He doesn't understand. Some people are just really transparent.*

Harry

Bea had seemed so uptight in comparison. Unwilling and judgmental and unaccommodating. A corpse in the bed. *Sleeping in a coffin.*

But Harry hadn't wanted Chloé to leave.

He'd liked the way she wouldn't let him say no. He hadn't minded paying for her services—he wanted to see her again. He'd liked it when she'd said horrible things. A new sensation. He knew she'd done it on purpose too. *A tactic.*

She seemed to know him better than anyone. She knew what he wanted. He hadn't had to write it down, or articulate it, or draw a diagram. He hadn't had to beg her to take off her flannel nightgown. There had been possibility, but there had also been a confirmation. That what was to happen was actually going to occur, and it was going to be real.

Would it be possible to live here forever? He was growing afraid. He would be home in less than a week, and he was afraid. Things had stopped making sense.

I just won't think about it yet. I have time. I have time! I don't have to burden myself with thinking of home.

He didn't have to think of his daughters. Not if he didn't want to.

Sometimes he wondered what their kids would look like. Sometimes he wondered who they'd marry. Sometimes he thought that Lilli would never settle down. Sometimes he thought that Vivian would be like Bea. Unconsciously, of course, but still like her.

But how would he know?

He wanted to say, "Look at who you're becoming. Do you like who you are?" *Because it's not too late. They're still young; they can change if they want to.*

I'll just stop. I have to. It's going to ruin my night. I can't let Bea ruin my fucking night. I can't let the girls . . . He took a long sip. He took another. He finished the glass. Asked for another. Did the same. Felt the buzz. Leaned his head back. Closed his eyes. His heartbeat slowed in his chest. His eyelids fluttered. He felt a slight numbness in his fingertips.

He felt *better.*

He would ask Chloé for her number next time. Her own number. *I want to take her out. I want to take her to dinner.* A prelude to the inevitable. And the inevitable did not seem like such a bad thing.

Beatrice

He hasn't called, but I know he wants to. He's really busy though. In Cleveland, there must be a million things he has to take care of. There must be a million things he has to do, and a million people who are counting on him.

Why should she expect that her husband would call her anyway?

"I know you're busy, Harry. I know."

She sat quietly. Dinner had been made and eaten. The table was full of platters and plates and dishes of food that were mostly untouched. She had worked hard. She had *tried*. She had really tried to make it good. She had eaten some. She looked around at the three empty seats, one of which was very much taken. One of which was important, and the rest of which were not.

"Oh Harry, I'm sorry. The meat was tough, I know. I should've gone to the market today, but I thought that these steaks from the freezer would be okay. I guess they weren't. I'm sorry."

She smiled into the emptiness.

"That makes me feel better. Thank you."

She began to clear the plates. So much food. Thrown away. Down the garbage. She used to feel guilty when she threw away perfectly edible food. *There are people all over the world without food. I know everyone says it, but it's true. It really is.* But it didn't seem to matter that much. She was throwing out as much food as her family would've eaten. That was no sin.

She had not seen her daughters in what seemed like a while.

They keep to themselves. I shouldn't worry though. Vivian may change her looks, but her grades will not suffer because of that. And Lilli, well, I have no control over anything she does. I have faith though. They're around. They're fine. But Bea still could not go into their rooms. They still would not come down for dinner. She still could not have a decent conversation with either one of them.

"I'm trying. I really am. Harry, I wish you'd come back, because they're not even *mine* anymore. I need your help. They need it." She strained to hear something through the silence, but nothing came. The hum of the radiator. The drip of the faucet. The whir of the dishwasher. The absence of something important.

Lilliana

She didn't usually drink in her room. But it was too hard to resist. She had been given a small bottle of tequila by some guy who liked her at school, and she sipped it slowly. *I'm not an alcoholic though. It's not like I do this all of the time. Vivi's the alcoholic. I saw her drinking at fucking lunch yesterday.* Lilli didn't really do this though. She almost never did it. She didn't even really *like* alcohol. Sex was her drug, or at least it had been.

So why wasn't it working?

She needed to call Paul. She had restrained herself, but she had to do it. The alcohol stung her lips. Maybe that was a reason to like it.

But she couldn't call him. Couldn't dial.

What the fuck. I really need to sit down and sort things out. This is stupid. I have no idea what is going on here. I can't even dial his number. I can't even call him! God! I mean, how dysfunctional can a person get? I've never been afraid of any guy before. Why do I get nervous around HIM?

It makes no sense.

She tried dialing again as she took another sip. Small sip. She didn't want to get drunk. Only alcoholics drank alone, and Lilli was not an alcoholic. It was just in place of something else. Because the thing that she really wanted was unavailable.

Still, she could not go through with it.

She laid down the receiver, laid her head in her hands. *God, Lilli, don't cry. Oh fuck.* The tears were streaming down her face. Streaking the remnants of the day's makeup. Ruining everything. Melting her confidence. Devouring the particles that comprised her last nerve.

It's just that I'm so confused. She crawled beneath the dirty sheets on her bed. She kissed the scars on her arm gently. She hadn't understood why she felt horrible after Nathan had gone. She didn't understand why she had felt like dying, why she had cut deeper afterward, and she didn't understand why the *thought* of Nathan sickened her. Made her feel worthless. And why the thought of Paul seemed the antidote to all of her pain, all of her troubles, yet a trouble within itself.

Vivian

How gross.

But fifty bucks felt good. Maybe too fucking good.

At least I know I'm not a fucking lesbian. That was disgusting.

Rick and some other people watching them go. Cheering and jeering and all that. She'd tried to get into it. She'd tried to seem into it. Their smiles had lit up the room. But all of the lights had been on anyway. *Obviously they didn't want to miss anything.*

Clicks and moans of the Polaroid camera. The buzzing sound. Clicks and zipping sounds and forced moans from Katerina's overglossed lips and the camera. All in unison.

And about five minutes later, Katerina had let out a long, high-pitched moan, toes curling, fingers gripping the sheets, signifying for Vivian to *stop.*

And then Vivian had run into the bathroom and vomited. Put on some lip gloss. Vomited again. Rinsed with water. And put on some more lip gloss.

But by then, Kat and Rick were already fucking in another room, and Vivian was already pretty drunk anyway. So she had a beer from the fridge and left.

At least they didn't see me naked. At least I didn't have to spread my legs like she did.

But she had taken off her top. *Big deal.* Toplessness was pretty much synonymous with Vivian now. *How long until everyone else finds out about this? And what would they think? If they're going to think that anyone's the dyke, it's going to be me because I had to actually fucking do it. And Kat is with Rick now.*

No.

Why did things like this always have to happen? Because Vivian trusted too easily. She was too trusting! And too skeptical about the wrong things. And too timid about the right ones. She befriended people who blatantly deemed her an accessory. She was risking a lot. She didn't even *like* pot. She didn't even like smoking! But she didn't mind compromising. The compromises she made, though, only benefited the other party. What a stupid smart girl. A desperate girl. Guarding the door for Katerina. Standing outside in the cold for her.

And no one likes desperate girls. *Don't you know that?* No one.

Whatever. Soon everyone will forget about this, and I'll lose my virginity and things will be better. They'll be all better.

She had been looking. But where? She had smiled. She had tried. *I want a boyfriend. That's all I want.* It was all she needed. To be completed. *I don't want to be a virgin anymore.* To be broken.

She had thought of it. She looked nightly at the box of condoms on her dresser. Untouched.

There were guys who would sleep with her. *There's no question about that.* They did exist. It wasn't as if she were completely undesirable. *Maybe I'm too picky. Maybe I should just be more accepting and lower my standards.* But the high-school boys seemed so juvenile, so childish—attractive, yet childish at heart. And she didn't know anyone else. She had nowhere to go to meet anybody. The bars were filled with seedy types who were so disgustingly aggressive that she locked herself up completely. Didn't belong to any clubs or societies. She didn't do any community service or take any classes outside of school. Anything that she was a part of was school-related.

There is just nobody. All of this change, and there's no one.

New and improved, and better, and the best.

And what did she get for it? *Katerina's fucking cunt in my face.*

This was not the Vivian who wore cotton briefs. This Vivian wore thongs. Or nothing. She ran her fingers through her pin-straight Little Mermaid hair and laughed at everything and everyone.

I guess I could sleep with someone in my class. It wouldn't really matter. The point is to get it over with. And I need to prevent people from saying shit about what happened. It would be nice if it was with someone I actually liked, but I don't know. I guess that could take second seat. I guess. Maybe.

Harry

Another meeting and another deal. Another cup of coffee. Another screwdriver. Another meal. Another restaurant. Another night in another place. Another smile or two. Another check. Another wink. Another "Don't worry, this one's on me." Another night of ass-kissing.

I hate my fuckin' job.

Sick. He was sick of it all.

I hate my fucking life. I don't care about this anymore.

"So Harry, I don't really understand what's been going on. You don't pick up your phone; you don't respond to messages . . . I mean, come on! I tried to help you out, buddy. It was a little deal between us, right? Just between us. Forget the business side. Remember? We're helping each other out . . . and look at you. You're a mess."

"I'm fine."

"I don't really get it. I did ask Serg about you though . . ."

"What?"

"I asked him. The wife is at her mother's house for a few days, and I was all in the mood last night, so. . . . Anyway, yeah, he said that you and this girl Chloé have been seeing each other pretty often."

"No, we—"

"And Sergeant doesn't lie. He may be frank, but he's one truthful fuck. Seriously, Harry. What's going on between you and this girl? She's just a whore, you know. I know you don't like your wife very much, but she's just a whore!"

"But Steve, I never said that—"

"You know, right after she does you, she's off doing somebody else. She ain't an exclusive bitch, that's for sure."

"I never said that she was exclusive."

"Just don't think that she ever will be. Once a whore, always a whore. Yeah, that's my motto. I can see it. You like her. Jesus, I can't believe it. Just because she's banging you, you like her."

"I never said that, Steve. Besides, this is private, and it's in my hands now . . ."

"Harry, listen. I'm going to lose a lot of money if this deal doesn't go through. You better get your ass into gear, Harry. At this point, I'm not afraid to call your boss. I don't need some infatuated fuck handling these fucking accounts. Yeah, I like helping people. You obviously don't know how to pace yourself. All I wanted you to do was chill out, partner."

"You see your girl a fair amount, don't you?"

"But I make it to dinner on time. I'd say I'm fairly considerate. Now I'm getting pissed. I can see you were really desperate though. Maybe this is why you can't get your own damned act together."

"I'm trying."

"Sure you are, Harry. Look, I know you. I know that your heart isn't really here. I don't know where it is, but it's not here."

"It doesn't have to be."

"What can I say? I'd love to forgive you. Technically, it's my fault for introducing you. I'm pretty stupid when it comes to women—you've already probably gathered that info on your own. Jesus, I thought this would help you work better! Become more passionate about this whole thing. Guess I was wrong. But I'm wrong about a lot of things. Hell, you know about my past. You should've been able to draw that conclusion on your own."

"I don't know."

"You don't know?"

"I've just got a lot on my mind. I'm sorry."

"We all have things on our minds. It's just a choice of whether we want to pay attention to them or not."

Lilliana

She had gone by the store again. She had waited again. She had seen him. He had been on break, but not for long. He had come back with a paper bag with a sandwich in it. She had said hello. He had said hello back. She had asked him to come give her a guitar lesson that night, and he'd said okay.

He's coming!

She didn't know what to do. She didn't know how to get ready. She had never paid too much attention to her looks. She was obviously attractive. She didn't need much makeup, and she didn't like to pile it on. She was skilled at showing just the right amount of skin, revealing the perfect pinch of cleavage, a thin sliver of abdomen that bridged the gap between her tank top and jeans. But all of this had been natural. She had never thought of it before.

But now she was thinking about it. More than anything else.

Lilli. Standing in her room, agonizing over what clothes to wear for her lesson.

Jeans and the black shirt? No. The white shirt? Maybe. The black pants? No. Well, maybe. The red shirt? The blue shirt? The orange shirt? I don't know! It had never been an issue. Clothes. It had always been what was under the clothes.

She was standing there in her underwear. Black underwear that was her own. She had kept the pair of ugly white panties squeezed in the back corner of her drawer. She took them out when she was in a strange mood. When there seemed to be no antidote to anything. When there were no answers. When she felt guilty. The white underwear. It made her feel all right.

Why do I feel so incomplete? Why do I feel like I'll never be good enough?

She grabbed a sweater and threw it over her bare shoulders.

He probably wouldn't like my scars. He probably wouldn't want to see them. She glanced over at the stain on her carpet, concealed by a stack of books. She had pushed her bloody tee-shirt to the back of one of her drawers. She had thrown a magazine over the stain on her sheets. But the stains on her body. How long could she hide *those?*

Harry

"Hello?"

"Hello, Harry!"

"Bea."

"Oh, how are you? I've been thinking about you so much lately. How is everything? How is Cleveland? How are your meetings?"

"I was asleep . . ."

"Oh, were you? Is it the time change? I miss you so much! Oh God, you have no idea."

"I—"

"So tell me about what's doing out there. Tell me what's going on there."

"I'm a little preoccupied . . ."

"That's all right. I don't think that I should be demanding anything of you. And I respect the fact that you're out there for work, and—"

"I have to go—"

"I know that you work hard. And that's what I respect about you, Harry.

I do. I really do. You know, I was looking at the blue dress. Do you remember that dress? Well, I was looking at it, and I just remembered that night. The night at the party where we met. I remembered how magical it was. And our wedding. I was thinking about it. You know . . . Harry? Hello? Harry!"
(silence)

Beatrice

A hasty phone call. But good enough for her.

It didn't take much of anything to please her. It hadn't mattered what words had been said, or better yet, what words hadn't been said. It hadn't mattered that his tone of voice had been monotone and drab. It hadn't mattered that he had bluntly avoided her questions, that he had let her talk and talk and talk.

Great. Fine. Superb.

Bea was happy. That was all that mattered.

Because every time I hear it . . . oh, it's heaven. I can't explain. You have to feel a certain way. You have to be so in love. And I was lucky to fall so in love so young. None of her friends had ever felt this way about anyone, at least not when they were in school together. They would call her crazy—affectionately, of course. In college, Bea was so lucky to be in love and getting married! They hadn't been envious of Harry himself, though they had wished for a love of their own. And Bea had owned love then.

But things had changed. There was no one praising her for *this*. No one except for herself.

I've grown up. We've grown up. I don't need silly comments from petty girls. I know what we have, and I know that we're lucky. Lucky. Of course. Because in Bea's world there were no arguments with her husband. There was no divorce, no separation. There were no prenuptial agreements. There was nothing that he could do wrong, and so she made accommodations for this. She took the blame. She tried her best. To shape herself around the hub of her world.

And it wasn't even that difficult. In fact, it was easy.

Vivian

And, yes, she was right.

Everyone liked talking about the new *lesbian* who had chilled with Katerina.

It's just a big, fat, ugly question mark. She's done more shit with girls than with guys. Look at her.

Yes, the girls would talk about this. And they were. Going and going and going.

And Katerina said . . .

She said, Leave me alone. And Rick looked good on her arm. And she looked good on his. She said, I already gave you the fifty bucks, so please chill the fuck out. Don't you have to get to class?

No.

I knew this was going to happen.

Katerina said.

She said, I have a boyfriend now and *a lot of stuff* that I need to take care of. Yeah, she said that. She also said, But it was fun chilling with you and all— maybe I'll see you this weekend at that thing. Oh yeah, thanks for the weed today. It wasn't bad.

And click.

She said all of that in front of everybody. Rick and everybody. *And I didn't even want to do it. She was the one. I fucking did it to stay friends with her!*

She was the one who fucking threatened me. . . . It's not fair. But the consequences were the same. Hadn't Vivian seen that? Hadn't she seen that Katerina was just going to turn around anyway? She hadn't seen that? *Oh God.*

But, maybe things weren't all bad. After all, people were talking because they cared. Didn't they care? *If they really didn't care, they wouldn't fucking talk about it.*

Harry

Let's pretend that the past doesn't exist.

Let's pretend that Harry is in love with Chloé.

He really did want to see her again. He didn't care what Steve had said. *Who the fuck is he to talk to me like that? He's not my fucking father. He abuses drugs. He's been married four fucking times! He does not get to dictate how many times I get to sleep with my girl. For every time I've had sex, he's probably had sex twenty times.* It wasn't fair. Hypocrisy.

He wanted to see her naked again. Unafraid and bold in the light. Voluntary.

He wanted to feel the sensations that he had only imagined. He didn't care if it was real or not, or if it was politically correct, or what Sergeant told Steve. He'd found his release. Steve had been right. This was a release.

And he was not going to give it up. He would not forfeit his rights and succumb to the masses again.

It's my right to be happy. And happiness isn't always practical. Extravagances were involved in happiness, its pursuit, one's ability to rear a piece of it. And domesticate it and make it accessible.

He owed it to himself. To be happy. Seek pleasure. Find the outlet that kept his mind from swinging from one painful issue to another. He would honor his wishes. He needed no permission. He didn't care anymore. *I don't care! I don't care about Steve. I don't care what he fucking thinks. I don't care, I don't care, I don't care. Everything is bullshit. It's just about which parts you want to believe.*

Harry wanted to believe. He wanted to believe the lies he told himself, and he wanted to disregard the lies that society told him. Happiness does not lie within the borders of conformity. Security, possibly, but not happiness. *And it's okay.* Because he was alone and ready—and because he could.

Lilliana

He had come and gone. Face expressionless for the most part. She had sat a good distance away from him. Wanting to reach out her hand. Wanting to silently take him into her beautiful, bloody sheets in her unmade bed. She had tried being blatant. She had tried being subtle. She had tried all of her techniques, and none of them were working. *I don't know. Have I lost it? Have I lost my touch? And if so, how do I get it back?*

But she had not lost her touch. She had changed.

She had slept with Nathan only a few days before. But this had brought her no pleasure. It had *hurt.* She had cried in bed. A little girl who was confused. No, she had not lost her touch. She had grown. Her life had been altered. What had been all right before was no longer enough.

The worst part was that while I was fucking Nathan, I couldn't stop thinking of Paul. She had opened an old scar so it would hurt more, bleed more, afterward. Paul was ingrained in her mind.

She had slipped on the old cotton panties after Nathan left.

Sat in her room silently. She had taken the nice pinpoint. She had thought of carving Paul's name into her arm. How nice it would look there. How nice it would be to have Paul's name permanently scarred onto her skin. She had wondered what she would think every time she looked at it. And she had wondered what he would think if he ever saw it. What would she say? What do you say to a person when you have made them a part of you without their consent?

Permanently.

But she was a perfectionist. Paul deserved no less than perfection, and if she were to carve his name onto herself, it would have to be perfect. Flawless.

She turned on his music. *God, he's so great. Oh God! Why have I never felt this way about anyone before?*

She looked at the beauty on her arm. She thought of Paul's boyish handsomeness. So unapparent at first. *He's so unconventionally attractive.* And she'd had attractive men. She'd had beautiful men. Like Nathan. Nathan was a beautiful man. *But Paul is more beautiful.* She thought of Paul's music, which she seemed to understand so well. She thought of wanting to please him, of how he was difficult for her to charm. Of how he ignored her and didn't care what she did. And then she realized.

She was in love.

For the very first time. *Am I in love with Paul? Is this what love is? Is this what love means? Is this why I want to wear his name? Is that why I don't care if he's not as beautiful as the other boys? Is that why I listen to him? Is that why I always want to talk to him? Not just sleep with him, but be with him? I want to exist with him. This is what love is.*

She had always thought that love would never happen. Not to Lilliana. Because she had fallen in love with sex. And she didn't know the difference. In love, hearts were broken. In sex, nothing was lost for her, but so much gained. She had had guys tell her that they loved her. She had laughed it off. She hadn't cared. But this was love. There was no way to dispute it. She had fallen against her will. "I am in love with Paul. I love Paul." The words sounded better than anything else in the world. The diagnosis had been discovered. Paul's music screamed in the background. Wailing. *And love is so good.*

Vivian

Brooding. I am brooding.

Lights were out, and she was in pain. *This is so lame of me. I can't just sit here. Maybe I don't need her anyway.*

She was enduring it. The rumors were not subsiding though. The halls at school. Straight out of a teenage movie. Girls and boys making equally lewd comments. Girls walked by and stared. They laughed. They shook their heads. They tossed their immaculate hair, and they sneered just enough to show their gleamingly straight teeth. Saying how they *always* knew that she was gay. Like, duh. Boys walked by, rubbing up against her. Demanding that she showcase her talents for them too. "Because it's not like she likes dudes anyway, so, like, it doesn't matter."

And what do I say back? What do I say to that?

Maybe nothing. *Just don't say anything. They'll get bored.* Yeah, bored.

Lesbians are never boring. Girls like Vivian are never boring. She would never be "boring" again. Because despite what she wasn't, she could never take it back. She couldn't ever change the past to make things work for her. She could never deny it. Why? Because there were witnesses. Witnesses. And there were Polaroids.

Don't they understand who she is? Don't they know Katerina and who she fucking is? They can't understand that she made me do it?

Whatever. At least I'm worth talking about. At least her name was on everyone's lips. Yeah, at least Polaroids of her were worth more than nothing. They wouldn't be discarded in the nearest garbage can. They wouldn't be forgotten about, carelessly left on a lunch table, a desk, wedged into a folder. These things were rare. Limited Edition. Those pictures were adorning empty wall spaces above beds, above toilet bowls. They were coveted. Yeah, no one had gone after Vivian before. No one had cared. No guys had made excuses to get close to her. And now they were. Wasn't this what she always wanted? Wasn't this what she had changed for? For attention. She had wanted attention. *And now that I have it, I can't complain. I'm such a fucking hypocrite.*

And it's not true what they think, and one day everyone will find that out. I know that it's not true, and they're going to figure it out. It's just a matter of time . . .

But I need to prove that I'm straight. I need to. I need to lose my virginity. At this point, I have no choice. I just need to.

Dying to get rid of it. Such a *burden* to her. Just aching to have it popped away, stolen in her drunken sleep by a stranger, or taken systematically and gently by a lover, or savagely ripped by someone who had no knowledge of her present state.

You just have to stop being picky.

"Just stop being so fucking picky."

Beatrice

Time. Aching like a bruise, pounding like a heart. Rhythm in a countless world. Meter in the slur of life. Because time had brought Beatrice and Harry together, and time would unite them once more. What she didn't realize was that time would tear them down. Destroy the fragile threads that had formed them into a unit. One from two.

And when he gets home, I'll make him a brisket. For the first night. I'll make it just for us. I don't care if the girls eat or not. It'll be our dinner for us. Harry and me. Us.

Pulsating and gyrating, the wheels in the clock. Ticking. Clicking.

"Doesn't the time go quickly? Don't you think it does, Harry? I mean, it seems like yesterday. Our wedding."

She smiled into the distance. Into his eyes. "How you held me in your arms . . . Time can never dull that." Bea didn't care who was watching, who was walking by. She turned unabashedly around and around. "And our first dance together that night." And around. And around. "And how you asked me . . ." How could she ask for anything more? She was ashamed of ever being discontented. She was ashamed of ever wanting anything more than she had. *How could I have ever been unhappy? How could I have ever taken time for granted?*

She had tried not to. *I always knew how lucky I was.* But it was impossible to appreciate *everything.* Every bite, and blink, and motion, and word, and sound, and expression. Impossible. But why? Did it have to be impossible? Why was it that she had never realized that she should have paid more attention? Why did he have to leave for her to understand?

I try. I try to. I always knew that I should appreciate the little things. Watch him more. Pay more attention. If that was possible. How much more attention could she pay him? How much more detail? "When you come home, Harry, I promise. Things will be better. Sometimes I'm selfish, but it won't happen anymore." She had learned. She had learned from the past. She wouldn't make the same mistakes in the future.

Harry

Maybe this is love?

Standing in the room looking at her, he could think of nothing else. But the question was prominent. She was bold but would obey. She listened, but she was defiant. Full of contradictions and animalism. And the fact that she didn't *need* him. She wouldn't die without him. There was no codependence.

"Will you dance for me?"

"Will you turn over?"

"Will you bend down?"

And the answer was always, "Fuck you." But Chloé would do it. And she would do it with enthusiasm. Sometimes he would just test her. Sometimes he wanted to spoil her. She was more than he'd ever expected. He'd expected a quiet girl, barely eighteen, to show up that first night. He'd expected someone else. Without a spine. Without a mind. Just someone. Just some pussy who would comply and not speak if he told her not to speak. Sit and drink champagne if he told her to sit and drink champagne.

Belligerence was a whole new concept.

"Hey, asshole, go fuck yourself. You wanna come and get me? Then get over here."

It was the oldest game and the oldest set of tricks. But they were tested with time, and that's why they worked. They really worked.

A part of him loved her. He really did think that at least a part of him did. *Because I don't think that I was in love with Bea. I think I was just young. And eager. I don't think I was ever in love with Bea.*

"You're the girl that I never had." And the best he ever had. The best brunette. The best. Prime. *I have to take her out for dinner. I want to know her.* "I want to know you." Her original purpose was bleeding beyond the parameters that he had set. He had been so faithful up until now. So faithful and complementary. *But I don't have to be perfect anymore. They're getting on without me. All of them. Bet the girls don't even know I'm gone.*

Lilliana

As if she'd been living in a dreamworld. She had waited for him outside the music store. She had beamed with her newfound love. She had not flirted with anyone at school. She had dressed nicely—for Paul.

She didn't know how she could see him and face him, and be with him and play for him. How could she do this? When she was in love with someone, how could she act as if he were just another person on another day? How could she refrain from telling him, from touching him? How could she keep it a secret?

She had never even thought of the fact that he may not have been in love with her.

But who would care anyway? Lilli was in love. And Lilli was some sort of goddess.

But how do I just sit there? How can I just sit there like I usually do? Just pay half-assed attention. I hate guitar. But I guess I only wanted to play it so I could see him. And I didn't figure this out until now! How stupid.

How stupid she had been. How stupid she had been before she had known what love was! She had not known, so she had not missed it, but now that she was in love with someone, she could not imagine her life without it. *It's so different. It's so much better. I wonder what it's like to sleep with someone you actually love. Just sitting with him would be enough though.*

That's part of the reason why it would feel different with Paul. I know it would.

She looked again at her arms. They were great to look at, really. Great for occupying empty, unchartered time. She was still thinking of how his name would look. Etched right into what was left of the peachy, unmarked flesh. She wouldn't do such a bad job, right? She was skilled at this, right? Wasn't she? Wasn't she great at cutting her own skin? Making emotions physical? Making mistakes stick?

But she didn't have the right tool. When she found it, she would know.

She didn't wonder if Paul had a girlfriend, or if he was interested in her, or if he knew of her love. None of this crossed her mind. Because Lilli had been entitled. Always. Lilli had always gotten what she'd wanted every time. So why should love be any different? Love was just like anything else, but more splendid, newer, different. The same rules applied. Didn't they?

Vivian

She had *eaten*. Gone through a bag of potato chips. *The real deal. Not the baked ones.* Half a pint of ice cream. Six pretzels. A chocolate chip cookie. An apple. Two bowls of cereal. And she was still hungry. *Why?*

Why was her body betraying her like that? She had been so good. Insanely good.

I haven't heard from Kat. Why won't she talk to me? I only listened to her. I only did what she asked. I don't get her. I don't get this! I followed the fucking orders.

"See? Now look what you've done." *Disgusting bitch. Fat disgusting bitch.*

"Who's going to sleep with you now? Yeah, guys just love those fat girls, don't they? Because all those supermodels are just fucking huge! Right?"

The *old* friends were "fat." "Normal," as they liked to say.

Vivian was not. Katerina was not either. *Her thighs make mine look huge. And look which one of us gets fucked in every way but one.*

She was wondering why her body was punishing her in this way. Why? Making her eat. Because she had held out so well almost all week, and the chips in the window of the grocery store had seemed too tempting to resist. And then the ice cream and all the rest came later. At home. And she had eaten and eaten, and finally fell back on her bed, exhausted. And cried. *I hope you gain fifty fucking pounds tonight, you fat fucking bitch! You deserve it. You deserve this.*

She pinched the skin on her stomach. She watched the glinting stone, watched the butterfly as it shrank and stretched with the breaths that filled her.

Fat. But it felt so good. To eat. To eat however much of whatever she wanted. And the chocolate had felt good sliding down her throat, and the salt from the chips burning her lips. And it had felt good to bite into the textures and flavors that she missed. And the richness that just couldn't be supplemented with apples and mints and water. Even the sweet, sweet apples were no comparison.

How could apples even begin to compare to chocolate ice cream in the first place?

But the damage had been done.

I should throw it up. I have to. I'm just so . . . tired. Her eyes were already fluttering closed. Her stomach, which had been so taut and starved, had begun to bulge with the bulk of food that she consumed. "Tomorrow, Vivian, you won't eat a thing. You can drink water, but you can't eat a thing." And she wouldn't. Vivian always kept her word. Always.

She would close her eyes as the Polaroids were passed around from girl to guy and girl to guy, and she would pretend that she was full of satisfaction. She could lie to herself behind her eyes. Tune out the laughter with headphones.

Disregard things. She could imagine what it would be like to laugh at Polaroids of someone else.

Yes, *she* was worth talking about. Her ass was worth staring at. Pictures of her were worth keeping. Maybe even jacking off to. Yeah, that's hot. But . . . *Why does it have to be like this?* Burn all of those pictures in a bonfire, watching the images crumple into charred pieces of nothing. It would take a forensic scientist to determine exactly what the ashes formerly were. Ashes. And then people could forget, because there was going to be something else next week. Another couple. Another "shocking" event. It was bound to occur that way. It was just a matter of time.

But if things were going to get better, if things were going to just blow over, why did all of this seem so permanent?

Beatrice

Days now. Days. Single days until his return.

She had had trouble getting out of bed again. She had become lethargic since his departure. Six-fifteen had come and gone. The alarm blinked furiously, and she forced her body up from the mattress, her eyes still blurred with sleep, her head still spinning. She went downstairs. The tiles were cold as always. She had started the stove up as always. Smiled as always. "Harry, I'm sorry I was late. I overslept. I shouldn't have overslept. Now I'm going to make you late!"

She hurried. Hurry, hurry, hurry. Can't make Harry late for work. Can't make Harry late for his big important meetings for the big important paycheck that goes to pay for big important things. She burned her finger on the skillet. "Bacon today. And toast. A bagel?"

The finger began to swell, but her movements were unfaltering. Faster faster faster! Watch Beatrice go! Watch Beatrice blink back the tears that the pain of the burn had caused. *I woke up late; I have to rush.*

And when it was done, she stood there. Satisfied. Staring at the empty seat and closing her eyes to imagine his body and his face and his eyes scanning the paper. His lips touching the rim of the teacup. His eyelashes fluttering, blinking up and down. *Just to watch him live . . . heaven.*

The burn began to sting angrily.

But she was too busy to notice. She was too busy to notice the obvious slam of the front door, which meant that her daughters were off to school again. She was too busy to notice that the food was growing cold and that his tea had stopped steaming. She was too busy to notice that the amount of food on the plate had not decreased, that the silverware and the napkin were untouched, and that the paper was unmoved and perfect. Too busy for any of that. All of that secondary nonsense.

What did all of that matter anyway?

Bea was getting on with her own life, just as anyone would do. She was doing nothing wrong. She was hurting no one except for herself. And she watched in admiration. In her own oblivious euphoria.

The tiles had grown warm under her feet. By this time, he would've been done. "Glad you like it." She murmured. *He can't hear you if you mumble.* "Glad you like it!" she chirped enthusiastically.

The burn had begun to shrivel and was clearly swollen.

Harry

He was doing this on purpose. Spoiling the whole plan.

Because I know what I want. And I don't care about Steve and what he thinks and who he thinks he is. I don't care.

And it was a conscious choice, so it was okay. Maybe. And why did these feelings have to happen now?

It didn't matter. *It doesn't matter. I want to see her, and that's my right. I'm paying to see her, and that's my fucking right! I have the same fucking rights that all of the other men in this world have. And I want to fucking exercise them.*

And when she came to the door, his heart was beating. His palms were sweating. He had been transported to a new age. "I want to take you out. I want to get to know you."

I want to know you because all of the other people I know are imposing things on me. She was very unthreatening in a threatening way. She didn't want to sit with him. She had never wanted to. She was on a schedule. People have schedules! People can't just turn their lives around because they feel like it. There *are* obligations. No matter how much we want to believe there aren't. "Please, let's go out. I'll pay for your lost time."

But lost time is irretrievable. It can't be saved up in a box or folded into an envelope. It's just gone. But Chloé felt sorry for him. Sorry because he was lonely and a widower. And she wasn't supposed to hang out with her clients. She wasn't supposed to get personal. But it was okay. Besides, she was hungry in more ways than one. And looking at him begging for her, she knew that she could crumple him up by walking away. She would eat with him. She would screw him. Who cares? She could see the desperation on his face. The agony. And she knew all the right things to say, and all the moves to make. She didn't have to cooperate.

Lilliana

He would be over in five minutes. Lilli didn't know what to do. *I'm in love with him! Now what? Now what do I wear? What do I say? Do I make my bed? Do I not? Do I clean up my room? Do I leave it messy? What do I do?*

Would he like her stains if he knew that they were all for him? *All for him.*

If she told him about her private things, what would he say? *If I wore a tank top . . . ?* If he saw that she could be vulnerable, what would he say? Would he say he loved her too? If she made herself human. If she lost her want of conquest. And exercise. Of prizes.

What would he say if she *could* play the guitar. *If I practiced at all.* Would he touch her? He sat so far away from her, always. Never touched her once. And he had backed away when she had touched his neck. He had refused when she had asked him to lay down with her. He'd left promptly.

She heard footsteps coming up the stairs.

"Hi, Lilli."

"Paul . . . hi . . . hey."

"So let's whip out the guitar." (silence)

"Okay, sure. Um . . . (silence) Paul, how's . . . college?"

"Yeah, school's fine. You know, a lot of work and shit, but still it's worth it. I'm happy that I switched my major though. It's so much better than premed."

"I bet."

"So how's the acoustic? Have you figured out the tuning?"

"Um . . . sort of."

"Okay, let's take a look."

"All right, uh-huh."

"Okay, it's pretty out of tune. Did you know that?"

"Wait . . . what?"

"Did you realize that it was really out of tune?"

"Um, yeah. I . . . well, sort of."

"Let me just play a riff or two on it to see if it's tuned better now, okay?"

"Okay."

"All right, perfect, or as close as I can get."

"So you like philosophy?"

"Yeah, I love it."

"Do you learn about Freud and stuff?"

"Well, not yet. We're doing the early Greeks. You know—Socrates, Aristotle. It's the history of philosophy for the first semester and a little of the real early stuff. Besides, Freud's more of a psychologist . . . at least that's what I believe. Yeah, he did have philosophies about psych, but I don't really think it should be taught as Western philosophy. His work with Jung just demonstrates that further. Besides, he's pretty modern, and the foundations of most of his ideas were based on the early guys anyway."

"Oh, I see . . . (silence) I'd love to go to college there."

"Yeah, it's pretty great."

"I really, really would. I should apply when I'm . . . Well, next year."

"Why not?"

"Yeah . . . (silence)"

"Let's get started, okay? Can you play that chord sequence I gave you?"

"I'll try . . ."

"Fifth fret."

"Yeah."

"Fifth from the top, Lilli."

"I . . . well, I need to practice more."

"I guess."

"It's true. I'll practice more. I really like guitar. I dunno, I just really like it, and I've just got a lot of work and shit. I know it sounds really stupid to you, but, seriously, it's true. And I just think that . . ."

Vivian

Walking through the hallways. Trudging from class to class, hauling her weight. The weight of her books, her body. Feeling the linoleum of the floor click under her shoes, her head throbbing. The Advil didn't work. She'd taken three in an hour, and the pain still stung her persistently.

Could it be because she hadn't eaten—in what? Something like twenty hours?

"Is she high or something?"

Nah. Fuck it. I'm not touching a thing. Not a bite. If you're good, Vivian, you can have half an apple after school. But not during. I have to work off all that junk from last night.

Was it honestly beautiful? To be trudging down the hallway with an "incurable" headache. Vivian thought so. Or at least it seemed that way.

"Eat something, why don't you?" people would say. Katerina turned her back. Clutching the arm of the boy whom she had so tactfully captured for herself. The old friends would glare. She glared back. *I deserve this. I deserve pain for all the crap I ate. I should've just puked then. Things would've turned out better.*

Looking at Katerina across the way. She was pressed up against him. His fingers were running through her hair. His lips were on her neck. She was laughing. They were an entity. Perfect in their shallowness. Flawless. All of the ugliness was just hidden by their desires.

But finally, Vivian was getting attention of her own.

Finally. Yes.

People knew her name. Calling after her, "Vivian, Vivian." *Attention.* Attention she had never gotten before, and now she had it. And with this attention, she was going to get rid of her virginity and become thinner and thinner and thinnest and eventually nothing. Which meant everything.

Constant images of her new, better self were reflected in shiny surfaces: car doors, windows, mirrors, of course. And she looked back, and waited, and smiled. How could she eat a thing if she ever hoped to redeem herself? How could she eat if guys liked skinny girls? How could she eat if the *old* Vivian had eaten and the *new* one didn't? Food had been lost with the old girl, along with the white underwear, and loose tee-shirts, and high-waisted jeans, and dirty Nikes. The absence of it had come along with the other lovely changes, the piercings, her new tattoo. *This* Vivian was strong because she had endured pain for her image. What had the old Vivian done? *Nothing. She did nothing. A fucking wasted body. A wasted life.*

Beatrice

She had nursed the burn on her finger carefully, holding a dripping ice cube against it, and then wrapping it in gauze and covering it with medical tape. *I hardly noticed. I was so busy that I didn't even notice that it had gotten so bad.* Yes, of course, she had noticed a slight tinge of pain; her reaction was, of course, to pull her hand up away from the heat of the stove at first. But then she had become wrapped up with Harry, and things had blurred. Bea had become less important. Her well-being was most definitely secondary.

But he was almost home. What was pain when there were so many more important things to care about?

Scouring, scrubbing, polishing more. She had tried to avoid her daughters' rooms. She didn't want to be confronted with the doors. The knobs. The frames. The slightly squeaking hinges. The lives behind them. The rooms that could tell her so much about them, about the people they were. The people they had grown into.

She had scurried across the hall, trying to divert her attention with other things. But passing the doors was inevitable. It was the only way she could get to her own room, her room and Harry's.

She had tried not to stop there.

She hurried away from the two doors whenever the girls were actually home. And when they were home, it meant that they were inside. She had stopped limiting visitors and visitation hours. *I tried. They won't listen. I tried. I have no control.* "I try, Harry. And I have no control. We need *you* here. And when you come, things will get better. And that's in only a few days! Can you believe it? I know, it's hard to be married and separate. Especially when we've been together so long, with a marriage like ours."

She had stopped nearly all conversation and confrontation with the girls, except for a word or two of acknowledgment in the hallways. She had stopped trying. In a way, she had surrendered. Given up. Stooping to their level, and further down still. Diminishing her authority. Lowering her stature. What was she now?

It wasn't that she didn't care. She did care. *I care. I do.* She hadn't stopped loving her daughters. But a mother's love was unconditional. She hadn't stopped worrying about them. She hadn't stopped wondering where they were at random intervals throughout the day and evening. But that question was easily answered. *Always in their rooms. Or they will be eventually.*

But it was true. She didn't have any control.

Could it be because she didn't have Harry?

Because if Harry were there, he would have *made* her function. He would have given her the enthusiasm that she asked for. He would have paid her the drab compliments, smiled at her in his drab way, gone to bed at night. It didn't matter about the sex—or the absence of it. That wasn't the reason.

What was Bea without Harry?

She cared. She loved the girls. But how could she know her place without someone else to tell it to her? Someone to tell her yes and no. What to do and what not to. Someone to make decisions and not leave everything up to her. She just didn't know where to begin. She didn't realize that not knowing where to begin was an automatic end.

Harry

He was trying. Living in fear. Living in fear of his wife's voice on the phone. Her breathing that he could hear on the other end. The heartbeat that would pulsate over the wire. Her warm breath on his face exploding out from the receiver.

He was trying so hard to block out those mornings at breakfast in the kitchen. *Her food was never ever good. I just said so. I just said it so she wouldn't get all sulky on me. The food was so bad. I . . .* And their silent evenings together. *How we never said a goddamned word to one another. She said it was some "connection" thing. I remember that. She said it in bed. I'd just fucked her. She said that afterward.* And their silent, vile dinners. And movies. And dances. And that blue dress. *Yeah, the blue dress. She looked okay that one night. Just that once. And I'd been fucking dared to approach her. The guys had given me five bucks because they'd heard she was a pill and a prude. And I guess I was blinded or something because I never stopped taking her out. Soon as I proposed, the dress doesn't fit anymore. She thinks that because she gets married she can gain twenty fucking pounds. Went all to her hips, the bitch.* And how they hadn't had sex in something like forever. *Not that I'd ever want to ever again. I would never waste myself on that worthless woman again. But still. Don't married people get drunk and fuck once in a while? She never drank. Never drank a sip of wine. Even when her husband wanted to get boozed up and have a little fun once in a while.* "It's always no, right, Bea? That's how it is? Well, I have someone *better* now. I have someone who's willing to . . . to . . ."

He hated crying.

He had not cried once while he was married to Bea. Well, maybe once, but he couldn't remember. He had never cried as a broken man. He had never cried because something irreplaceable was broken inside of him, and because he didn't know how to feel, or how to erase, or how to care about his daughters anymore. When things change, it's difficult to understand the things that don't.

Everything is affected by change though. In some way, that is.

Lilliana

I choked. He thought I was an idiot. I *sounded like an idiot, I looked like an idiot, I acted like an idiot, I was unprepared, and I fucked up. I wouldn't be surprised if he thinks I'm just some juvenile wannabe loser.* She *had* been unprepared, immature, clumsy. Her mystique had fallen away. She had been frazzled. She had not known how to *talk* to the person she loved, much less play for him. She had not known how to keep the conversation casually rolling. She had not known how to restrain herself from touching him.

She had tried edging casually closer to him, but he had taken no notice. She had tried slyly smiling at him. Laughing off her mistakes. Flirting with him to the best of her knowledge. She had almost forgotten how to flirt at all. She had almost forgotten how to flirt when the objective wasn't actual sex. Just recognition would've been nice.

She had gotten no recognition.

If anything, it had been dismissal.

He hadn't been in a good mood. He hadn't been receptive to her comments or questions. He'd been brief. *Maybe he just IS brief. He's never really gone into a lengthy explanation of anything. Has he?*

My hints just aren't working. How do you tell someone something like this?

She looked at the clean patch of unscarred flesh on her arm. She'd been saving it for him. She'd left that space blank. She'd used the X-Acto to open up old scabs in order to avoid running over the boundaries. This space was reserved. For Paul's name.

She didn't think that it was crazy. *When you're in love with someone, you should want to do this. This is what lovers do. Right? Isn't it?* She'd been planning it in her mind. A prominent fixture on her forearm. Something that was obvious—and calculated. Something insane done by a "sane" person. A regular person. A regular teenage girl in love.

Because love changes you.

And change affects everything, no matter what. No matter how small.

How nice would those four letters look arranged just right?

It wouldn't be difficult for her. She'd make it as perfect as it could get, and she'd cut when she was calm and not frazzled or upset. She'd do it with a clear head. *I'll do it when I want to. When I can do a nice neat job.* She knew that with a little patience she could do it correctly.

What would he do if he saw his name on my arm? Not like a tattoo. But like this. My own. What would he say? And was this the only way that she could say the inevitable?

Vivian

Standing in her room in her underwear once again. Picking out her flaws as if she were holding a magnifying glass to her reflection. Glaring at the girl who stood there. Watching. Examining herself meticulously. A red-haired, pierced, newly tattooed girl standing in her room, looking for all of the little things that had gone wrong along the way.

But these things were all fixable.

And Vivian liked fixable things. *I was ugly before, just plain ugly, and I fixed it. I was unpopular, and I fixed it. I had bad clothes; I fixed it. I don't want to be a virgin anymore, and I'll fix it. I wanted a tattoo and a piercing; I got them. I bought things. I can do this. I can fix whatever I don't like. I can mold myself in whatever way I deem necessary.* Because impermanent things were fixable. Because Vivian was pliable. Penetrable.

And Vivian was not fat. Or a lesbian. Or a prude.

Was it really asking too much? To want thinner thighs and tighter abs? She didn't think so. After all, America was becoming obese, and she refused to follow *that* trend. No one had naturally crimson-purple hair, but she wanted to be herself. No one had a butterfly tattoo, did they? Or a belly-button ring? Nobody had those things, right? That made Vivian unique. *Because tattoos are unique. They are! And Mom would hate them. If she cared, she would hate them. Who gives a fuck though? What's she going to do, punish me? I'll be eighteen soon.*

Eighteen and a child.

Was she being childish? To want things and get them? Was it childish that she wanted things to be beautiful and perfect, wanted to regard yesterday as nothing and the future as everything? No, no, Vivian was being *mature.* And this is what mature people did, didn't they? They found flaws and fixed them.

And she was far from there. Maybe she would never even come close.

I need to fix so many more things. There are so many little problems. So many little things that I could get rid of if I had the chance. And so Vivian's pursuits were justified, as she sat on her bed, gently running her fingers over her body. In quest of pleasure? No. In quest of perfection? Yes.

Beatrice

"There are times, Harry, when I can't believe that you're mine. When I can't believe that we're married at all. When I can't believe how lucky I am . . ."

It was nice talking. Feeling the warm air hit her lips and teeth and tongue. Feeling the false intervals of heat and air from the vents in the walls touch her face and pass over her. *In this house. That Harry and I bought together. How he kissed me that day, on top of the stairs. In front of the real estate agent and everything. I was so embarrassed!*

But talking was second best. And Harry wasn't there to kiss. And even if he were there . . .

Who was she to say anyway? Every day is a new day. Right?

She walked upstairs, carefully. Averting her eyes and turning her head away from the doors. Both of them shut tightly. Was there anyone behind them? Was anyone living there? They could've moved out for all she knew. She imagined opening the doors and finding the rooms bare and stripped entirely of their contents. The furniture would be gone. The posters too. And all of the clothes. She walked quickly past.

And then she was in her room again. Staring at the dress. The beautiful blue dress. And she was gently touching the worn taffeta with her fingers. And then she was examining the worn zipper, trying to pull loose threads out of the teeth, so it would glide smoothly up and down. When she'd zipped it up that night. Just like when she'd worn it at the party. Just like when she'd seen the man who she was destined to love, for the first time.

I don't think that a more beautiful dress could exist. I don't think that a more beautiful dress has ever been made. She had seen the Academy Awards, the period costumes of movies, the flashy dresses of the early decades. Pictures of her mother's wedding. But never had she seen a dress so lovely as the blue one. A plain dress. A plain, worn, blue dress. Worn too many times. Exercised past its prime, and then left alone as soon as the seams could give no more. As soon as they could bear no more weight. And then its simplistic beauty had been retired to the closet.

And now it was out in the open again.

"See, Harry? Don't you just love this dress? When you saw me . . ."

Harry

Business. It kills everything.

Passion. Lust. Happiness. Everything. Killed by the pursuit of material wealth. Of money. Killed by lack of time. By time taken away. By time diverted. By time stolen. By time kept, locked. Shut into hours. By time organized. Counted. Calculated. Definite. And gone.

How long has it been since I fucked Bea? Two years? Something ridiculous. When I was still "in love" with her. I'm not anymore. I don't need her. I wouldn't do it again.

Business had taken his time from the girls. It had made him unavailable on Friday afternoons, Saturday evenings, Sunday mornings. He had not seen them off to kindergarten. He had missed a handful of school events. He had not been available for questioning. He had never talked to his daughters about sex. He probably wouldn't have wanted to talk to them about it anyway. He would've panicked. *But they hadn't even asked. They never asked.* He had no reason to panic.

Business had taken his bank account and made it bigger. Business had added onto the house that one September, when he and Bea decided that a new garage was needed, and that it should connect to the kitchen. It had bettered their reputation in the neighborhood. It had looked good on his card. It had looked just great, handing his name out to people. Printed. Business.

It was all the fault of the business. Wasn't it?

Business had bought Christmas presents. Paid for birthday parties. Car rentals. Cosmetics. It had replaced lost items, keys, credit cards. It had been there. Almighty. Constant. Just as everything else was.

Fuck it. I won't let business ruin THIS.

Lilliana

She had sat on her floor, gently etching the *P* into her flesh. How nice it had felt to her! How lovely the pain had felt. Because it had a purpose.

When she was done, she let it bleed for a while, and when it started to run onto the carpet she held a towel over her forearm for a while, and sat and stared at nothing until it began to scab and tighten, and take form.

Welcome something new.

And looking at the *P* with pride, she wondered if it could be misconceived. *What will people think if I just walk around with a goddamned P-shaped scar? What'll they think? What'll they say?* She didn't want a *P*; she wanted a *Paul*. In all caps. Controlled but meaningful. Beautiful. Her own. His own. Their own.

A gift.

Or something.

Will he appreciate it? She started on the *A*. Slowly. Pressing down hard. Making it hurt an extra lot, so she could remember it and it would stay with her and stand out. So it wouldn't be like just any other time. *It's not like any other time. It can't be.*

It was beautiful in her bed with the candles burning. Lights set low on their dimmers, silence making soft music. And the beautiful liquid, wet and crimson like lacquer, like a fabric almost, seeping out. Freshness. Newness. To have your life's liquid escape. To have it come *out.*

The *A* was finished.

She blotted it with the towel and examined her work. It was there. The *A* in *Paul.* Perfect.

She had planned to go slowly. She had *planned* to do something rational, like a letter per day. No. Now she could not stop. She looked at the newly graffitied arm and stared at it in disgust. *PA.* She vigorously began to shape a *U.*

The simplest letter so far. So easy. So round, curved. She could practically do it in a single stroke. And then, quickly, messily almost, she shaped the hard corner of the *L*.

And she sat. Blinking at the pain, wide-eyed and amazed.

She let the cuts drip for a little, and then watched them scab. The letters, so desperate in their message. Had she been thinking? Had she even considered the consequences? Had she considered that Paul might not reciprocate? That he didn't seem to show her any sign of his interest? Did she consider that she would have to spend the rest of her life walking around with Paul's name engraved on her skin? On her arm, for the world to see? For everyone to know?

But things were too good. At that moment.

In that moment.

She wouldn't realize the magnitude until later.

Vivian

"Vivian? How do you get your stomach so *flat?*"

Lucky Vivian.

Look how her popularity soars!

Look how pretty. Look how loved.

Her image is known.

She's famous! Fame. Isn't it just so . . . cold?

"Such a fucking slut. Look at her. Who the hell does she think she is?"

"Whatever, she thinks because she gets pierced she's all that. She's just an insecure, slutty, white-trash, anorexic bitch. Have you heard what she's done? She's, like, evil."

"Just a wannabe. That's it."

"I just feel sorry for her. So pathetic."

Lucky Vivian.

Katerina looked on. Whispering, "I always knew she was a dyke. She was always, like, coming onto me. She was always trying to get me fucked up on weed so I would hook up with her."

It seemed so nice. All of the attention. It was more than just stares now.

Now *she* was reciprocating. Because she could. Vivian didn't realize that she was now powerless. At *their* mercy. But she was trying to prove people wrong. At least get them to think that she was bisexual rather than purely gay. She flirted overtly with just about anyone who wasn't ugly and had a penis. She was very physical. She was a show-off. *A kiss is just a kiss.*

Still not as good as her sister though. Not as good as Katerina either. *I'm never going to get her friendship back. But I don't know what I did! I listened to her! Still different. And I'm not trying to be like Lilli. I never wanted to. I don't understand why people are saying that or thinking that.* She just had to focus on other things. She would get into college. *I'm sure I will. Please! No one else is interesting. Extracurriculars hardly determine a person's value. I used to do community service and shit. So what? What's the big deal? I never felt good or anything.* Just the same.

How boring.

To be one person. To be one person and not long for constant change. What a travesty. *I'm just growing, for God's sake. I'm just growing up. It's not such a monumental thing.* What a travesty.

Harry

I like her.

He liked what she did to him. He liked the kind of person that she had helped him become. *It's important to care about myself. I never cared about myself.*

Bea had forced him to be selfless. He didn't think that selfishness was a virtue, but never before had he really considered his own needs. His needs. Harry's needs. He had needs like everybody else. He sometimes needed certain things that she could not provide. *People need more than dinner to be happy. They need other things.* It wasn't even about him anymore. It was *her.* Bea. Doing everything that was so right that it was wrong. She had her own concerns too, didn't she? Didn't she have the right to say she didn't want to be naked in the light? That she didn't really approve of giving oral sex? She'd tried it for him. Trying should count.

Sadly, no. It doesn't. It didn't.

All of Bea's problems had been counteracted now. Now those problems didn't exist. He'd had his fill of home-cooked meals. He'd had his fill of romance. *What the hell is romance?* These things. They'd become such banal factors of existence that he'd chosen to regard them with nothing more than a nod. They'd become peripheral. He'd let them blur and didn't care.

But Chloé had eaten with him. He had taken her out to dinner.

He never took Bea out to dinner. She'd always been too worried about expenses.

But Chloé had sipped fine wine and eaten filet mignon—*and* she'd jacked him off under the table with her bare foot. Toes curling, lips stretched into a smile.

He'd paid extra for *that*, of course. And she'd smiled the whole time. "When are we gonna fuck, Harry? This is so damned boring."

Bea would've never done that. Never! Not in a million years.

And Chloé was so warm. In bed. On top of him. Beneath him. It was so easy. "Bet your wife didn't do it this good." *No, that's right. She didn't. She didn't do it at all. It was awful, just awful. Now that I'm here with you, I never want to see her again. I never ever want to go back again . . . I never . . . I think I love you.*

He just really liked her. Maybe she was just a better alternative. Had he forgotten? He already *had* a family. He had a normal house in a nice neighborhood and two seemingly normal teenage daughters. And he had paid off his mortgage years ago. Everything was *his*. At least most of it.

Sort of.

He caught himself wondering about the girls again. *How do they live there with her? I wish I knew them better. Like I used to.* Because it was true: he didn't really know them anymore. He knew that Lilli was a vegetarian. He knew that Vivian got good grades, dressed conservatively. He knew that Lilli was not a virgin. He knew that his daughters were in high school. He knew that Lilli was sixteen. And he knew that Vivian was seventeen. Their birthdays were April eighteenth and October seventh—or April seventh and October eighteenth. But what else did he know? He didn't know their likes and dislikes. He didn't know their friends. Or what they did after school. He didn't know what books they'd read or hadn't read. He didn't even know if this information was valid anymore. The things he knew. *Are they even true anymore?*

He also knew Bea's birthday, but he didn't want to get into it.

Beatrice

And there she was again. Standing in front of the doors. The doors that were vehicles to unknown places. For if she opened them, she would see unknown things. Discover secrets. Become acquainted with reality. For once.

Though her hand would not reach out. Her fingers would not curl. Bea was not even able to touch the brass. She was unable to grip it as she had done only days before. *But everything will be all right. When Harry comes home, everything will improve. I won't have to stand here. He could go in if he wanted.*

Maybe I just don't want to go in at all. Maybe that's why it just won't work.

She turned away. Quickly. Trying not to remember the days when she had freely entered and exited the rooms. When she had scrubbed the floor of the adjoining bathroom. Made their beds, pulling their spotless sheets tightly. Creaseless. Absolutely perfect. Flawless little rooms, with meticulously vacuumed carpet and with little neatly folded clothes stacked in their drawers and in their closets.

It couldn't have changed that much. They were always a little messy. I'm sure it hasn't really changed.

"I'm sure the girls haven't changed that much. Don't you think, Harry? I think that they're just the same. The thing with Vivian is just a phase. I know it'll pass soon. She'll be back to normal when *you* get here." She smiled. "I know it. You just wait." She turned back again. Looking at his placid face. "And Lilli seems the same. She'll always be the same."

She went downstairs to the kitchen. "Ha-ar-ry!" she called up the stairs. "I want to know what you want for di-in-ner!"

Vivian

Standing in front of her mirror, brushing her purple-red hair. She had a "date." With a male. Someone had asked her at lunch. Someone who was either intrigued by her past exploits, or who had ignored the rumors altogether. Did she want to hang out tonight? She had complied. *Why not? He was semi-attractive.*

I wouldn't sleep with him, but still. . . . I can occupy my time. Because she would *know* when it was really right. *Because I would know that second. Like lightning. I might as well fuck him on the spot when I meet him. That's how fast I would know.*

Such a broad prospect: hanging out.

Vivian colored her pale lips purple. Lined her average eyes to make them large. Extended her lashes as far as possible, and curled them perfectly. Made her cheeks rosy. Her complexion appeared perfect. Ran her fingers over the jewelry, over the things that made her new. And smiled. Or practiced smiling.

And she'd gotten very good at it. She tried to smile like Katerina had.

There were certain smiles that meant more than others. And Vivian had become well versed in this field over the course of her metamorphosis. She practiced the one with the squinty eyes. The one with *a lot of teeth. Like, molars.* The one with closed lips. The one with medium teeth and tilted head. With wide open eyes.

She also practiced laughing. Laughing was more difficult. Especially if there was nothing to laugh at. But she had noticed that laughter was the best icebreaker, silence filler, and mood inducer.

She mouthed the words to a popular song.

She agonized over her top.

I like this. This is fun. This is what high school should be.

What's his name again? He must have told her three times. He must have written it down somewhere. He'd written his number on her hand. And she'd worn it all day. Flashing her graffitied flesh at the other girls to make them jealous. *Dan? Dave? Greg? God, I have no idea. Whatever. I probably won't even need to say his name. I mean, it'll just be him and me. Whoever he is.*

But his name didn't really matter. He was "hot." He used to date someone named Kelli something. He lived in a huge house. His parents had money. He drove a Mazda.

And that constituted a worthwhile male. To date. To hang out with. To use for practice.

But first and foremost—most importantly—*he's a guy. And people are going to hear about this date. And I'm going to shove it in their faces until they realize.*

She slipped on her thong. *If we do do something, I want to look nice and all.*

Her skirt was slit up to *there*, revealing a nice slice of her gradually shrinking thigh. She decided on her purple cutoff tank top. Deep purple. It brought out the purple tones in her hair and lipstick.

People say it's not natural. I don't want it to look natural. Don't they get that?

Because people didn't like *natural* girls. Look at the celebrities. *Do they look natural? I don't think so. They don't.*

She smiled again. Closed her eyes. Tried to remember his name. Tried to forget the stares. Tried to pretend that she had never done what she'd done. That she'd never fallen for Katerina's bullshit. She'd been taken advantage of. She had been naive and juvenile and no better than anybody else. It could've been anyone, but it wasn't.

"Fuck you, Katerina. Go fuck yourself, you selfish cunt. If anyone's the dyke here, it's you."

And she tried to remember his name.

Lilliana

The beauty was covered in a long, navy blue sweater-sleeve. And it *itched. Like a motherfucker!* But pain, discomfort, whatever she felt, had been dulled. Transported to some sort of lesser place. Because her perspective had changed or had been warped, or dulled, or magnified. Now Paul inhabited a substantial portion of her mind, her thoughts, her time, her desires: soaking up a significant portion of her energy.

But now what?

What was she supposed to do after the fact? Was he supposed to see it? And what would he do if he did?

She had been almost afraid to look at it afterward. She had been almost afraid to see the work that she had done so meticulously. Fueled by adrenaline then. And after the feeling had gone, there had been the pain that she had vied for. And then the silence. And the fear that she had denied had ever existed.

But cloaked in the blue sweater, it seemed to burn more. To be more visible.

Paul. *I love him. I'm in love now. With Paul. There's nothing wrong with that. This is what I've been waiting for. I'd never been in love before, and it's true. Everything does change. And this changed. Is that a problem? It shouldn't be.*

But how is a person supposed to show it? *I need proof.*

She didn't know how to express love. This feeling. She didn't know how to tell him. Didn't know how to justify the sex in her past. What *had* it all really meant? So this was the result. *PAUL.* On Lilli's arm. And Lilli, confused about everything. *What does it all mean?* What did sex mean in the context of love? And what did love mean in the context of sex? And if sex had been so physical, so animalistic, so meaningless in the past, then how could it become all of the opposite qualities? Did Lilli know *how* to love? Did she know how to be in love?

Paul.

Harry

He was walking because he didn't know when or how he could ever visit Cleveland again. Surely not with Bea that coming summer. Surely not with the girls. Maybe he would never see Cleveland again. Before he died, maybe he would never set foot in Cleveland.

Did things have to be that final?

Did it all have to end so predictably?

Everything was calculated. Two weeks could only last so long. He would get on another plane soon. He would go *home.* He would have to see Bea. He would have to forget. *I could never forget.* He would have to pretend that his time in Cleveland had been successful—in a traditional way, of course. Pretend that the boss had been proud of him, that the Verchon deals had been closed, that his head had been dizzy with dreams of Bea and that his heart had held on to his daughters throughout the whole tedious, fucked-up thing.

How could he just go back and live on? *I know why I want to live now. I know why I want to be alive. I've found what had kept me from living.*

Maybe it doesn't have to end this way. It doesn't have to because it can't!

Because Harry was afraid. He was afraid of his past. Afraid of the girls he no longer knew. He feared his wife. Bea. And if he could just run away from it all, it could be so much better. Fixed.

He could be free. He would never have to face his problems again. Of course, *they* would be alone. Alone and left to fend for themselves. *Could they do it?*

Maybe it doesn't have to end this way.

Maybe it did.

The girls would need him. *What would they do without a father? What would people say?* They would be known as the girls with the father who left home for two weeks and never returned. He wouldn't be invited to their weddings. They would have no address. His girls would hate him. Bea would be dysfunctional. *They would have no parents. They'd be orphans.*

But Vivian was almost eighteen, and Lilli was almost seventeen, and they were almost adults. Couldn't they take care of themselves?

What would happen if I just stayed for a few more days? Or another week? Or a month or so? Would anything happen? I don't think so. They wouldn't miss me that much. Hell, I haven't even spoken to them in two weeks. I hardly speak to them when I'm there. They wouldn't miss me.

But Bea would be impossible. No matter what Harry did, she'd never be happy until he was there.

The selfish bitch. All she cares about is her own fucking self. No one else. Sure, she cares about me, as long as I'm making HER fucking happy.

Nothing was going according to plan. Everything had taken on a different shape. New factors needed to be included in the equation. There was a new variable. There was Chloé. And there was Harry and his own life and his own views and his own happiness. And everything had been hidden until now. A jolt—and repression was over. Movement began. Those times, that time . . . over. Beat on the doors until you get what you want. Beat on the walls until your fists bleed.

Vivian

It had gone well. Vivian's date. She'd been drunk half the time though. And the memories of it all had melted together into an endless stream of time with significant pieces missing. *His name was Dean something.*

He'd taken her to some coffee place. Some pizza place. Some movie. Some bar. They had had some fun and some conversation. There had been some silence as well. There had been some contact. There had been no disagreement.

Driving and driving in his Mazda. And laughing! There had been music on the radio. His hand had rested on her bare thigh, she had opened the window, and her purple-red hair had billowed like a cape. *But I wouldn't want him for a boyfriend. He was okay for a date.* And she remembered how her old self used to look. What she would've been doing on a night like the night before. *Probably studying for some fucking test. But not anymore! I don't even know what work I have. I haven't even started, but who cares? You're only young once. Right? You only live once.*

He was a pothead. *He'd taken twelve fucking hits before the movie.* He'd hot-boxed the car, and they had sat there. She could taste pot on his breath when he kissed her. *That was all though. We just kissed.*

But if that had been the best she could do, any guy was better than no guy. And he had been any guy. Just the same, average, suburban druggie. The same I'm-so-fucking-fed-up-with-everything type. He'd talked about the virtues of video games and his parents' liquor cabinet for over an hour. And Vivian had just smiled her nice, new, lipsticked smile. And agreed, and laughed, and nudged, and squeezed. "Oh, I *love* that game!"

He was nice. For one date. Because girls dated these types. And it wasn't a problem. Or shouldn't be. *And everyone's going to find out.*

And his parents really had a lot of booze. He'd poured her tall screwdrivers without ice, made from Tropicana and lukewarm Smirnoff. He had done shots of Jack Daniels, and they had sat on the floral living-room furniture, each of them closing their eyes to pretend that they were somewhere else. *But he was already pretty gone anyway.* And suddenly, they'd been together. But she'd left, stumbling down the street, and called a cab before anything drastic had happened.

A perfect date. A normal date.

And she felt fine. Better than fine. She felt good.

Beatrice

The sunlight that illuminated Bea's face seemed to take ten years off her. She wasn't really *old*. She did, however, have the beginnings of wrinkles, crow's-feet, laugh lines. She could get them fixed. If she wanted to. She didn't. *Aging should be beautiful, shouldn't it? People should just age naturally.*

But sitting in the sunlight, Bea looked like a different person.

And it was the morning.

The steam from Harry's plate of food curled up into the air vent in the ceiling. Bea looked at the burn from a few days before. Smiled at it. "See, Harry? I didn't even realize, isn't that funny? I was making you breakfast, and I didn't even realize."

She got up from the seat slowly, and she moved out of her brightly lit place. The wedge of sunlight remained on the table. She turned around abruptly. "Is there anything wrong with it? Too salty?" She paused and smiled. "Oh."

She walked over to her chair again. Sat down. "I love you, Harry. I do. I swear." She felt his two sad eyes on her; she saw his simple self sitting there. She saw him grab his paper. Smile at her. Smile at Beatrice. Make Bea happy.

And I am happy. Just sitting here. Living. Here.

She thought she heard a shuffling in the doorway. But her placid grin could not be removed. It would not turn into a grimace. It would not fade. And Harry, or her notion of him, would not suffer.

And Bea was still in the sunlight.

And under her eyelids, she was wearing the blue dress. And turning and turning, with Harry's strong arms to support her and his strong gaze to keep her alive. His words were there to nourish her. They were moving to the music in that dance hall. The loud music. Watched by friends. And now she was slipping.

I always wanted to go back there. To that room where we met, Harry. I always have. Maybe someday.

And then a shadow cut her spotlight in two.

"You should be at school. Shouldn't you?"

"At eight forty-five."

"Oh, that's late."

"Juniors and seniors get to go in late."

"Um, can I ask you a question?"

"What? I'm in a rush. Have you seen my brush anywhere?"

"No. Um, Lilli, have you been eating?"

"Yeah."

"Because you haven't been coming to—"

"I know. I've been busy."

"What about Vivian?"

"I dunno."

"Oh."

"You're sure you haven't seen it? Maybe in the living room or something?"

"No, I haven't. You should get to school."

"I know."

"What time do you have to be there?"

"At eight forty-five. I just told you. I just said it. Literally."

"Oh, right."

"Jesus, you never, ever listen to me or—"

"I . . ."

(silence)

Lilliana

She hadn't cut herself since. And that was a long time. She had stopped by the store again. Waited for him. Again. *Like a goddamned groupie. That's what they think I am. A fucking groupie. A Paul groupie. And not for his band.* He'd obviously had other girls. He'd obviously had other girls like Lilli. Gullible, vulnerable, younger girls. Pure girls and nymphs alike, strutting their smooth teenage limbs up and down the aisles and waiting for him. Tossing their hair and pretending that they were "just browsing." Maybe that's why the salespeople laughed. Did she ever think of that? *I know that he's had girlfriends in the past. I've had boyfriends, sort of. I've had other people too. It's not like I'd expect him to be a prude. Or save himself for me or something. That's just stupid.*

But who *wouldn't* fall in love with Paul? A musician. A *deep* musician, who plays guitar, and can teach, and who is a philosopher in the making.

Who wouldn't? But Lilli had been contaminated already. She had knotted herself into his life and knotted him into hers. She thought about him. She cared about him. She liked the fact that he was an intellectual. That he wasn't conventionally attractive. *Not Nathan handsome.* She liked how he played the guitar, wrote music. That the music he wrote seemed to have been written for her.

It hadn't been written for her.

But thoughts are thoughts. And wants are wants. Needs are needs, and so on.

While she was waiting, she touched her nice "Paul" scar through the thickness of her sleeve. *So personal.*

She smiled beneath the smirks of his coworkers. Smirking at the girl who skipped seventh and eighth periods to stand there like a fucking groupie nerd. And they never said exactly where he was. It was always "he's on break." That only narrowed his whereabouts down to about a thousand possible places.

But I like it in there. I don't mind waiting. I like music. And if you love somebody, you'll do anything. For them. For him. Lilli paced and smiled, looking up whenever the door to the store opened or shut.

He didn't arrive for two hours.

And she had been greeted with a cold shoulder. But she had persuaded him to come over that night at eight. Because she hadn't forgotten how. Because she could.

Harry

"Hello?"

"Harry, it's Chad. Did I wake you up or something?"

"Uh, Chad, no. I've been up."

"Well, you sound sort of . . . groggy."

"No, not groggy, just—"

"Look, let's cut to the chase here."

"All right."

"You've been missing meetings, lunches, engagements. What's up with you? Steve called me yesterday. He said you missed several scheduled meetings. . . . He said he talked to you about it. I really don't understand why you're fucking up like this. See, Harry, I was under the impression that you were a trustworthy guy—"

"I am a—"

". . . and I hope you haven't been dicking around out there because I don't like getting calls. How are we supposed to gain clients who trust us if our employees are out screwing things up?"

"I *am* trustworthy."

"Good. I thought so. Don't fuck this up, Harry. I know you've missed more than three meetings, including one that was supposed to start right now. Ten-thirty. With Verchon. You think the clients don't call when something is fucked? They do."

"Yeah, Chad, I know."

"So tell me. Is there a reason why you've been missing these engagements? Find a new girl or something? Huh? You can tell your good ol' boss. Stayin' out late in those good ol' Cleveland bars? Fuckin' around behind the wife's back?"

"God, no. No!"

"Haha, just checking."

"Good. Because I'm not."

"Right. Yeah, you've been married forever. I guess there's a time when you just don't want another girl, right? How is the wife? What's her name? Becky?"

"She's fine. It's Beatrice."

"Right. Yeah. So anyway, I'm just giving you a heads-up. And just letting you know that if you fuck it up again, there will be consequences. But I shouldn't have to give you all this shit. You're a smart guy, Harry. You should know this. You knew it before I called."

"Yeah, I know."

"Anyway, I'm trusting you with Verchon. Remember, don't fuck up. He's a fucking huge client, and if we lose him, we lose you. Got it?"

"Right."

"I'm gonna let you go. Don't have too much fun out there. It's only Cleveland. And you'll be back in a few days anyway. Clean it up. Especially for the finalization with Verchon tomorrow. You've already missed three with him, remember. You'll have to cover four times as much info in one quarter the time. Don't fuck up."

"Right. Bye, Chad. Thanks."

He felt his chest heave. *How quickly time goes.* How his concept of time had been lost, along with his grip on reality, which he had formerly appreciated, and knew so well. And it wasn't because he didn't care. He *cared.* He cared about his fucking mediocre job as the underdog, and he cared about Verchon and all the other clients, Chad too. And the family. Because society had forced him to care. Because underneath it all, he hated everything. Because it had been forced upon him. Because it was all for the family that he hardly knew, and the family that hardly knew him. And for Beatrice. Of course.

Because all he wanted now was something that was silly, unheard of, taboo.

Because every fucking thing is for Bea. And what do I get in return? A fucking dinner plate.

Chloé. He didn't need her to pretend anymore. He just liked her. He liked the way she walked into his room and held her own. She was good at what she did. He was done with emotional stuff. With Bea. But there was a mystery about Chloé, *the whore.* It made him want to know her.

Was it possible not to care about anyone or anything? To be just a motionless, senseless *thing*?

No. It was obviously impossible.

And I love her, and I don't love Bea. "I swear. I wish I could tell her. . . . But you're different. You're . . . someone else." He smiled. Fully. Maybe he was there already. Maybe he'd made it. Maybe he'd made it beyond the denial, the slander, the hatred of it all, and come to some other state of being.

But how good it felt to tell Bea to go fuck herself. And how good it felt to shout anti-Bea obscenities in his drunken escapades until he fell asleep to the sound of his own empowering, musical cant. A symphony of power. *She can go fuck herself. She needs it.*

I'll make the Verchon meeting tomorrow. I'll hammer out a goddamned deal. That's what I came here for, right? But sometimes unexpected things happen. *But for now . . .* Her beauty was suffocating.

Vivian

I should get a job. I need money. But she had no interest in working at so many of the places that employed seventeen-year-old high-school seniors. Dairy Queen. Burger King. McDonald's. *Food. All fucking food! Isn't there anyplace nice? Where I don't have to be surrounded by greasy obese people all day long? Where I won't have to wear a fucking apron?* It was unlikely that she would be able to meet any guys that way. Highly unlikely. Even if she wore a really short skirt, they wouldn't see it if she was standing behind a counter. *Stupid fucking counters. Stupid low-wage jobs. Doesn't anyone ever think about what it is that people want?*

Mr. Bently's Ice Cream, ShopRite, concession stand operator at Southport Cinemas, hot dog vendor for minor league baseball games, waitress, Candelabra, Lynne's Gourmet, Dane's, Spade's . . . Jesus, there has to be something that doesn't involve food. I can't be around it. Because if I am, I'll fucking eat it. I'll have a huge binge. I'll be tortured. She could just imagine herself wolfing down croissants. Gradually loosening her apron just a bit every day. And then one day it just wouldn't fit at all. The circumference of her body would exceed that of the apron. They'd have to make one specially for her. She swore. She was sure.

She threw down the paper. *I guess I could live for a few more months.*

She ran her fingers gently over her taut abdomen. She'd been doing sit-ups. Crunches. Push-ups. Jogging two miles a day. She had lost seven pounds. She had been trim before.

And now she was *thin*.

She closed her eyes. The room was very quiet. She wasn't expecting any calls. Katerina surely wouldn't phone. At this point she knew that. *I get it. Okay?* Neither would the other night's date. No one would bother her. No one would inquire about her. Not her mother and not her sister. Her father was away, and she had not heard from him. *But it's okay. I like it in here. I like my privacy.*

And soon I'll lose my virginity, and things will really change. Really. And there will be no trace of the lesbian rumor. I'll be just like Katerina. The straight girl who is unafraid to mess around. That's the best situation, I guess. Because everyone thinks you're free and hot and modern and okay with stuff. Easygoing.

And it was true. The rumors were dissipating. A little. The date the other night had helped. She'd been right. Too bad he lied and said she'd given him head in the car. *Whatever. That's better than everyone thinking I'm fucking gay.*

Virginity was a burden to Vivian. A thing that was keeping her from so much else. *Lilli. God, she lost it so young. I wish I didn't have to worry. I wish I didn't have to wonder.* A thing that was preventing her from living the truth. Living the new identity that she had created. The identity that had been created for her. The rumors that sped through the hallways. So fast! *Well, it has been practically lost for me.*

I'm just being too picky. That's why it never gets done. That's why I never get anywhere.

But she had time. And time was important. Because now the old friends and several others believed that she truly was a slut, whatever that meant. Nothing could change that. *So I might as well do what I want.*

Beatrice

I hate talking to them! The girls. Hate it. *I always have, always will. I hate it!* "I told you, Harry. They need *you*. You know what you're doing. You could talk to them. I can't even get a straight answer to a question. I don't know what they've become. I don't want to know." She sighed and began scraping the dinner plates with a knife. "But you'll be home soon. And things will fix themselves."

In a few days, she could go back to the routine. Everything would fall into place. Everything would be just fine.

Wouldn't Harry make it all better?

Harry, who was so in love with her, who was so sure of himself, who praised her, complimented her, smiled at her, touched her. This was the answer. Harry was the person, the thing, the factor, almost, that would and could make the difference. Harry was a god.

You are a god to me. Bea closed her eyes, inhaled the aroma of detergent, and heard the running water and the scraping of metal against china that were so comforting to her. This is what Bea was in love with. She loved her house. She loved Harry. She loved the simple pleasures. The simplicity of it all. When she was in the kitchen. When she wasn't thinking about the girls—or the people that they were becoming. When she was alone with Harry. That's what she loved.

I still love the girls. They're just so . . . burdensome. I never thought that being a mother would be so hard. I always thought that they would never change. The girls as babies. So difficult. So easy.

If she just didn't think about them, things could be easier still. Easy not to think about people you rarely see, people who rarely see you. People you'd rather not see because seeing them would hurt, touch things, grate against nerves. Even if they live in your house.

Because she rarely saw the girls, she had no desire to question them. She had stopped demanding to know their whereabouts. They had a curfew at midnight, but she was usually in bed and asleep before then, and she knew that they would not obey it anyway. But what could she do? *What do you do when you have no power? What do you do when your rules have no power?*

Her reactions were dull now. Bea could not muster the strength to yell at them. Their schedules did not match. The girls hardly stopped by the kitchen in the mornings. Neither of them came to dinner, for undisclosed reasons. It didn't matter that they were under the same roof. They might as well be living in different states. None of them could communicate. But this was a family nonetheless. This was a family, and this was just how things were. *How things are. Just the way they are.*

Lilliana

When do you tell somebody that you love them? And how? She'd hidden the *Paul* scar for days now. The pain hadn't fully subsided, but the danger had. And she liked the pain. The constant, relentless, throbbing pain. A heartbeat. Paul's heartbeat within her. A heartbeat she had created.

I did it for him.

But would he like to see it? Would he be appreciative? She couldn't predict his reaction. *When you love someone, everything changes. Everything.* She had to show him. *I have to. I did it for him. Not for me. For him.*

He had been there last night.

Sitting on her bed, on her carpet, on her floor. He had sung and played. She had stared, mesmerized. Transfixed. Watching his lips move up and down, shaping words and releasing them. All for her. *As if all of his movements were for me.*

Then he left. And nothing had happened. He was no different, and yet he had changed so much.

She looked into her mirror. "I have to tell him. I have to show him." *I will.* Because she had worked so hard. She had tried. And she had done something that was unselfish. Something that was for someone else. Broken the pattern. She had stepped out of the routine for a single brief moment. She had caused a change.

And then, she sat on her floor, and let the tears come down fast. There was no competition there. Just being. Living. Alone. And she was reveling in it. Loving it. "I'm going to fucking tell him. I'll let him fucking know that I love him, and nothing can change that. And he'll love me too." *Tomorrow night.* She picked up the phone and began to dial.

Harry

Why am I going to the meeting?

To make money.

For who?

For the family. For Bea.

And why do you want to do that?

I don't know. Maybe I don't. Maybe I don't care if I fucking lose my job. Maybe I don't care about making money. Maybe I don't care if Chad's pissed. Maybe I don't care about losing the damn Verchon account. Maybe I don't care about hearing about Verchon's fifty fucking failed marriages. Maybe I don't care about anything anymore.

Relief was only a phone call away. He hardly had to do a thing.

No. He would not go to dinner. He would not ever see Steve Verchon again. *I'll probably lose my job. I'll probably get a call in the morning. Chad'll say he wants to see me ASAP when I get back to the office.* And he paused. *If I get back to the office.*

Did it all have to end in the morning?

Does it all have to end in the morning?

Vivian

Soon.

Soon. Sooner.

Sooner than you think.

Sooner than she thought.

Eyes open, lips open, arms open. Arms. She will dance like a big girl. Spinning and spinning for everyone else. She'll bend down on purpose. She *wants* you to look. She is telling you that *maybe you could be the lucky one.*

Come on, take the fucking joint. And she did. Take the bottle. Drown your inhibitions in booze. Make them alcohol-soaked, twisted up, shaken on the rocks. Stain them and darken them and put makeup on them and blend them into the background. Maybe then they'll all stop looking at the wrong thing(s).

I can dance. She let the music enter through her pores. She understood that there was a yesterday and a tomorrow, but that *right now* was impermanent.

So she'd better make the best of it.

Every moment was a new moment. Every moment was a missed chance.

Each one could've been something special. *And each one can fucking be special. I can do what I want. And fuck anyone who tells me I can't. Fuck all of them. Fuck everyone who doesn't believe me. Fuck you, Katerina. I hope you get fucking herpes from your sick, disgusting boyfriend and your fucking manipulative ways. I hope you get it all over your face.*

Soon. She could turn nothing into something else. She could intoxicate, exercise, flex her muscles rapidly. She could have power. *And I will.*

Beatrice

When the alarm rang, her eyes were already open. She pulled on her robe and hurriedly descended the stairs. Because it was the day. The day that Harry would come home.

Bea pulled out the slices of bread, the potatoes, the large bottle of slippery oil. She heated the skillet. "Harry, I love you so much! And tonight I'll make a brisket, all right? You still like that, don't you?" She smiled. The sun slanted through the drapes, illuminating her face once again. Peeling away the years. Bea was young again.

A brisket tonight for Harry. I'll make a brisket.

Swimming in sunlight. A new body in the morning.

She glanced back at Harry's seat. Felt his presence. How the air *changed* when he was there. How *things* changed when he was there. And *change affects everything. Harry affects everything. He pulls us all together.*

She listened to the hissing sound of the potatoes in the pan.

She beat the eggs for the French toast.

She loved this. This is what Bea lived for. *This.* She wanted nothing more. Nothing less. Just this. Just the sound of potatoes frying, and just Harry sitting dutifully in the kitchen, staring at her in the old way. Complimenting her. Remembering her in the blue dress. The dress that now hung on their bedroom door.

The potatoes were done.

She poured them out of the pan onto his plate. More food going to waste. More more more. *It's okay though; he'll be home tonight.* Now the toast was sizzling as well. And she was happy. More than happy.

She had heard the girls go off to school. *They probably won't return until late tonight. He probably won't see them until tomorrow.*

The girls. *So difficult, so easy.*

But it was a happy day, and nothing could change it. No darkness could dampen that morning. Nothing could dull it. *Maybe it wouldn't hurt if I had just a bite of the potatoes. Just one bite.* She had been good all week. So good. She'd had almost nothing caloric or fried. But today was a holiday! *The day that Harry comes home.*

Bea picked up a small, hot potato with her fingers. Tasted its texture, its flavor. *Oh God, this is so good.* She took another. Another. Another still. Then she put a plate in front of Harry.

Another still. Another piece of potato. She turned around rapidly. Saw his smile. That smile, the weary smile she loved more than anything on earth. And she laughed. She tossed another potato in her mouth, and . . . *Oh . . . oh God, I . . . I . . .*

Two of Harry's hands squeezing Bea's heart with one solid motion. Increasing the pressure. How much do I love you?

How much does he love me? Like a cage. A vise.

So much love that she couldn't breathe. In his eyes. And in her own mind.

She backed up against the cabinets. She tried to speak. There was no "Glad you like it." The morning was not complete. Today's speech was inaudible. *I . . .* She felt the nice, white, polished wood of her cabinets against her back. The handles. Her hands wrenched onto the marble counter. The things they had bought together, she and Harry. She clutched her chest, just as she had during the proposal. So desperate, thinking that she could never do enough. Never feel enough. And now she was feeling something more.

She tried to grasp the one last thing. Those beautiful kitchen smells. The detergent, the potatoes, the soap. The mixture that she loved so much. The things she lived for. These simple pleasures. So easy to please.

She couldn't.

Change . . . She let her legs begin to give . . . her knees bent. Letting her body slide down to meet the tiled floor. Let her eyes linger still, on Harry's seat. So still. And she let her mind go blank, didn't think about the girls, didn't think of the fact that they might not find her lying there. That they would probably return home later not noticing the closed kitchen door, the complete absence of life behind it. She was not thinking of the chill of the tiles. She was not thinking of the whirring of the ceiling fan, of the concave dip in Harry's seat that she loved so much, of the blue dress, the party, how warm he had been that night when she had given herself to him to keep, and the sunlight afterward. She was not thinking of their wedding. She was not thinking about the girls when they were born, when they had been babies. Simpler times. When she had had no troubles. She was thinking of none of this.

She was just thinking of how easy it was, how fast things come and go, how easy it is to slip in and out, barely noticed. . . .

What about me? What about ME?

Lilliana

He had said that he was coming. Coming over to Lilli's house to sit in Lilli's room and hear what she had to say. *He thinks that it's just a normal day, but it's not. It's not a normal day. Because this is when I confess. Because this is when I show him how much he means to me. How much I love him. How in love with him I am!*

She had called late.

He hadn't sounded surprised.

Could he please come over tomorrow? She had tried to sound calm. She had tried to sound poised. *Normal.* But it was so different to conceal this. It was so difficult to be normal when the situation itself was so far from normalcy. *Because love isn't normal. It's not just like every other thing!* Love was not casual, or silly, or petty. *Love is real. Just like my scar. That's what love is. That's what it does.*

But she didn't want to seem desperate. She didn't go by the store.

Thoughts of him, thoughts of Paul. His imperfect perfection. His unconventional attractiveness, his intelligence, his will, his musicality, his artistry. All of this embodied in one man. In one near-perfect specimen of life. All of this in one person, and only one. Paul. The person whom Lilli loved.

And today, when he comes over, I'll roll up my sleeves and show him. Because he deserves to see. Because I did it for him, and he should know. It was the day that she would reform her old ways. The day that the lover of sex would confess her love of another. A day of reform. A day of change.

She had told him to come early. He would be waiting when she arrived. *Always keep them waiting. I always, always like to keep them waiting.*

Vivian

She had smiled at herself again. Brushed her long, red hair, and stared at her own exotic beauty again. Stared at her own taut skin again. Stared at the box of condoms on her dresser again.

Something fateful will happen. It's all up to me now. It's in my hands.

She loved being alone like this. With herself. Because she could make herself believe anything. She could make herself believe that she was fat. Or beautiful. Or hot. Or disgusting. Or grotesque. Or wonderful maybe.

And it always worked, because she believed so easily. So trusting.

And now I'm almost done. I'm almost there

My metamorphosis is almost complete. She had the jewelry, the tattoo, the color, the makeup, the desire. The need. And soon she would become a woman. *A real woman.*

And it was a beautiful day.

So nice being alone in this room, alone in this house.

No one to bother her. *Lilli isn't home. Mom is, well, out, I guess. Or in the kitchen. And Dad is away. And I'm just here.* And ready. She had been ready for so long. She had been waiting for forever, it seemed. And now she sensed it. She would no longer be the red-haired virgin who dressed like a whore. She would be the red-haired nonvirgin who was free, and truly the person that she had waited for, longed for, wanted to be, and had finally become.

She heard the doorbell ring downstairs.

"Hi . . . um, is Lilli here?"

"No, sorry, she's not home yet."

"Oh well, do you know when she'll be back or something?"

"Sorry, I don't. Maybe when school gets out. I guess around three-thirty, three forty-five? . . . (silence) You can come in here and wait if you want."

"Thanks. That would be great. . . ." (silence)

"You play the guitar?"

"Yeah, well, bass."

"Oh, are you in a band?"

"Yeah, actually. You know, just college crap."

"What are you guys called?"

"The Box. I didn't pick it . . . (silence) By the way, I'm Paul."

"I'm Vivian. Lilli's older sister."

"Yeah, she's talked about you."

"Really? Anything terrible?"

"No, haha, no."

"Seriously?"

"Yes, I'm serious. Just a few mild complaints here and there. Nothing incriminating or anything, haha."

"Hahaha . . . Wait, I know you from somewhere."

"I work at Max Records, and—"

"Yes! I swear you must've helped me, like, a billion times."

"That's funny; you look a little familiar too, but—"

"Yeah, well, I've changed a lot lately. Recently—"

"Change is good."

"Uh-huh . . . So, do you want a drink or something?"

"No, well, I'm actually okay right now."

"Well, there's really nothing to do down here . . . so do you want to wait in my room upstairs?"

"Yeah, sure, why not?"

"She should be home soon."

"Yeah, let her take her time. Your little sister has quite a reputation, you know."

"Yeah, she does, doesn't she?"

"I don't think she really likes the guitar; I need the teaching experience though."

"Well, I doubt she likes it too. Haha."

"So you have this house all to yourself?"

"Well, I guess so. My mom must be out or in the kitchen. She doesn't bother me."

"Always a good thing. So are you in college or something?"

"No, I'm a senior. Can't wait to get away . . . out of this fucking house. Do you want some of this if you've changed your mind?"

"God, I felt the same way. Yeah, thanks. I can't say that I know many high-school girls who keep Jack Daniels in their rooms. Prying mothers, I guess."

"Well, it's for times like this. Getting to know people, you know? And I don't have to worry about that. She never comes in here."

"That's how I like it."

"What's your major?"

"Philosophy."

"My favorite. Plato's *Republic* is, like . . . well, I really think he got the whole idea of how a society and a government should be, you know?"

"Haha, touché."

"Well . . ." (silence)

"I can't help wondering . . . you don't seem like your sister at all, but what's with the blatant box of condoms?"

"Oh, haha, you know—"

"Is that like an invite or something?"

"Are you saying—"

"Are *you* saying—"

"I—"

"All I'm saying is that when a really attractive girl invites you up to her bedroom when no one's home, and she gives you a bottle of Jack, and she's got a box of Trojans on her dresser, I think it means something."

"You think I—"

"Yeah."

"I know we just met, but, well—"

"Do you feel something here?"

"I seriously do. You don't know how much I've wanted this. From the second I saw you, I just thought that . . . I mean, I've been waiting for this and—"

"Me too."

"Can I ask you one question though?"

"All right."

"Why didn't you just fuck my sister? I'm sure you had the chance."

"Why would I ever sleep with her when I knew that she had a sister whom I was dying to meet?"

"Haha, so what the hell, right?"

"Yeah, what the hell!"

"Hey, would you mind pressing Play?"

"What?"

"On the CD player by your foot."

Harry

He stood in front of the bed. The television screen. He looked at the plane ticket in his hand. As he tried not to think of Bea. Of Chad. Of Steve. Of anyone. Except her.

So hard not to.

But maybe things don't have to end now . . . here, like this. Maybe things could just *be*. Maybe he would never really leave this place, and Chloe would stay with him, steadfast and strong. And touch him, open his eyes, shut out the parts that hurt.

This hotel room. Sad hotel room. Where he had screamed obscenities, loved tremendously, hated, despised, detested, drank, slept, and awakened. Where he had died and become new. Where his guilt had subsided and turned to its antithesis. Where he had become part of a whole. Made a realization. Made many realizations.

But this can't be it. I can't leave this place. The hotel was empty. He was sure he could book the room for another week. He wouldn't have to tell anyone. He could just do it. Be impulsive. On a whim! He was young again. Doing things on whims. Asking girls in blue dresses to dance and marrying them. Whims. All whims. Some turned out for the better, some for the worse. *This is for the better.*

He had already called *her*. But *it's not for good-bye*.

He grabbed his coat, searched frantically in the pocket for his ring. The ring that had once held so much meaning. Would it ever bear so much weight again? His finger had stopped missing it. The indentation had gone away. It was almost as if he'd never been married at all.

Yes, he had called her, and she was coming.

Coming for Harry. *But I'm not going anywhere. Today is the start of a new life. A new era.* Poised in his hand, the dull gold seemed to glint in the light. He silently began to rehearse what he was going to say when she came. He wished he had a box for it. This was not an impulse. *I'm clearer than ever. This is being done out of clarity. I've considered everything.* This was no longer Harry's ring. Finally, a deed that he could be proud of. A crescendo. Finally, repentance.

Acknowledgments

Jennifer Weis: For taking on *Shut the Door* with unparalleled enthusiasm. Without your work, this book would never have been what it is now.

Arthur Klebanoff: For taking a chance on a fifteen-year-old kid, and for being the quickest reader yet.

Mary Frosch: For making me want to be a writer. Your class is still my favorite. I wish I could go back to sixth grade so I could do it all over again.

The Professional Children's School: For teaching me what I'm *supposed* to know.

Dr. James Dawson: For foreign hellos.

Abby: For going first, for dinners at Orlin, and for being the best occasional neighbor a gal could ask for.

Caroline: For long days and nights on the town, pseudo-French cuisine, loud music, and summertime. Nobody can pull it off like you can.

Dennis Anderson: For putting up with me for ten-plus years.

Laurie Hurt: For getting me off my ass twice a week—and for listening to me discuss this project forever.

Dominique Plaisant: For making Tuesdays exciting.

The Strokes: For music worth writing to.

Special thanks to Stefanie Lindskog, David Hoffman, Evan Marquit, Stephen Merrow, Teresa Reichenbach, Elena Shahin, Tracy Gallagher, Nina Hurwitz, Andrea Marquit Clagett, and Café Orlin.